Hot Zone

There had been a flash of light, Erik remembered as he crawled along the floor. A flash of light, near the ceiling. It must have been the explosion. The explosion had come from above.

"Bomb," Erik croaked, and looked up, through the soot and shadow. Now, at last, he saw the source of the tearing metal sound. The shadowed mass of the great casting cauldron hung crazily on its track, its angle all wrong even to his non-expert eye. As Erik watched, the cauldron rocked a bit and tipped. A curved line of brightness formed at the vessel's lip, as its contents shifted and seeped over the rim. The brightness was the glow of liquid metal, seeking release from its prison.

The bomb had wrecked the cross-track and maybe the motors that drew the cauldron along it. Tons of white-hot molten metal hung precariously above the foundry floor, with only a damaged track and vessel holding it there. If the cauldron tipped more, if it came free . . .

Erik tried to move faster.

Ace Books by Pierce Askegren

HUMAN RESOURCE
FALL GIRL

FALL GIRL

PIERCE ASKEGREN

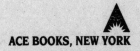

ACE BOOKS, NEW YORK

THE BERKLEY PUBLISHING GROUP
Published by the Penguin Group
Penguin Group (USA) Inc.
375 Hudson Street, New York, New York 10014, USA
Penguin Group (Canada), 10 Alcorn Avenue, Toronto, Ontario M4V 3B2, Canada
(a division of Pearson Penguin Canada Inc.)
Penguin Books Ltd., 80 Strand, London WC2R 0RL, England
Penguin Group Ireland, 25 St. Stephen's Green, Dublin 2, Ireland (a division of Penguin Books Ltd.)
Penguin Group (Australia), 250 Camberwell Road, Camberwell, Victoria 3124, Australia
(a division of Pearson Australia Group Pty. Ltd.)
Penguin Books India Pvt. Ltd., 11 Community Centre, Panchsheel Park, New Delhi—110 017, India
Penguin Group (NZ), Cnr. Airborne and Rosedale Roads, Albany, Auckland 1310, New Zealand
(a division of Pearson New Zealand Ltd.)
Penguin Books (South Africa) (Pty.) Ltd., 24 Sturdee Avenue, Rosebank, Johannesburg 2196,
South Africa

Penguin Books Ltd., Registered Offices: 80 Strand, London WC2R 0RL, England

This is a work of fiction. Names, characters, places, and incidents either are the product of the author's imagination or are used fictitiously, and any resemblance to actual persons, living or dead, business establishments, events, or locales is entirely coincidental.

FALL GIRL

An Ace Book / published by arrangement with Albe-Shiloh Inc.

PRINTING HISTORY
Ace mass market edition / July 2005

ISBN: 0-441-01297-3

ACE
Ace Books are published by The Berkley Publishing Group,
a division of Penguin Group (USA) Inc.,
375 Hudson Street, New York, New York 10014.
ACE and the "A" design are trademarks belonging to Penguin Group (USA) Inc.

PRINTED IN THE UNITED STATES OF AMERICA

10 9 8 7 6 5 4 3 2 1

CHAPTER 1

.

THE treaded surface that lined the big exercise drum helped her run, but the smartshoes on Enola Hasbro's feet helped more. Big and clumsy with thick soles, they had been made not to look smart, but to *be* smart. They knew when to cling to the lateral treads and when to release, simulating Earth-normal gravity in a way that was incomplete but still helpful.

Enola ran. One after another, she put her feet down, and one after another, the smartshoes gripped. Each was equipped with its own Gummi-Brain, matched miniature semiliving data processors that had been preloaded with task-specific brainware. The Gummis read the actions of her muscles, so that the shoes knew when to release and move on to the next step. In between, the shoe-soles clung to the wheel's surface with enhanced friction. The exercise drum helped, too, working against her as she ran, making her work harder to force the big wheel to spin on its axis so that the tread-lined surface moved through her field of view. One side of the wheel was open. Through the other and anchored to the wall, a curved crossbar projected. It traced, more or less, the drum's axis.

Enola held tight to the bar's textured grips as she ran. With each step, she made headway against the exercise machine's hidden works, and with each step, the wheel adjusted itself and the resistance increased. Enola's heart raced. The grips read her respiration and metabolic data and presented consolidated values on the crossbar screen for her consideration. The numbers crept higher as she picked up relative speed. She glanced at them and smiled. Even the numbers she didn't understand looked impressive.

Without the shoes and the cross-brace grip, she wouldn't have been able to run. The force of her steps would have thrown her up as well as forward, to carom and ricochet in the big wheel's interior. With the shoes and the grip, and with a little bit of conscious effort shaping her stride, she could.

Working out was work, hard work, but right now, she liked it. She had a good sweat going, but the clinging material of her sweat suit—much smarter-looking than the smartshoes—wicked most of it away so that her scent hung in the air. The cooling effect nicely offset the burn that built in her muscles and joints, and she felt the flesh of her legs and abdomen pull closer against the bones beneath. She gulped air and picked up the pace.

It was a perfect moment, or nearly perfect. Her body seemed to guide itself along its course, without conscious direction on her part, and for the first time in days, she felt at peace. The worries of her world had fallen away, and things felt right again.

She ran a bit faster, lifting her feet higher, coming down on the toes only instantaneously before moving on. The smartshoe soles were of memory plastic and reconfigured themselves incrementally, responding to the changes in her pace by making a more efficient grip with each footfall. The numbers on the display crept higher. At the edge of her field of view, the lateral treads had begun to strobe, shiny metal strips and black plastic ones merging into a restless blur that seemed to move and stay still at the same time.

She was free, she was flying, she was soaring, beyond even the Moon's weak pull. Her troubles were behind her.

"Hey, Hasbro. Go to Mesh. Check the Project Ad Astra feed."

The voice in her ears was one that she had heard too many times before. It belonged to Crag Fortinbras, working his upper body on the resistance machine. He was from Purchasing and had never shown himself to have any shortage of mildly suggestive comments and invitations.

Would Enola like to go the casino? Was Enola interested in the new Australian holo-sculpts? Did Enola know that there was a new nouvelle Korean restaurant in the Mall, and did Enola like *nakji-jeongol*? Would Enola like some guidance on how to avoid muscle cramps after long workouts with deep-body massage therapy? Because if she would, or if she was, or if she did, Crag would be more than happy to join her.

In the office or in the gym, or almost anywhere else, he asked her things like that almost constantly. He had done that for as long as she had known him, and today was no exception. With equal constancy, she had been screening out his comments. Practice made the process easy.

She could have turned off her phones, she supposed, but that would have been rude. Fortinbras worked in the same Duckworth Foundries offices as she did, in that company's sprawl within the Villanueva lunar colony's deepest levels. As a coworker, he had her codes. For some reason, he thought that entitled him to more. Enola thought differently.

Of course, Fortinbras wasn't likely to be a part of her life for much longer.

She tried to ignore him and concentrate instead on running. She was leaning into the curve of the exercise drum now, the crossbar having shifted to accommodate her new posture. Inside the smartshoes, her toes dug into the yielding inner soles. As the shoes' lining shifted in accommodation, her toes remembered what it had been like to run in sand, in dirt, back on Earth. That had been a world away and a lifetime before, though, and right now, Enola didn't appreciate the reminder. She tried to ignore the feeling that percolated through her nervous system, just like she tried to ignore Fortinbras.

She tried, but it was futile. The moment of quiet perfection perished even as she tried to keep it alive. The rhythm fled, and her feet, so fleet a moment before, suddenly felt clumsy and heavy. She had lost her pace; the number readouts changed less steadily, and the sliding blur of the strobe-effect treads began to resolve itself into alternating bands of black and silver.

She didn't feel free anymore.

"Go to Mesh," Fortinbras repeated, almost commanding. "You'll want to see this." The resistance machine was a dozen meters away, but his words sounded clearly from her earrings and this time, there was nothing bantering about his tone.

Enola wished fleetingly that she had turned off her office phone, but it was too late for that. The compact device had a manual switch, and she couldn't press it without releasing her grip on the crossbar. Besides, no one ever turned off the phone. Not really.

It didn't matter anymore. The moment was gone. Working out had become just work again, the mundane process of pushing her body to make it maintain muscle tone and bone mass. It was work, and it was important, so she continued her run, but her heart was no longer in it.

Without bothering to answer Fortinbras, she shifted one hand just long enough to shift the crossbar screen from diagnostic to Project feed. She blinked as the numbers faded and a remembered face condensed into high-definition reality. Square-faced and impassive, Erik Morrison was instantly recognizable.

"*—no real evidence that there's intelligent life involved at all,*" he was saying, in response to some unheard prompt. He was on a newsfeed, Enola realized. "*Let's be realistic. We don't know what happened.*"

Enola blinked again. She hadn't seen Erik in more than three years, and at least five had passed since they had done more than exchange greetings. Enola wasn't sure why anyone would want to wear the years, but Morrison seemed to do it as well as anyone could.

Never one for cosmetic appliances or grafts, Morrison had aged gracefully. Faint new wrinkles fringed his eyes and mouth, and the neatly groomed hair that framed his square features had gone completely gray, instead of what Enola's mother had called "salt and pepper." Also new was a narrow scar at the edge of his left eye, just big enough to notch the eyebrow above. The slight disfigurement flexed slightly as he spoke. On most men, Enola would have presumed that it was artificial, a bit of pretentious self-characterization. On Morrison, however, she was sure that it was real. At some point, something had cut the man, and he hadn't bothered to fix it, not with surgery or an appliance or even the Mesh mirage system.

For some reason she didn't understand, Enola almost liked that. Morrison had always seemed authentic to her, in a way that most men and women weren't.

"I think I am *being realistic,"* the newshead said. Enola needed a moment to recognize the unattractive woman as Sarrah Chrysler, yet another in the parade of on-Mesh personalities that had been moving ever more quickly of late.

If Enola found Morrison's approach to personal appearance oddly reassuring, Chrysler's baffled her, especially coming from a media figure. Dun-haired and drab, the woman was plain rather than attractive. She had enlarged pores and sharp, angular features. Worse, to Enola's practiced eye, the problems would be easy to fix. Of late, Mesh productions had trended toward an oddly defined pseudo-reality. Personalities were being cast to simulate the kind of authenticity that Morrison achieved effortlessly. Enola found the fashion distasteful, but too many others seemed to feel differently.

"We've committed tens of millions of new-dollars—" Chrysler said. Her tone was as sharp as her chin.

"Most of which derives from new taxes on the ALC," Morrison said, interrupting quickly. His air of impassiveness

flowed seamlessly into utter self-assurance, but stopped just short of condescension. He was really very good on camera.

"Taxation was a condition for the charter renewal," the unattractive woman said implacably, but she seemed startled by her guest's interjection. *"So was competition. And most of the money goes back in construction—"*

"Goes back," Morrison said, snorting. Again, the comment seemed reflexive. *"Back to Earth."*

"What a gopher," Fortinbras said, startling Enola. "Prime feed, and he can't even stay on script."

"Hush," Enola said, and shot a brief, poisonous glance in his direction before returning her attention to the display. "I want to see this."

"I thought you would," Fortinbras said, pleased.

"Millions of new-dollars," Chrysler continued. *"And now the reason is in doubt?"*

"The reason for the current program is, in the last century, the old NASA sent an unmanned probe with Mankind's name and address on it out past Pluto," Morrison said. He sounded as if he had said the words many times before. *"About six years ago, a Duckworth prospector found pieces of that probe scattered across the surface. Something had sent it back to us."*

"Duckworth," Fortinbras said softly, and the name sounded like a cheer.

He was very loyal.

"Hush!" Enola said again, snapping the word this time. Her attention drawn by the Mesh, she had unconsciously slowed her pace. Now, around her, the exercise drum was coasting to a halt. She matched her pace to it.

"Something, or someone," the Chrysler woman said. *"That's my point."*

Whoever was in charge of the Mesh production booth chose that moment to be clever and miraged something new into the picture. It was something with too many tentacles and even more eyes, and a cruel, fanged mouth that dripped saliva. Scaly skinned and ominously drooping, the apparition seemed to loom behind her left shoulder, and it reached for her with an illusory tentacle. The words SIMU-LATED IMAGE appeared on the screen.

Enola nearly laughed at both the picture and the term.

Chrysler didn't play along with the display, though. Her only reaction was to glance angrily at someone off camera. After too long a moment, the monster evaporated.

"Or someone," Morrison said, apparently oblivious to the picture-play. No one was tinkering with his feed. He spoke with an air of easy pragmatism, and a stray bit of his published biography drifted up from Enola's memory. Morrison had been an engineer once, a career that suggested a practical man. *"The real point is, we don't know. That's why we're going out there."*

"At considerable expense, I note," the woman said. *"Public expense. The deep space initiative is EnTek's biggest single reported profit sector in more than twelve years."*

This time, Morrison didn't say anything, but his expression spoke for him. Annoyance, faint but undeniable, flowed across his features.

"Everyone's biggest profit sector," Fortinbras said. "Especially the Feds."

The exercise wheel halted completely now, and the crossbar unit finished downloading data files to Enola's personal directory. Without looking away from the screen, she reached for her necklace. Nimble fingers found the pendant switch and squeezed it. The Duckworth channel on her phones went dead, and Fortinbras's interruptions died with it.

"You were part of that discovery, weren't you?" Chrysler asked.

"A very minor part," Morrison replied. As he spoke, he shifted slightly in his chair, made of cobweb-fine steel filaments in an elaborate basket weave that gave with the movement. A scrolling data display appeared behind him, offering financial and Project status details, but Enola didn't bother to access them. She was still watching Morrison

attentively, and again, she wasn't certain why. Their acquaintance had been brief and casual, and was long over. *"I brought it to the attention of upper management,"* he continued.

"That was good for your career," Chrysler said.

Now, a caption appeared beneath his image: "Erik Morrison, director of communications, Ad Astra." The letters flowed and shifted, moving from one character set to another, but in any language, the words were the same. That was what the Allied Lunar Combine—Villanueva's founders and owners—used as a euphemism for "Public Relations." Morrison seemed entirely too direct a man for that kind of role, Enola thought. He was undeniably articulate and informed, but his words lacked the frictionless quality she associated with spokespeople and newsheads.

Perhaps the fashion for apparent authenticity went further than she had realized. Maybe people wanted to hear about business from genuine businessmen.

Or perhaps it was just the mode of the day.

She watched the familiar face for a moment longer, then shrugged, and shut down the feed. She had never known him particularly well, and seeing him had reminded her of happier times, but there were other things she had to do.

She and Fortinbras were the only two using the minigym at the moment. It was one of the dozens that served Duckworth personnel, and like many counterparts, it was hidden discreetly in a "found" space left over from the colony's first wave of construction. After the voluminous hollows had been blasted into being below the dead world's cold crust, after walls had been framed and cast and placed, odd spaces had remained unassigned. In the ensuing years, they had found use. This one, a ragged wedge-shaped hollow, held a half-dozen exercisers, a bank of lockers, a refresher station, and little else, all in a hidden nook that exited to an aroma gallery and a commercial file repository. To reach that exit, Enola had to walk past Fortinbras, something she would very much have preferred not to do just now.

"Hey, Enola," the purchasing agent said as she neared, his words punctuated by a gasp as he pushed again on a spring-braced resistance armature. The exercise wouldn't have the long-term metabolic benefits of running, but his arms and chest were building up nicely. Crag was at least a dozen years older than she was, but managed not to be obvious about it. "Phone problems?" he asked. "My department's looking at some new ones. I could bring samples by your desk. When are you due back?"

She favored him with a baleful glance, but nothing more as she paced past him. For this kind of pace, the smartshoes made no real difference. Her body had long since learned the shuffling pace that worked best under low gravity.

Fortinbras gasped again, pushing the resistance bar up and back. He shifted slightly in the resister's saddle, and she knew that he was doing it so that he could see her better. Enola's experience with Fortinbras was that he looked at women whenever convenient and at her whenever possible. Now, with perspiration gluing the sweat suit's fabric to her body, he was obviously working very hard on maintaining a good view.

"Or after lunch," Fortinbras continued. "Have you eaten? Do you like—"

Enola had finally heard enough.

"I don't like octopus, Crag," she said sharply, not even breaking stride. The past weeks' stresses lent more venom to her words than she had intended. "I don't like octopus, and I really don't like *nakji-jeongol*. And I'm not Korean. Neither were my parents. And I'm just not interested in you."

It was the most she had ever said to Fortinbras at one time, and it was enough to make even the persistent purchasing agent blink in surprise. The stunned expression made her aware of just how loud and angry she sounded.

"I'm sorry, Crag," she said, awkwardly. She paused. "I'm just not."

"But," Fortinbras said. "But, you have to be interested in me. You're interested in *everyone*."

Enola's hands balled into fists so quickly and so tightly that her perfectly maintained nails dug deep semicircles in the heels of her palms. She scarcely felt them. Fury and embarrassment ripped through her, overwhelming almost any other consideration, and the irritation of a moment ago faded into insignificance. Blood fled her face, leaving her features the color of old ivory. Her teeth gritted, and her lips formed a pale, straight line as she glared at him.

Fortinbras cringed, literally. She had never seen a man do that before. He clearly knew that he had said too much, but also knew that there was no way to take back his words.

Tears were forming in the corners of Enola's eyes, but she would not let him see them. Instead, she spat in his general direction, without caring whether she hit him or not. Then she found she could speak again.

"You're lucky," she said. Her words had the flat, uninflected tone that came with utter fury, and her body quivered with tension. "You're much luckier than you know."

Fortinbras still didn't say anything.

"If we were in the office," Enola continued. "If I didn't have other things to do, and I've got friends who—"

But they weren't, and she did, and she knew that soon, she would have no friends at all.

Enola spat at him again. She turned away and walked as fast as she could toward the refresher, leaving Fortinbras and his stumbling apologies behind her. She stumbled, too, tripping as she kicked free of her smartshoes and threw herself into a shower cubicle. The unit was a no-frills, utilitarian model, and she had to operate the controls manually, but it worked well. In seconds, the shower nozzle bank hissed to life. Needle-like sprays of cold water were stabbing into her before she even thought to undress.

It didn't matter. She wondered how much longer anything would.

Even so, after a long moment, enough of her anger had faded to leave room in her mind for other considerations. Almost without conscious thought, she unfastened the sweat suit closures and peeled the waterlogged garment off

her trim body. It was heavy now, doubly drenched with her
sweat and shower spray. Even in low gravity, it tried to pull
free from her grip. Rather than let it fall where it could
block the floor pumps that labored to drain away the
shower's sluicing blast, she hung the suit on a conveniently
placed hook. Her undergarments followed.

Enola closed her eyes and presented her face to the
shower's cold spray. Tightly focused water stung her brow
and cheekbones, then ran along the smooth contours of her
body below. She could feel the sweat slide from her skin,
taking with it those first, tentative tears that she had been
so desperate to hide from Fortinbras.

How could he have *said* such a thing?

And how much longer could it matter?

Water was coming into the shower stall faster than the
pumps could take it back out, and it was pooling at her feet.
The echoing splashes sounded in her ears, and the cold
wetness made her toes curl, but the hydraulic massage
made her feel good. She moved to let the spray find first
her collarbone and breasts, then her stomach.

Enola had good coordination and an excellent sense of
her body's physical presence. She did not need to see to
move, at least not in the cubicle's close confines. Eyes
still closed, she turned, careful not to slip on the slick
flooring. Shower spray found her hair, long and dark, then
her back, then the long muscles of her legs, still tight from
exertion.

The twin heats of exercise and emotion faded, and the
water's stinging bite grew cold. She did, too. It was time to
finish here. She opened her eyes to look for the soap controls, and saw something else instead.

The Duckworth logo had been perma-printed onto the
back of her now completely sodden sweat suit. Metallic
gray, the distinctive insignia confronted her now. Even in
the fog of shower mist, the famous trademark's lines were
sharp and distinct. For most of her life, that logo had
summed up her identity and career, her very reason for being. But now, today . . .

Enola felt new tears come, and this time, she let them flow.

"—NO mirages," Sarrah Chrysler said angrily. "I mean no mirages!" She was looking in Erik's direction as she spoke, but her words did not seem to be directed at him. "I want to know who did it!"

Around them, the production area had become a bustle of man and machine, often working at cross-purposes as they moved to dismantle the set they had constructed mere hours before for Chrysler's interview feed. Somewhere near the bottommost threshold of audibility, hidden motors hummed, indistinct but persistent. Cameras and lighting arrays retreated along gossamer-fine guide cables. The set's few physical components—backdrop, chairs—repositioned themselves neatly in appropriate storage slots. Access panels clicked open and shut again. As the low table that had stretched between him and Chrysler receded, a stagehand moved just quickly enough to reclaim the pitcher and glasses it bore. Ice clinked softly as he snatched it up.

"You needed something," said a man whose name Erik recalled as Bainbridge. He had drifted up behind Chrysler, and his words startled her. "Some bright."

"The herd doesn't want bright," Chrysler said crisply, anger and sarcasm giving a different kind of edge to her words than they had possessed during the interview. "Not today. They want *real*."

One hand, dainty and well manicured, rose to her face. The nail of her index finger dug into the skin at the corner of one nostril. It dug deeper and twisted, and the nose seemed to come away, revealing another proboscis hiding underneath.

"No, Sarrah, no, don't," Bainbridge said. He sounded like he was in agony as he watched.

Chrysler smiled at Erik, but it was not a nice smile. The bit of ersatz nose she held flickered and faded away, leaving only a scrap of nearly transparent film. It drifted with consummate laziness to the studio floor.

"Please, please, please," Bainbridge said. He was a big man, tall and with bulky muscles. Erik was not small himself, but Bainbridge towered over him, taller by at least a head. Right now, however, he seemed like a pleading child, his hands clutched in prayer. "Please, wait for the crew."

Presumably, the crew was the two desperate-looking women who had joined the grouping. Chrysler waved them away with casual hauteur and tugged at her left ear. More facial appliances came free and then died, and their miniature Gummi processors lost connectivity.

The appliances that she was destroying so casually were masterworks of custom-programmed professional-quality image-casting technology. They were wafer-thin arrays of semitransparent cells that issued and shaped holographic images sufficient to convince even a Mesh camera's demanding gaze, even on the highest resolution display. Usually, their job was to enhance appearance and make the wearer more beautiful, but standards of beauty had become remarkably varied of late, and what the public wanted to see didn't necessarily conform to any of them.

"I want the beast deleted before rebroadcast," Chrysler said.

Bainbridge did not seem to hear. "That's hundreds of new-dollars," he said. "The nose alone. Thousands—"

"Delete it," she said again, more sharply.

"You're going to give him a heart attack, Sarrah," Erik said mildly. The sympathy he felt for Bainbridge was less pronounced than his own relief that the interview was finally over. The air in the studio was dry to the point of aridity, and a faint, very faint scent of ozone tanged the air, offered up by the various electrical components. He would be glad when he could leave this place, but he was willing to be patient rather than rude.

Chrysler shook her head, but paused in the dismantling of her face. "You're still a groundhog," she said. Her laugh was like silver bells. "You still think like you're on Earth.

No one has heart attacks on the Moon. You should know that by now."

Erik almost laughed, too. The judgment sounded almost silly, coming from her. He had been in Villanueva for nearly six years; Chrysler had been there less than six months, mere Mesh talent imported from Earth.

"Please, ma'am, I insist," one of the two crew members said. She ran a wand along Chrysler's left cheek, moving the instrument with quick confidence.

"Get that away from my face," Chrysler said, in the voice of someone who was accustomed to obedience. She wasn't laughing anymore. "If you touch me—"

"Guild regulations insist, too," the other woman interrupted, in a less conciliatory tone than her partner used. "The same guild as yours."

That caught Chrysler's attention. With a shrug, she dropped her hands to her side and said, "Go ahead. But do it here."

Bainbridge positively moaned with relief as the two subordinate imagineers went to work. Chrysler had already destroyed two of the three largest appliances, but the one on her right ear remained. So did the less-elaborate applications that gave Erik's hostess's face a slightly corrugated look. One by one, the wispy bits of cosmetic magic came away, and one by one, they were stowed neatly in their designated containers.

Chrysler looked again at Erik as her real face emerged slowly from its packaging. "Well?" she asked.

"Very nice," Erik said, made awkward and uncomfortable by the direct question.

Chrysler gave a snort that was neither delicate nor ladylike. "Not this," she said. "The interview."

"Oh." Erik's response had been sincere. "Sorry."

"I know it's very nice," Chrysler continued. She had good features and sparkling eyes, and her own skin, newly revealed, glowed with health. "Genetics helped, but I spend a lot of money to look like this." She glared at Bainbridge. "And now Zonix is spending more to undo it."

"Trends," Bainbridge said, in a matter-of-fact tone. "It's what the herd wants." Now that his inventory of facial appliances had been nearly completely reclaimed, he seemed much calmer. "These are very expensive, Sarrah. We'll need to discuss budget later."

"We need to discuss more than that," Chrysler responded. "And as for the herd," Chrysler continued. She rolled her eyes. "They think they want real."

"They want what they think is real," Erik said.

Chrysler returned her attention to him and nodded, pleased at the turn of phrase. " 'What they think is real,' " she quoted. "Good."

Erik didn't say anything.

"What do you think?" Chrysler asked again.

He thought a moment. "Repetitious," he said. "I had covered most of what we talked about before. More than once." He didn't point out that those interviews had been with Chrysler's predecessors.

Chrysler nodded. "It's a ten-year project," she said. "At least."

Her words rang true. Constructing the deep-space probe would take an absolute minimum of ten years, according to the current schedule—a schedule that Erik did not trust. Even with all five ALC companies working together in seamless partnership, there were bound to be delays. The Ad Astra Project was a unique endeavor, with many engineering and logistical challenges. Too many things had to happen for all of them to happen right the first time, and on time.

To build a deep-space ship, capable of supporting multiple generations in a journey to the outermost solar system, was daunting enough. To make that same craft self-sufficient, and to make the crew able to act on what they found, if necessary—that was a challenge that could take longer than even the most favorable projections. Erik was sure of that. That such an effort was so immediately vulnerable to the opposition or even disinterest of a fickle public infuriated him, when he let himself think about it.

"We have to keep reminding them," Chrysler said. The imagineers had finished reclaiming their tools, and she was dabbing at her face with a cloth now, removing the last of the adhesives. As she did, Bainbridge moved with surprising delicacy to remove her ear- and throat-phones. She did not deign to notice as he went to work. "It's part of the cost of business."

If he liked nothing else about her, Erik could admire Chrysler's directness and focus, at least about most things. Her values weren't his, but he approved of the way she pursued them. Certainly, she was easier to deal with than had been any of her predecessors in the newshead's chair, and she seemed to do her job well. He could understand her recent popularity.

He wondered if she had any idea at all that she worked for him, when all was said and done.

"Good business practice is always a good driver," he continued. "But there are others, just as good." Five years before, he would have been surprised to hear himself say the words, but time had a way of changing a man's views. More than half a decade of increasingly responsible roles in the Ad Astra Project could change views even more.

"I'll settle for business," Chrysler said, still seeming not to notice the attendants who had gathered around her. Now, they were changing her clothes, swapping one breakaway Meshcast outfit with another, equally breakaway ensemble. There was nothing erotic or even particularly revelatory about the process. Chrysler's attendants moved in a matter-of-fact way that allowed for total modesty and did nothing to stimulate or excite. When it was done, Chrysler was no longer in a Zonix Meshcast uniform, but wore more casual gear instead. She looked at a convenient monitor array and nodded in approval as she continued speaking. "Ratings," she said. "Audience, endorsements."

"There's nothing wrong with any of that," Erik said, still speaking easily.

"Good," Chrysler said. An image technician had reapplied a watch to her left index fingernail. She glanced at it now and nodded again. "Lunch," she said. "Care to join me?" Her features, reserved and aristocratic, abruptly became elfin as she smiled. A picto-tooth image of Marilyn Monroe, diagrammatic and precise, glinted out at Erik from behind perfect lips. "Do you like Korean?"

She reminded him of someone, he realized, but he couldn't decide who. The resemblance was too subtle to be specific, and expressed itself instead as an easy familiarity.

In some vague way, that worried him.

ENOLA'S heels clicked on the plastic walkway as she walked briskly along a crowded concourse in the Duckworth corporate sector. She moved with grace and precision, her gaze locked dead ahead, and scrupulously avoided making eye contact with anyone. Even so, it seemed to her that every eye in the bustling swarm was trained on her.

That was ridiculous, she knew. Most of these people had no idea who she was or why she was here. Fortinbras's comment, however, so casually cruel, still rankled, and added to an already grinding sensation of doom and presentiment. There was nothing she could do about that, though, not even drive it from her mind.

She hadn't bothered with lunch, at the Mall or anywhere else. Her knotted stomach wouldn't have allowed it. Instead, she had made a brief visit to her quarters and changed into something less casual. A matching top and skirt, both in patterned gray, both in conservative cuts. The colors weren't her best, but that didn't matter. They were Duckworth's, and that did.

Even so, she had chosen accents with equal care. She wore dark turquoise phones and nails and eyes, and sleek flats nothing like her clumsy smartshoes. They were finished in black gloss, but indigo glints seemed to appear deep within their polished surfaces.

The basic outfit was Duckworth, but the accessories were entirely Enola.

As Enola entered the primary Duckworth offices, she

could see that the receptionist wore gray, too. That was to
be expected. Gray was the color of iron, of the bones of
Villanueva, and Duckworth had taken that color as its own.
Most associates dressed accordingly, if only to please the
deeply conservative management.

Elegant and neatly composed, the other woman was as
much a part of the foyer furnishings as the utterly empty
reception desk she sat behind. The desk had been surfaced
to resemble matte-finish steel, as plain and undecorated as
the surrounding walls that supported an absurdly high
vaulted ceiling. The net effect of the entire tableau—cavernous space, formal receptionist, Spartan furnishings,
subdued lighting—was chilly but impressive, and Enola
knew it was deliberate.

Duckworth Foundries and its subcompanies had performed most of the heavy construction of the Villanueva
colony, and the rest had been done by subcontractors under
Duckworth's direction. Corporate management liked people to remember that. The dramatic, obvious use of real
space in the Duckworth offices, and the contents of that
space worked together to remind visitors of an important
truth. Their host had built their world.

The receptionist smiled at Enola and greeted her in cool
tones colored only faintly by condescension. She was there
as an emblem of the company's prosperity, a trophy attendant paid primarily to look pretty and to impress, and she
filled her role well.

"Hasbro," Enola said. "I have an appointment." With
some effort, she kept the emotion from her voice.

The receptionist nodded. She had carried the gray motif
much further than Enola ever would have, adding silvered
highlights to her lips and hair, and they glistened as she
spoke. "Chesney," she said, with no obvious reference to
screen or calendar.

Enola nodded. She was nervous and worried, and far
from sure that she could keep emotion from her voice.

"He's waiting," she said, then corrected. "Human Resources, third door." Now, she spoke with a hint of sympathy

coloring her tones, and some tiny increment of her professional reserve faded away. Enola knew why. They both worked for Duckworth, after all, and that meant both knew one thing full well.

A summons to Chesney's office meant trouble.

CHAPTER 2

THE house specialty, *nakji-jeongol,* was spicy and rich, but too hot for Erik's tastes. He filled a spoon, lifted, then let the thick stew spill back out. Broth and vegetables and octopus rained down at about one-sixth the speed they would have exhibited on Earth, tumbling and cooling as they fell some twenty centimeters back toward the big soup bowl. At the last moment, Erik's spoon interrupted the journey, matching velocity to minimize back-splash as he intercepted the food. He raised the spoon to his mouth and ate. The bits that needed to be chewed, he chewed, and then he swallowed, savoring.

"You're not supposed to play with your food," Chrysler said, watching him. She had also watched, with fascination that bordered on the grim, as the smiling waiter had prepared Erik's meal for him.

Erik shrugged. After years on the Moon, taking advantage of low G was second nature to him. "It's too hot," he said. "Not easy to do here."

Traditionally, the viscous dish was assembled and simmered at the table, to be enjoyed immediately. But the lower pressure of Villanueva's artificial atmosphere meant a correspondingly lower boiling point, and it was difficult to coax liquid temperatures to the appropriate levels. The remedy was simple: Cook the dish in a sealed vessel with release valves. He had never before seen it done at the table, though, and had watched the process with some fascination.

Erik ate more. Between mouthfuls, he cleansed his palate by sipping from a very untraditional accompaniment, a flute of French-type white wine. The food and drink both were of absolute top quality, and he was very pleased that Chrysler had suggested the place.

"What do you think of Bainbridge?" she asked abruptly.

"He seems competent," Erik said. He was not a man to hand out praise without measuring it very carefully, but he didn't like saying anything that might impact another man's employment, at least, not without cause. The producer had seemed to know what he was doing. "A little bit nervous, but competent."

"I'm going to get rid of him," Chrysler said. "Would you like to try some of this?"

She was working her way though a modest serving of red, fragrant *patbap*. It was a simple, even a staple dish, and Erik was willing to bet that the rice and beans were genuine and local. The gingko nuts, however, were probably counterfeit, the product of genetic wizardry. Erik shook his head.

Chrysler continued, "How is your octopus?"

"Very good," Erik said, aware that she was watching him carefully. "Hot, but good." He felt vaguely rude for not making a reciprocal gesture, but he was enjoying his own meal too much to share it. "I like cephalopod." He felt almost silly saying it, but it was true. Octopus, squid, cuttlefish—they all appealed, no matter what the specific cuisine. "Low gravity and farm cultivation does something for the texture."

"That's right," Chrysler said. "You cook."

Erik nodded, surprised at her easy knowledge. "When I have time," he said.

"Historically, *nakji-jeongol* is a communal dish," Chrysler continued, pointedly. She fluffed her *patbap*. "One large pot would serve a family."

Erik sipped wine and ate a rice cracker while he waited for his entrée to cool. The flavors went well together. "Most Korean dishes are," he said lightly. "And this is a small pot. What issues do you have with Bainbridge?"

"You saw the mirage," Chrysler said. To accompany her meal, she had ordered the menu's biggest surprise, New England–style cornbread. Now, she took up a yellow cube from the platter that stretched between them and nibbled at it, then smiled in wordless approval.

Erik shrugged. "He overstepped," he said. "If he does it again, or if he doesn't make the edit—"

"No," Chrysler said. She shook her head, but not enough to disturb her short-cropped coiffure even slightly. "It's my program."

Actually, it was Zonix Infotainment's program. Biome and EnTek worked together to build and implement the lunar Mesh, but Zonix had a near-total lock on content. He supposed that it was possible that Chrysler's superiors would choose to indulge her. That didn't seem likely, though, if Bainbridge was any good at his job. A single skilled technician, even with quirks, was worth any number of interchangeable newsheads. That Chrysler didn't realize that fact surprised him, but that she was so confident in her presumption of authority surprised him even more. He said so.

"I have a commitment from Arreigh," Chrysler responded. "That was part of our agreement."

"Aarray?" Erik asked. His dish had cooled a bit. Following the example she had set with the cornbread, he chose a few additional items from the multisectioned platter between them. Scallions, cucumber slices, and radishes made little splashes as he added them to his stew, then stirred. The *nakji-jeongol*'s aroma became even more appetizing.

"Arreigh," Chrysler said. She pronounced it the same way he had, though. She ate red rice and beans with elegant precision. "Keith Arreigh. He's a subcontractor, packaging

Mesh for Zonix. He's new and enthusiastic, and he's eager to please. He'll remove Bainbridge for me."

Erik nearly flinched. He glanced from side to side, without being obvious. Despite the excellence of the food and service, not to mention the immaculate table settings, the restaurant Chrysler had chosen was otherwise dingy and dark, lit only by simulated oil lanterns. Walls paneled in what looked like wood were dark with what looked like age. To judge by appearance, the place could have been scooped up whole from Seoul's worst neighborhood, disassembled, and transported. That was deliberate, he supposed, yet another manifestation of the recent trend toward antiglamour.

The important thing was, the place was nearly empty. Only a few other tables with patrons enjoying late lunches, he noted with relief. That was good. He didn't like talking about bad turns in another man's career, and he especially didn't like talking about such things in public. It wasn't good business.

"This Arreigh must want you here, then," he said, noncommittally, still uncomfortable at the bent the conversation had taken.

Chrysler was making admirable progress on her food, taking spoonfuls that were small but many, and fast. Swallowing yet again, she said, "My résumé is why I'm here. Keith is just part of it." The last bit of playfulness left her voice. "Thirty-seven reporting awards in the last ten years, thirteen of them major citations," she recited in methodical tones. "Personal awards, not joint efforts. Arreigh wants to upgrade the news Mesh content, both local and Earth-relay, so he wants me."

"Arreigh is back on Earth?" Erik asked. There had been a time when he would have said, "back home," but that time had passed.

"My audience is on Earth, but the stories are here. And so are Keith and I," Chrysler said. Something in her tone reminded Erik of a prospector announcing a water strike, or a Gummi technician reporting the isolation of a new processor gene. She sounded like someone who had made a discovery of great value, or thought she had.

Erik drank some more and let the bright taste of the wine linger. What his glass held was a Moon-local product and Heaven only knew what had actually gone into its making, but it reminded him of his years in France and of the French countryside. It bulged up slightly in the glass, hilled a bit where surface tension and low gravity intersected. A few years before, the sight would have troubled him. Now, he scarcely noticed such things, but there were times when he missed Earth.

"And you?" Chrysler asked.

"I'm a businessman. The business is here. And so am I," he said, half-smiling as he half-quoted her words of a moment before. His mind was on other things, however. The stew was very good, but the cornbread tempted.

She shook her head again. "No," she said. Her spoon struck her bowl and made a sharp click. "There's more. I've read your résumé and watched seven years of backgrounders. You didn't come here because you wanted to. Nothing you did on Earth leads logically to what you do now."

The cornbread abruptly lost its appeal. "Oh?" Erik said, his attention commanded. "I thought the interview was over, Sarrah."

"Not an interview," she said. "Just curiosity."

"It's an interview, then. You're a newshead. Curiosity is your job," Erik said.

Chrysler smiled. She picked up a glass filled with mineral water, pushed aside the fruit that garnished its rim, and drank. Bubbles hissed and spat. "You started out as an engineer," she said. "And you've been with EnTek ever since."

"I started out as a games-tester, when I was still in school," Erik corrected. "And I don't work for EnTek anymore."

"Not directly," she said. "Detached duty."

"I work for the ALC itself," Erik continued as if she had not spoken. "Over-Management, they call it."

"They," Chrysler stressed the single word. *"They call it.* You might say you're Over-Management, but you're still an EnTek man. I can tell."

Five companies, each of them superconglomerate in scale, had come together to form the Allied Lunar Combine. The ALC, in turn, had exploited an opportunity embedded somewhere in international law and done what the old space programs of a dozen different nations had failed to do. The ALC had established a working colony on the Moon.

Other factors had conditioned that success, of course. There were new technologies that had been outlawed on Earth for safety or commercial reasons, but which were perfectly legal on the Moon. There were economies of scale and economic principles too arcane even for Erik. In the end, however, commerce had taken the lead where government had faltered, and to Erik's way of thinking, it was business's grandest accomplishment.

"It's a figure of speech. I work for the ALC Over-Management, now," he told her again. "I transitioned four years ago. But old habits are hard to break."

"Corporate loyalties run deep. Your quarters are still in EnTek spaces," Chrysler said. She made a great show of selecting just the right pickled radish and began to nibble. Tiny, precise bites shredded the purplish root rapidly. The Marilyn Monroe picto-tooth, a famous face reduced to little more than a stylized logo, peeked intermittently from behind her lips.

"Old habits," Erik said again.

"Arreigh wants a profile series on historical principals in the Ad Astra Project," Chrysler said. She spoke with a shift in tone and expression, as if changing the subject, but that was just a feint. Her ultimate point in the conversation remained the same. "Start in the present and work backward through the major names. You're one of them."

"I'm just a man doing his job," Erik responded. Even though the conversation had moved in some unwelcome directions, he felt no urge to leave. His bowl was empty, his spoon set aside, and the *nakji-jeongol* sat comfortably in his stomach, but wine remained.

"Historically, that's not true," Chrysler said. "You found *Voyager.*"

"I brought the *Voyager* find to management's attention," Erik said, patiently. It was a correction he had to make often.

"That's close enough." Chrysler started on another radish, making little crunching noises. "That makes you profile material."

"I'm really not interested," Erik said. He grinned with self-consciousness. "And I'd be surprised if anyone else were."

He meant it. The very idea that anyone might be interested surprised him. For years, even decades, Zonix had made most of its Infotainment division money at the entertainment end of the scale. The Villanueva division of the media conglomerate had focused on producing, packaging, and exporting heavily fictionalized versions of the lives of the lunar colonists. Pedestrian events like the installation of a new sewage processor had been charged with false drama and then Mesh-fed to enthusiastic audiences on Earth. Trends came and trends went, but such content had always enjoyed a reliable level of success. It was staple programming, pure and simple.

The vérité that Chrysler now proposed was something new. New in Erik's experience, at least, but it comported well enough with the recent antiglamour trend. Erik didn't like it. He liked it less as he remembered Chrysler's questions during the on-Mesh interview session. Prescripted and preapproved, they had been nonetheless well founded and probing and had earned careful responses. If this was how Chrysler did business, life promised to become more difficult. Facts were almost always harder to control than fiction.

He began to wonder just how much backing she had, and how high in Zonix management her sponsors were. Zonix's inner management structure was the most fluid of any of the ALC companies. Lines of authority were shaky and erratic. Even then, they were unreliable and confusing. Authority was defined in terms of success, and success was defined in terms of end-audience share. To make things more complicated, up-and-comers came and went at Zonix with alarming frequency. Infrastructure employees and allied subcontractors were fluid categories, blurring into each other with none of the defined boundaries Erik preferred.

Erik wondered a bit about this Keith Arreigh.

"I'm serious," Chrysler continued. "We've polled. People are interested, here and at home. We could work together on shaping the topics, but the questions and answers—"

"I'm not interested," Erik said again. The last of the wine was gone, but he didn't gesture for a refill. This was not the time for drink.

"But I am," Chrysler said. "I told you, I've watched your backgrounders, and I was watching the monitor, too. You're a natural for this. The cameras love you."

"Now that's ri—"

She frowned slightly, a tiny moue of irritation, and reached across the table. "This is the kind of look they're trying to shape for *me*," she said. Her cool fingertips found the scar near his left eye and then traced the line of his cheek and jaw. "Weathered. I hate it on me, but it looks good on you. You don't wear any appliances at all, do you? Not even hair."

Erik pulled back reflexively at her touch, but managed at the last moment to turn the instinctive move into a head-shake and shoulders-shrug of disagreement. "No," he said. "No, I don't. I've spent too much time outdoors over the years to bother."

Apparently, he had not covered for his reaction well enough. Chrysler looked slightly chagrined by his rejection, but it didn't show in her words as she continued. "That's right," she said. "Hiking, fishing, hunting. Ten weeks a year, taken in two five-week segments. One with your sons, one alone. That's your arrangement with EnTek, isn't it?"

"I won't ask how you know that," he said. This time, he spoke with mild emphasis. The casual expertise she displayed about his personal life and history annoyed him. "But the word is, 'was.' I don't work for EnTek anymore."

"The transition must have been difficult," Chrysler prompted.

"Not really," Erik said. "The low gravity was the hardest—"

Just in time, he caught himself.

"I didn't mean the transition to the Moon, Erik," Chrysler said. She tapped one ear, indicating the tiny silver phone clipped there. "My researchers are working on that. I'm curious how you felt about moving into Over-Management, when—"

"This isn't an interview," Erik said, for what felt like the tenth time. "I'm not interested in a profile." He permitted a precise percentage of authority to enter his voice. "And I • can keep it from happening. That had better not be a recorder."

He could make things difficult for her, if it were.

Chrysler dimpled at him, gracious in defeat. She touched the ear-clip again. "Understood," she said. "But how about dinner? Dinner and an evening?"

Erik grunted in surprise, not sure what to say. She was easily fifteen years younger than he was, but didn't seem to be the sort that was drawn to authority or power.

"I'm serious. We've done the interviews," she said, then corrected her own words. "The *interview*. Singular. We've had lunch. You smiled several times. It seems to me, dinner and an evening come next."

Despite himself, Erik smiled again.

"There," Chrysler said. "And you've been here longer than I have. I'd like a tour. Dinner and an evening?"

"An evening, at least," Erik said, still smiling. "Would you like to attend a get-together in my quarters next week?"

* * *

LYLE Chesney was probably the fattest person Enola had ever seen, even in pictures, and certainly the fattest she had seen on the Moon. Half-memories of her childhood on Earth held images of flab and chubbiness, but nothing on the scale of the corpulent man who sat behind a cluttered desk in the Human Resources office. Heavy people were rare in Villanueva, made scarce by the need for near-constant exercise and scarcer still by social pressure.

Neither factor seemed to have had much effect on Chesney. He was enormous, easily 150 kilograms/lunar, and she had to wonder if he could even have stood upright under Earth gravity. He was so obese that he seemed to have grown a second chin. Even seated, his shoulders sagged and his belly pressed out against a tunic that would have draped like a maintenance shroud on a person of normal girth. Chesney's face was full enough to make his head nearly spherical, and he had done himself further damage with an unfortunate style of facial hair. Even worse, he wore personal one-way data displays, lenticular units in frames. From his viewpoint, he could read information feeds; from Enola's, they made his deep-set eyes appear almost buried in the surrounding flesh.

Enola tried to cover her shock and distaste, but she tried too late. Chesney's humid eyes fixed her with a glance that fell just short of a glare. "It's glandular," he said. "And, no, the gene patches don't help. At least, they don't help me. Not anymore."

The best response that Enola could manage was to look puzzled and oblivious, as if she hadn't even noticed the man's sheer mass. "I'm sorry?" she said, but then she realized that the choice of words probably hadn't been a good one.

Chesney limited his response to a shrug and a snort. "You're Hasbro," he said, and gestured. "Sit. Thanks for coming." He didn't sound very grateful at all.

Enola perched on the edge of a visitor chair, a delicate

looking spiral of spring-steel strands so gossamer-fine that
the cushion they held gave slightly even under her petite
form. In finish and design, the seat matched Chesney's
desk, but not his chair. His seat was big and stolid, with a
bulk that comported well with his own. Even so, the piece
of furniture groaned slightly as Chesney leaned back so
that he could look at her more directly.

"Do you know why you're here?" he asked. He wheezed
a bit as he spoke, and Enola could see that sweat and oil
from his skin had lightly fogged his data lenses.

She shook her head, but at best, her denial was only
technically true. She had seen the signs over the previous
several months, and she was savvy enough to recognize
them. Her assistant had been just a little bit too inquisitive
about the specifics of their work, and her superiors had
been just a little bit too dismissive of her opinions. A
missed deadline the previous week—almost without prece-
dent in her career, really—had prompted only an eye-roll
from her team leader and a rebuke that had sounded more
resigned than irritated. She and a coworker with similar
duties had both requested new field modelers, but only the
other woman had gotten one. No one invited her to lunch
anymore, and no one asked if she wanted something
brought back.

"We need to discuss your future with the company,"
Chesney said, confirming her worst suspicions.

She nodded in response. If she spoke, she knew, her
voice would break.

The big man rummaged through the half-dozen or so
computers that rested, unfolded and open, on his desktop.
They were disposables, little more than flexible film displays slaved to the local Mesh. He handled them casually,
making them rustle as they slid along one another. Chesney muttered something Enola could not hear as he looked
for, then found, the specific sheet of Gummi membrane he
sought.

"Here," he said. The other computers made a heap at
one end of his desk as he swept them aside, not bothering

to shut them down. One of the flimsy sheets overshot the edge and drifted lazily to the floor, but Chesney made no move to retrieve it. "I knew I had opened your file. Lot of activity."

Enola nodded again and nibbled nervously on her lower lip. She was very conscious of her body now, of her entire being, but it was a curiously remote sensation. It felt as if she had stepped outside of herself somehow, to experience things from a viewpoint once removed. Events were moving forward, implacably, and dragging her with them.

Chesney unfurled the computer. Slight clicks sounded as the device's corner fasteners engaged the desktop. He gazed into its depths, then looked up again. When he spoke, he was surprisingly gentle. "This is never easy," he said.

The four words made a difference. His new tone made another. Enola's teeth released her trembling lower lip and the aching tension that filled her ratcheted back a tiny increment. The worst wasn't over, but the anticipation was, and she felt grim resignation about what she knew would happen next.

"You've been with us for ten years," Chesney said.

"Sixteen," Enola corrected.

"Ten as direct staff," Chesney said. "Six before that, as a contractor."

"I consulted on an Earthside multimedia package while I was still in Academy. I was a legacy. One of my mothers was with Duckworth Micronics," Enola said. "She gave me my start."

"Well, we're not concerned with the contracting now," Chesney said. There was an insulated mug at his elbow, with a cat imaged onto it. The cat danced madly as Chesney lifted the cup and sipped new-coffee, then calmed as he set it down again. "Ten years as company bones."

"Yes," Enola said. "And I think I've—"

This time, Chesney interrupted. "You're not recording this, are you?" he asked and she shook her head. "Because you can't. Your clip won't work here, but I'll see to it that you get something for your files."

From there, the interview and Enola's world went into a slow-motion plummet, as slow and implacable a fall as Chesney's computer's had been. Did Enola know that the win rate for the last thirty-two proposals she had worked on was only 30 percent? Was Enola aware that a client had complained about her demeanor during a recent program review? Did Enola have any explanation as to how proprietary specifications from a project of hers had ended up in another task-team's efforts? Did Enola really think it was appropriate to store personal imagery in her professional Mesh-space? Had Enola not seen the last iteration of Duckworth's *Apparel Guidelines* and if she had, had she bothered to read them?

Methodically and with more precision than she would have expected from one with his appearance and workspace, Chesney plodded through the questions. For most, she had answers. For some, she had good answers, but only for some.

Her group's win/loss ratio had slipped because of increased competition in her subsystem specialty, and that was because of charter changes the UN had forced onto the ALC. The complaining client had mistaken her for a Zonix "professional mistress." No, she didn't now what had happened with the data, and no, she didn't think it was a very good idea, but everyone did it. She hadn't seen the document in question, but she would be happy to reference it in the future.

With each exchange, another vestigial bit of desperate hope drained away. No longer worried about posture or appearance or eye contact, Enola slumped in her chair. Her mind raced frantically to find the best responses to Chesney's patient accusations, but she knew that it was no use.

She was doomed.

"—severance terms," Chesney finally said. He spoke with no rancor or menace in his tone. His words were chilling enough.

"Severance?" she said, gasping. Even anticipated, the

words were a shock. "You're *terminating* me? But, probation, suspension—"

Despite all her mental preparation, the news was unthinkable. She was actually being fired. No one got fired, not after ten years of faithful service. Not for infractions as minor as those that Chesney had listed.

"It's not my decision," he said.

"But—demotion, or even transfer—" Enola began. She was desperate, willing to make any promise he wanted to hear, ready to bargain for any alternative.

"It's not my decision," the fat man said again. He sounded regretful enough that Enola suspected he was sincere, not merely playing a role. "Standards have changed, since the Ad Astra Project, and—"

Standards. A snippet of half-remembered news feed drifted up and into Enola's mind. The ALC's charter agreement with the UN included population requirements for Villanueva. Even without those requirements, the more people who lived in the lunar colony, the greater was the enterprise's standing in world courts. The Ad Astra Project had brought a new stability to Villanueva's legal status, however, and created new opportunities for immigrants. Over-Management's need to boost population, and thus satisfy the terms of its charter, was no longer quite so overwhelming.

"But . . ." Enola said. She wanted to say something more articulate, but the words would not come.

"Here are your terms of separation," Chesney said. He indicated a list in the computer display. "You'll find they comport with your original employment agreement and include a generous compensation component. You'll have two standard months for genetic regression therapy—"

"I—I have to go back to Earth?" Enola interrupted. The idea horrified her.

Chesney's beady eyes peered out at her from within the folds of his face. "We have no place for you here any longer," he said. "On Earth, things might be different. I can't promise you anything, but I've been told to tell you that if you apply for a consulting agreement, Engineering will try to find something for you."

Enola started to cry. Hot tears finally found their way from her eyes, and ran in burning streams down her cheeks. She did not try to stop them, but the embarrassment made her cry all the harder. Her greatest fears had become real, and the reality was more awful still. She sobbed, her shoulders shaking.

Chesney reached for a tissue. His fingers, thick and clumsy, found the dispenser easily enough, but they also found and struck his beverage. The cartoon cat writhed in dismay as the mug toppled. Brownish new-coffee flowed in all directions across the desktop. Chesney moved with surprising speed for such a big man. He blotted swiftly with one wad of tissues even as he handed a second to Enola for her tears. Obviously, he was practiced in the maneuver.

Enola paid him scant attention as she dabbed at her eyes and cheeks. In a strange way, the tears helped, just as her earlier outburst at Fortinbras had then. Her emotions, tightly contained, found release and fled. By the time she folded the damp tissues tightly and dropped them into a recycler, she was more or less calm again.

Chesney glanced at her, his cleanup completed. After a long moment, he nodded. "Now, as to the disposition of your lodgings and personal effects," he began again, his voice carefully neutral.

This time, Enola did not cry.

CHAPTER 3

WITH easy confidence his only companion, Hector Kowalski moved through a world that most did not even realize existed. Phones off, computer closed and de-linked, the wiry man walked behind the walls of Villanueva, hidden behind plastic paneling, stone blocks, and structural braces. The very things that gave Villanueva form served double duty now by providing him with privacy. He whistled softly while he walked, confident that no one could hear him.

The colony was basically a place of chambers and corridors that had been blasted and bored into the lunar crust, but its boundaries were less clearly defined than most occupants realized. Behind walls, above and beneath the living and working areas, stretched a pressurized tangle of service and maintenance spaces, of tunnels and crawl spaces and access ways. Together, they formed an incomplete, three-dimensional shadow to the labyrinthine habitat. Some of those passages saw occasional or even regular use, by the men and women and machines whose efforts kept Villanueva and its occupants alive. Some were almost habitable, finished and well lit, with framed walls and dropped ceilings. Others were little more than raw bores, and walled only by rock that was naked but for polymer sealant and sprayed insulation, or by construction members and modular panels. Not even the relative few who labored in the utilitarian area realized how extensive it was.

Hector Kowalski did. He had made it his business in recent years to explore and map the hidden corridors. Originally, it had been a matter of indulging idle curiosity, expedited by the privileges and authority he commanded, but his studies had fast become more than that. It was useful for someone working ALC Security to know of ready places of concealment or subtle ways of getting from one enclave to another.

Some of Hector's research had been Meshwork, patient ransacking of archives and file repositories. More had been undertaken in person, yielding notes and memories that filled gaps in historical records. Engineering plans never precisely matched reality, neither before nor after construction, and Hector had found more than a few discrepancies.

He did not know the service network in its entirety, but he knew parts of it exceedingly well. The route that he followed now was one such segment. Well within the erratic boundaries of the EnTek sector, through a service tunnel that was poorly lit but spotlessly clean, he moved with easy grace. Hector had spent much of his life on the Moon, and his body had long since adapted to the rhythms and techniques necessary to move with measured, reasonable speed.

Low gravity could be more hindrance than help. Long, forceful steps too often meant a loss of balance between strides and could make stopping very difficult. Running was impossible; each pace launched the runner from the floor completely. Smartshoes helped, but they were for tourists or newcomers. Without them, something more like ambling was best. Hector moved in a gliding shuffle that lifted his big feet only centimeters from the floor before plopping them down again.

The shadows and gloom that surrounded him did not impede his progress. He was familiar with this trail, and he had excellent peripheral and twilight vision that were only slightly augmented by artificial means. Though widely spaced, the long-life, low-output illuminators cast a subdued glow that was more than sufficient. Not even the occasional shadows offered any real inconvenience.

The passage turned sharply, bending left then right twice and then left again to accommodate a massive vertical foundation brace, Duckworth work. Getting past it was a tight squeeze, but the landmark meant that he was nearing his destination. The hidden corridor widened abruptly, and he saw, once more, a rack of excavation tools and an emergency pressure unit, walled away years before and forgotten. He nodded at the familiar signpost, turned another left, and then started up the angled ladder waiting there.

For a man his age, born on Earth and relocated to the Moon just after adolescence, Hector was of precisely average height and build. These qualities, too, had proven useful. He could be remarkably nondescript when he chose to be, and the world often seemed to have been built for him. Certainly, the ladder did, with rungs and risers spaced to fit his reach and stride. He climbed rapidly and easily, still whistling.

He liked this. He liked walking, and he liked climbing, and he generally preferred physical exercise that was productive and not merely staged competition with gymnasium machinery. Even the public areas of Villanueva had been designed to encourage exercise, with pedways and foot-tubes and ramps being key components of most routes. A man who planned his day properly never had to bother with a stationary bicycle or lateral treadmill. He could get his daily quota of exercise while going about his business.

Halfway up its length, the ladder angled past an access panel hatch that was listed only in a very few records, and listed in those as sealed. It wasn't. The lock was old and out of date, but its override code still worked, and the panel glided aside on perma-lubed guides. A stooping, sideways step and a half-hop later, and he stood in a kitchen's maintenance closet, slamming the hatch shut behind him. A moment after that, having rinsed his hands in the kitchen sink and tidied his longish hair, he ambled into the adjoining executive dining room. Now, he walked without whistling, and with some effort to be silent.

That effort was wasted. Erik Morrison was already seated at the long, low table, the remains of a light snack lingering before him, and a computer unfolded in one big hand. As Hector entered, Morrison barely glanced in his direction, then blanked the computer and set it aside. "The kitchen, eh?" he said. "Did you see anything you liked in the icebox?"

"Icebox?" Hector asked, puzzled. The term was unfamiliar.

"An old name for refrigerator," Morrison said. "Early twentieth."

"I didn't even look," Hector said, honestly but with sudden regret. His stomach reproached him slightly as he settled into the chair opposite Morrison. He rested half-folded forearms on the tabletop and leaned forward, an amiable note in his voice. "And since when are you interested in history?" he asked.

"Just since I started living in it," Morrison said. He unfolded the computer, prompting its display to flare back to life. *Counter-Outreach: A Study in Historical Isolationism and Its Impact on Modern Initiatives,* the title field announced, followed by lines of scrolling text, punctuated by images. "I'm told it's the definitive work," Morrison said. "Evidently, not everyone is interested in what lies beyond Pluto."

The book held no interest for Hector. He scarcely glanced at the display. "I wanted to give you an update," he said, mildly disappointed by Morrison's equanimity. "I know we don't have an appointment, but—"

"But you looked at my personal calendars, and you

knew I was free," Morrison said, interrupting, still unfazed. He spoke as if quoting, a habit that Hector found singularly annoying. "And you wanted to see if you could surprise me. You never like coming in through the front door if there's another in back."

This time, Hector smiled, if only to mask his increasing pique.

"I'm too familiar with you for those games to work," Morrison continued. "After years of coming home to find all my Mesh links reset, or my refrigerator empty, I'm convinced. You've proven your point. You know all and see all, and can go anywhere. I won't even ask how you got into the kitchen."

Hector laughed, genuinely amused now. "But I really do have an update for you, though," he said. "More of Scheer's agents are leaving us. It may even be the end of the network."

"That's good news," Morrison said. He refolded the computer and set it aside. "But you've said so before. Are you sure this time?"

The question didn't have an easy answer. For several decades, the commercial Villanueva and the much smaller federal Armstrong Base had been neighbors on lunar shores. Villanueva was a business enterprise, a test bed for experimental technologies and a tourist trap and a first step in the exploitation of the near-virgin Moon's considerable resources. Armstrong was a scientific enclave, home to Project Halo and a steadily dwindling portfolio of research, technological exploration, and SETI, Search for Extraterrestrial Intelligence efforts. Villanueva's core function, if not goal, was to usher earthly life into outer space; Armstrong's primary mission was to determine if life already existed out there. Their agendas had been at once opposed and complementary. Their relationship had been a wary one, with the vastly less wealthy Armstrong piggybacking on Villanueva's more established presence.

The months following the *Voyager* find had laid bare the extent of that wariness. That was when the Scheer network had come to light, a system of informants and surveillance agents stationed in Villanueva but reporting, however indirectly, to Wendy Scheer, a high-level Armstrong official. Most of Scheer's operatives had not even been aware that they worked for her. Members of a system organized on the classic, three-member cell model, with each member knowing only identities of a very few others, many had thought of themselves merely as industrial spies. The ALC companies kept close track of each other's activities, after all, and rivalry among various subcontractors was intense. Surprisingly few of Scheer's people had realized that they reported, ultimately, to the federal government. Other factors had been at play, as well, further complicating the situation.

"It seems likely, but I can't be absolutely certain," Hector said calmly. "You know that. I have to be discrete. And most of the traces I would use don't hold in this situation."

Morrison grunted in reply, clearly irritated. This was a point that they had argued more than once in the past, and Hector decided not to argue it again just now. There was a reason that dismantling the network had proven to be such a lengthy process. Scheer's unique techniques made her influence difficult to detect.

He continued. "I've identified and engineered the removal of another twenty-three persons who have—*had*—suspected connections to Scheer," he said. "They should be off local payroll by the end of this week, and off the Moon within two standard months."

"Anyone important?" Morrison asked. He leaned back in his padded seat. The possibility was a personal nightmare for both men. A prominent corporate officer in Scheer's thrall could do untold damage and be difficult to eliminate.

More to impress than inform, Hector recited the names from memory. The exercise was easy; he had spent weeks dealing with these people and their situations, and the facts came with little prompting. "Kahn Souphanousinphone, imaging specialist, Zonix, came into a small inheritance and will relocate to ancestral holdings in Laos," he said. "George Perez, bioengineer for Biome Consumer Products, has been promoted; his new billet is in Manitoba. Aelita Hanover, also Biome bioengineer . . ."

He spoke without effort, almost without thinking, nearly by rote, as if reading the specifics from an invisible list without bothering to understand them. The report unreeled easily from his lips and into the dining room air. He had nearly half-finished when Morrison interrupted.

"Enola Hasbro?" Morrison asked sharply, sitting at attention now.

Hector had to work his way back down the mental roll call to confirm. Irritated, he said, "Yes. Enola Hasbro, Duckworth proposal modeler. Terminated for poor performance."

"Terminated?" Morrison said.

"You seem surprised," Hector answered. It didn't surprise him that Morrison evidently knew the Hasbro woman, but his reaction was still unexpected. "Does that matter?"

"Probably not," Morrison said. The fingers of one big hand drummed on the tabletop. "Tell me more about Hasbro."

"There were performance issues," Hector said. It wasn't hard to summon up the information from his excellent memory, but it wasn't as easy as reciting the list had been, either. "Minor ones, but enough to move her off payroll, especially in the current operations environment."

"Full termination?" Morrison asked. "I wanted these things to be gentle."

Hector shrugged. "That was the easiest way to work it," he said. "Her quarters are part of her compensation. Fare home is part of her severance package. The books balance."

"Not very gentle," Morrison said.

"My options in her case were limited," Hector said. He shrugged again. "The jelly-belly in Duckworth says that she'll be welcome with the groundhogs. Not as company bones, but as a consultant. There's good money for people with lunar experience."

"And you're certain that she was working with Scheer?" Morrison demanded.

"No, I'm not certain," Hector said. "I can't *be* certain. Not in cases like hers, and not when I uncover new connections so often. But I can prove that they met at least four times over a two-year period, and the work-quality issues included file security problems. *Genuine* problems," he concluded.

Morrison glanced at his blanked computer, then at the remains of his meal, then at the otherwise empty tabletop, as if hoping to find something else that would command his attention. He didn't.

"Is there a problem?" Hector asked, in carefully neutral tones. He knew that Morrison could be squeamish about these things. "I mean, I know that she's cute, but—"

"We have to be sure," Morrison said, as if speaking to himself.

What he said was accurate, though. Hector had undertaken the slow, thorough dismantling of the Scheer network happily enough, but it had been at Morrison's direction. Both men understood its importance. Scheer herself was supposedly no longer an issue, but it made no sense whatsoever to leave her information-gathering forces in place, especially not with the Ad Astra Project moving along so quickly.

"I could probably change things, if there's a reason to," he said. He didn't like mentioning the possibility. It would mean calling in a favor, and those were in short supply these days. Worse, it would mean yet another compromise to a policy he had personally proposed. "On probation, perhaps."

After a long moment, Morrison shook his head. "We have to be sure," he said again. "Let the process take its course."

"Eight weeks, then," Hector said.

"Send me a summary, though," Morrison said. "A current one."

Hector glanced at him in agreement. He paused a moment, thinking, and then began his recitation anew.

"Daniel Tezuka-Jones, Zonix Human Organic Reclamation System, terminated for incompetence. Mildred Aovergine, Biome med-data archivist . . ."

Morrison listened without further interruption, but his attention seemed elsewhere.

DEAD inside after the interview, Enola didn't feel much like walking, no matter how good for her the exercise was. She took the commuter shuttle instead. Many in the Duckworth workforce ended their shifts in early evening, and she thought that she might feel better being surrounded by them.

She didn't. Perched on the edge of a plastic-padded seat in a crowded car, surrounded by men and women who only hours ago had been coworkers, she felt as if everyone was looking at her, or was about to. She was certain that she could feel pity in the air, mingled with the smell of sweat and the murmur of conversation. It was as if everyone knew who she was and what had happened. She sat bolt upright, her eyes trained dead ahead, and stared without blinking or seeing. Too sick at heart to read or listen to music feeds, too acutely self-conscious and ashamed to think clearly, she did not know what else to do.

The case made it worse. If her fellow riders didn't recognize her, surely they recognized the type of cumbersome, wheeled case that rested on the floor between her feet. Utilitarian and ugly, marked only with a generic and nonanimated Duckworth logo, Chesney had given it to her as she left his office. It was the kind of employer-issued luggage that staff used when relocated or reassigned. The fat man had assured her that it held the entirety of personal items from her workspace and private locker. Then, without pause, he had corrected himself and said, ". . . everything that Security would release today, that is. Anything else will follow."

She wasn't even allowed to say good-bye to anyone. She wasn't at all sure that she would have wanted to, but she wished that it had been an option.

Now, Enola was irrationally certain that her fellow passengers could see the case for what it was—her personal mark of shame. She tried not to touch her burden as the shuttle glided smoothly through its tunnel, but starts and stops made that impossible. Each time the car paused to admit or disgorge passengers, the cheap carry-on rocked slightly, bumping one of Enola's perfect knees, then the other. Each impact reminded her of how completely and suddenly her life had changed.

"Hello, Enola!" someone said, from within the surrounding throng. Startled, Enola shifted her gaze to see that Narçissa Esposito, a casual acquaintance from Accounting, stood only a meter or two away. The short, squat Hispanic woman waved happily, pleased and surprised to see Enola. "What are *you* doing here? Don't you usually take the pedway?"

"Um, hello, Narçissa," Enola said. There seemed to be no way that she could not respond. "H-how are you?"

Narçissa wrestled her way closer. "I am fine," she said cheerfully. She was nearly always cheerful. Narçissa spoke with a very slight Nordic accent, the result of a youth spent in Continental boarding schools. She was an older woman, with a deteriorative disorder in her ankles and knees that had made her transfer to the Moon's low-gravity working environment an eagerly sought goal. "You never came back from your workout," she said now, in mock accusation.

"Uh. I had an appointment," Enola said nervously. She tried to smile. "I had to . . ."

The words trailed off as Narçissa's expression changed. The other woman had finally noticed the wheeled case, and it had been enough to confirm the rumors about Enola's afternoon absence that were no doubt rife at their workplace. Her eyes widened in shock. "Oh, Enola," she said, just loudly enough to be heard. "I am so sorry."

She knew.

Just in time, the commuter shuttle paused in its headlong flight, giving Enola an opportunity to end the awkward conversation before it could truly begin. They were at a major stop, with many connections. The thronging passengers, made anonymous and nonconfrontational by their numbers, carried her along in their sudden, surging exodus. Spared, for the moment, the mixture of pity and revulsion that she knew was to be her lot in life now, she let herself be swept out onto the station platform.

Termination's stigma was terrible and complex. Enola knew that it would be her companion for some time to come.

Made clumsy by emotion and shock, she stumbled as she stepped onto the platform; stumbled, but did not fall. She threaded her way through the crowd, dragging the case behind her, with her head down low and her eyes averted. Her path was shaped more by luck than by conscious effort, but she made good progress, and in moments she was on an up-spiraling ramp that led to her home corridor. Another moment, and she stumbled again as she lurched over the threshold and into the sanctity of her private quarters. This time, the misstep was worse, and the heel of Enola's left shoe broke with a loud snap.

"Good evening," her apartment said, and announced the time.

Enola ignored it. She kicked off both shoes. Her apartment's carpet was deep and cool, and her newly naked feet liked it, even if the case's wheels did not. They caught in the luxurious pile, caught and dragged, and Enola had to fight to wrestle the recalcitrant baggage into the receiving room and onto the couch. A fingernail caught and tore sideways as she opened the piece of luggage, but the injury comported so well with the rest of her day that she scarcely noticed.

Inside the case was her life at Duckworth, or most of it, and tears filled her eyes yet again as she took hasty inventory. Gummi-frames set to display images of her parents and several former lovers. A crystalline teardrop vase, once her birth mother's, badly chipped now by someone's sloppy packing. Her personal Zonix dancing cat mug, its display dark now. A deluxe scent synthesizer, awarded her after a proposal imaging competition. The toiletries and facial appliance she kept for emergency use, and the extra pair of shoes. A rack of data modules, five when there should have been twelve, back-up copies of various projects that she could be certain had been purged of all that was proprietary or unique and interesting. Worst of all, and least welcome, was a sheaf of hard-copy forms and datadumps that summarized her rights and nonrights as a now former Duckworth employee.

What was she going to do?

What *could* she do?

"You have messages," the apartment's housekeeping system continued. It spoke with the voice of her sister, Donelle, dead so many years. Enola had scavenged it from family files and brought the voice forward as brainware engrams. Whether she had sought to console or remind or reproach herself, Enola had never been sure. *"Four messages, all personal, none flagged priority. From last to first—"*

"I don't want to hear them just now," Enola said, as she continued to root through the case. There were too many other things to do. "Please update and assess my personal finances, for later review. Correlate them with current market trends and cost-of-living indices, Earthside. Inventory my private files and start moving them to outboard media. And run a systems check on my personal presentation modeling kit." The possibility, however faint, of finding another job in eight weeks was tantalizing.

"Financial review is in-process," the apartment said. Its speakers were hidden somewhere above the ceiling, but shaped acoustics put the familiar voice close to Enola's ears. She liked hearing Donelle's echo, but was careful never to address the housekeeper by her sister's name.

Still unpacking, she made a sound of misery. Whoever had packed her things had broken the expensive scentthesizer, too. "Update my calendar, too," she said in her command voice. Tomorrow—"

The apartment interpreted her troubled pause as an

interrogative. *"You have a noon appointment at Regenics,"* it told her.

Regenics. That was a Biome subsidiary. Chesney must already have scheduled her genetic regression therapy. Enola didn't want to think about it.

"I'll hear the messages now," she said.

Another pause, then another voice filled the air, different but still familiar. *"Enola?"* Crag Fortinbras asked. *"Are you there? I hope you're there now, Enola. I've been calling all afternoon, ever since the gym."*

She rolled her eyes as he continued and found that the reflexive flash of disdain took the edge off her misery. Some people just didn't seem to understand the word "no."

"I'm sorry to keep pestering you," Fortinbras's recorded tones continued, punctuated by an embarrassed, rueful laugh. *"I guess I've been doing that for a long time now, and I didn't realize it until today. I'm sorry. For everything."*

He sounded contrite, Enola realized with some small pleasure—more than contrite, really. Fortinbras's voice held unreserved apology and embarrassment, more intense than she had heard from any man since her teens. She wondered if he had heard about her termination. The "for everything" sounded ominous.

"Look, I'm sure you'll say no, but I'd like to make it up to you," Crag continued. *"If you're free this evening, if you'd like someone to talk to, let me know. Please."*

Enola rocked back and forth a bit on stocking-clad feet. She thought. Remnants of a broken career confronted her from the open case. Crag Fortinbras's recorded pleas and apologies filled the cool apartment air a second time, then a third and a fourth, as the housekeeper scrolled back through her messages. The hours of the evening yawned emptily before her, and she could think of nothing to fill them with but misery and self-reproach. Dead Donelle's recorded ghost voice waited patiently for instruction, and Enola thought some more.

"Get me Crag," she finally said, and shrugged. What could it hurt?

* * *

AFTER his workday, a fast forty minutes in the executive gym and a quick visit to his favorite designer grocer left Erik Morrison feeling better physically and emotionally, if somewhat the poorer financially. The loosely woven fiber mesh bag that he held in his right hand as he ambled home held prosaic goods like soy flour and fresh produce from one of the nature habitats that helped to refresh Villanueva's closed-cycle atmosphere. Its partner, gripped securely in his left, held a more specialized inventory of imported caviar—flash-frozen—Peruvian spices, and absurdly expensive veal brains. But the prize was a single bottle, swaddled now in antishock foam and with a certified history of having been shipped only in climate-controlled cargo holds.

It was Kentucky bourbon, traditional and pure, aged in oak and bottled in bond. He could have directed his housekeeper to place an order and receive his goods, but treasures such as this were one reason Erik preferred to do his own shopping. The whiskey boutique's owner had assured him that this bottle was the only one of its type on the entire Moon.

"Erik," his apartment said as he entered. The recorded strains of a Sibelius concerto welled up from discreetly placed speakers. *"Hi, there. Welcome back."*

One of the first things that Erik had done upon his transition to Over-Management and a much higher income had been to remodel his original, EnTek-designated residence. He had secured several neighboring apartments, adjacent and above alike, and thrown them together. The dividing walls and ceilings he had mostly sacrificed in favor of open space, so that the new place was not only big, but *felt* big. It was big in terms of real space, not the trompe l'oeil display-paper that sufficed for the majority of Villanueva residents. The ceiling of the receiving room alone vaulted more than five meters above the carpeted floor. More than one visitor had accused him, only half-joking, of "going

Duckworth," but Erik liked the effect. He was a pragmatic, even utilitarian man, but not without a sense of drama. He knew the value of making a strong impression.

Built to his personal specifications, the kitchen was more of a functional space than a discreet room. An apse, a hollowed half-dome, it sheltered appliances and cabinets and opened onto the receiving room area. Erik went to it now and set down his burdens on the island counter there. He began filing the food away, opening and closing various cupboards and drawers in rapid sequence. He was pleased that the impromptu run-through also indicated that Hector Kowalski had evidently not, in fact, made any clandestine raid of what was already on hand.

"You've got messages," the apartment housekeeping system continued, in tones that were polite and pleasant to hear, but otherwise completely devoid of any human character. Another of Erik's little luxuries for himself had been to upgrade the housekeeper artificial intelligence and optimize it for conversational discourse. At the same time, he had been careful to keep it clear of any kind of simulated personality, preferring to avoid that particular illusion. *"Seven data loads, nine business messages, six personal. Nothing very important, but for one. Janos Horvath would like you to call, when you get a chance."*

"Message him that I will," Erik said. "And offer my regrets." Horvath was his former superior and his current advocate in EnTek's top management, back on Earth. His specific authority over Erik's current activities was limited, but even so, he merited reasonable courtesy. "Anything else?"

The housekeeper paused for a moment, as if in contemplation. *"The data loads are all work stuff. None of the business messages are marked time sensitive, and I've summarized them for your files. Of the personal calls, two are from a Sarrah Chrysler."* The housekeeper's Gummi paused again. *"I don't believe I know her, Erik. Is she someone new?"*

That was almost enough to make him laugh. "What about the business messages?" he said, as he configured the appropriate refrigerator compartment for the veal brains and put them away. He wasn't planning on making dinner tonight, but they had been too tempting to ignore. "Is there anything from Kowalski?" he asked.

"Just one," the apartment responded. *"A backgrounder on Enola Hasbro."*

Erik paused, then. He thought about an evening some seven years before, when he had danced, however briefly, with Enola Hasbro. She had made her way across a crowded dance floor to where he stood, for the moment alone, and insinuated herself into his arms. They had waltzed to something by Strauss. He remembered how the trim Asiatic woman's body had felt against his and how her dark eyes had shone as she smiled up at him. He had encountered her other times, before and since, but for some reason, that single dance together was the moment he remembered best. The moment stood out in his memory. That, and how bright and alive she had been. Now, he had condoned her destruction.

He sighed, feeling suddenly very old.

How could Enola have gotten involved with the Armstrong people? *Had* she gotten involved with them? There was no way to be certain, especially at this late date, but Kowalski's policy was the right one. Err on the side of caution.

"That can wait," he said, snapping the refrigerator shut. "File it. File them all, for later review." He unwrapped the bourbon. Melancholy faded as the perfectly pellucid glass bottle and the dark amber liquid it held came into view.

"Of course, Erik," the housekeeper replied. *"That's why I'm here."* Again, it paused, and then said, *"Incoming message. Personal, referred from outdated codes. I haven't flagged you as home, yet."*

"Who?" Erik asked.

"Wendy Scheer," came the announcement. *"She's recording now, but I can interrupt."*

"She can wait," Erik said grimly. That wasn't a name he wanted to hear, or a person he wanted to talk to. "Take a message, but file it for later review."

He decided that the whiskey could wait, too.

CHAPTER 4

AWAKENING in the simulated sunrise of a prerecorded dawn, Enola felt as though someone had urinated on her naked brain. It hurt. The rest of her hurt, too, every square centimeter of skin, every muscle and bone and joint, from the top of her head to the tips of her toes. Her ears rang and her eyes stung. Other than the headache, no single throbbing twinge was particularly intense. Together, however, they almost overwhelmed.

"Good morning," the apartment annunciator said.

Enola moaned. It shouldn't have been possible, but the housekeeper actually sounded cheerful, and there wasn't much room in her world right now for cheerfulness. She tried to slither from beneath the bedsheets, but they seemed to have grown muscles, and they fought her efforts tenaciously.

"Your Regenics appointment is in one-point-five hours," the apartment said.

The calm words took a moment or two to make their way completely through the itchy morass inside Enola's throbbing head, but once they had, she panicked. She kicked and flailed desperately. This time, the tangled sheets gave way and released her. She dragged herself to the edge of the bed.

Reporting to Regenics was imperative. The genetic regression treatments were essential to her health and well-being if she went back to Earth. Even more important, they were part of her separation agreement; if she forfeited them, she forfeited the rest of the package, including room, board, and severance, everything but passage back. If she went back without the therapy, her current problems would seem small, indeed.

With great effort, she lurched to her feet. The room— the entire world, really—lurched and spun sideways. The pounding in her head worsened, and nausea swept over her as the contents of her stomach tried hard for a sudden, violent escape. She leaned on the nightstand and trembled, her legs rubbery.

"Oh, God," she muttered, as her too-dry eyes took in the chaos that had been a neat and tidy bedroom only the previous day. The mess was made more stark and surreal by the light of the wallpaper's rhododactylous dawn. "What happened last night?"

The apartment housekeeper offered no reassurance. Instead, it played back a recorded snippet.

"Hey, Donelle," the Enola of last night said. Drunken and slurred, it remained recognizably her command voice. *"Give a girl some privacy!"*

The Enola of this morning, naked and miserable, shuddered. She covered her eyes with one hand. "That's enough," she croaked. "And turn off the damn Sun."

Obediently, the wallpaper's dawn simulator shut down. Normal illumination took its place. Enola, tottering, made her way to the bathroom. She ransacked the shelves there with trembling hands until she found a bottle of blue liquid, much beloved of bartenders and partygoers alike. The dosage guide called for a few cubic centimeters for someone her size, but Enola was desperate. She swallowed half the mint stuff in a single gulp.

What exactly had she done the night before?

That was the easy question, really. The hard one was, why the hell had she done it?

The answers to both were distressingly obvious, even if only half-remembered, but her personal standards required that she ask such things of herself. Enola's approach to her social life was robust and even aggressive, but incidents like this were few and far between.

It wasn't as if she even had particularly *liked* Fortinbras. And thinking about him now, she was reasonably sure she liked him even less today. She wondered if he would be a problem.

"Messages?" she asked, as she collapsed in a nerveless heap on the covered commode. She leaned against the washstand for support. Already, the world had righted itself a bit, but not nearly enough. It would be at least a minute or two before she could even consider braving the shower.

"Three," the housekeeper said. It spoke in Donelle's re-membered voice again. Enola had made no effort to in-clude a personality module in the system—the voice was reminder enough of the dead past—but even so, it was too easy to hear a note of reproof in the revenant's tone. *"Re-genics confirmed your appointment. Lyle Chesney indi-cates that your business e-mail and Mesh accounts have been closed and Security is reviewing all personal files prior to forwarding them. And a Keith Arreigh of Zonix In-fotainment recorded a personal message."*

She supposed that a message from Fortinbras would have been too much to expect, but the one from Chesney just made her feel worse. She was glad she had missed talking to him directly again. The last name was com-pletely unfamiliar, though. As her stomach settled, Enola muttered, "Who's Arreigh? What does he want?"

"Hasbro! Hey! That's Korean, right?" Chipper and cheerful, the unfamiliar voice the apartment played back now was that of a man, and apparently of a man who was very pleased with something. He spoke with an enthusiasm that Enola, at the moment, found alarming. Whether it was

talking to her that delighted him, or the world in general, or even just the experience of being Keith Arreigh, she couldn't guess. *"You don't know me, but have I got news for you! I want to—"*

The cheerful tones grated. "Stop it. Delete the call," Enola commanded, and the message died. She was in no mood for a man who spoke entirely in exclamations.

"THIS place is an acoustical nightmare," Bainbridge said. Standing near the center of the foundry floor, he spoke loudly, to emphasize his point. "And it will be worse when we're working, because they'll be working, too."

His words bounced from one hard, high wall to another and then down from the segmented, retractable roof of the casting room. They found heavy banks of machinery that surrounded him and bounded off of those, too, so that each syllable came back in time to overlap and obscure the one before.

Also surrounding him were perhaps twenty production crew members, exploring the place's nooks and crannies. They scuttled about the industrial space, clinging to wall handholds and swinging from roof stanchions as they took readings and strung support cables for cameras and other equipment. They chattered among themselves as they worked, further polluting the sound landscape.

Despite the background noise and concomitant reverberations, Sarrah Chrysler could understand Bainbridge well enough. That wasn't because she could hear him clearly; she couldn't. It was because she had heard him deliver much the same speech in much the same timbre several times before. The content was sufficiently familiar that she could recognize each of his specific complaints by duration and tone.

He was right, though. Mesh production in the foundry *would* be a nightmare. Steelwork was not a quiet process, but one of hammering thunder, roaring motors, and hissing spills of molten metal. The cavernous confines, surrounded only by native stone, would catch those sounds, and the foundry apparatus's complex surfaces, all of them potential reflectors, ensured that those echoes would interfere with one another. The ambient noise alone would be terrific, and echoing cross-talk would make it worse.

But that would be Bainbridge's problem.

"Use suppressors," she said. Her words, too, bounced and slid around the walls that surrounded them. Not particularly wanting to, she moved closer to him as the conversation moved into new areas. She needed to be sure that he heard her clearly. "Use lots of them," she continued. "There will be a booth, too. And baffles."

"I could use suppressors and the booth and foam every surface and member in here," Bainbridge said snappishly. He was obviously tired and had long since become tiresome. "It wouldn't be enough. The only solution is to set the cameras for backdrop info and then mirage you into the feed."

"We're not going to do that," Sarrah said. She looked herself today, fine-featured and attractive, even in mufti, clad in a bulky jumpsuit that did little to flatter her body. She didn't mind. Though relatively newly refurbished, the casting room was a bit chill, and test pours had left the place masked with soot and dirt. Anything that protected her from the cold and the grit was fine with Sarrah. "The audience wants to see me sweat."

It was cool in the foundry, but Sarrah knew that the temperature was only temporary. The injection cauldron that hung overhead was proof of that. Huge and heavy, it swung on gymbal-mounted moorings from the track that ran the length of the big room. The vessel's spouted lip was stained and eroded, marked by past pours. In use, that same vessel would glow white, heated by the liquid alloy intended to form engine casings for the first deep space probes of Project Ad Astra. Those were the engines that could carry mankind into trans-Plutonian space. When that first Pour happened, mere weeks from now, the air here would be thick with thunder, heat, and soot.

Bainbridge rolled his eyes. By his standards, Sarrah knew, sweat was no indicator of authenticity or realism, but an imperfection to be miraged out. Personally, Sarrah tended to agree, but she didn't say so.

"I'm not a tyro," she said instead, permitting herself to sound a bit testier. "And I've seen the production budget. We can do this. You can block out most of the ambient noise before it reaches the sound pickups and condition the rest out of the feed."

"It's not the right way to do it," Bainbridge said. "We can achieve greater image fidelity and audio accuracy—"

"With mirages?" Sarrah interrupted. She allowed herself a laugh, a short, sharp sound that carried well. "What do you think a mirage *is?*"

Bainbridge didn't respond.

Sarrah sighed. "Here," she said. "Let's see how it looks, at least. Or plays." She moved to a likely spot and gestured to a point ten or twelve meters farther away, but facing her. She waited patiently until the production specialist positioned himself where she had indicated, in a fair approximation of a likely camera stance. She nodded and clicked on her phones. What she was about to record would be useless for any Mesh purposes, of course, but it would give Bainbridge a rough—very rough—idea of what she wanted.

The world seemed to retreat a bit as Sarrah took a deep breath and centered herself. Almost without conscious effort, she composed her unadorned features into a mask of earnest professionalism. With the ease of long practice, she made eye contact with a camera that was not there, looking past it to engage with her future audience. The first lines of a tentative rough draft drifted up from the depths of her memory.

"This is where it will happen," she said, gesturing for emphasis. "Here, in a place of fire and steel, humanity will take the next step on a long road to the stars."

* * *

"YOU like alcohol, don't you?" Dr. Huerta said. "That can make this more difficult."

"I don't drink very often," Enola said, lying reflexively. It sometimes surprised her how often she lied to figures of authority. She blinked, then winced. The insides of her eyelids felt rough. "Does it have to be so bright in here?" she asked.

.Huerta laughed. "I didn't ask about frequency," he said. "And you don't need to answer. I ran a full scan on your liver. You consumed an inordinate amount of alcohol within the last eighteen hours."

Enola had barely made it to Regenics in time for her appointment. The following session had been an insane crush of events. She had removed her clothes, drunk fluids, had sensors glued to her head, breasts, and other body parts, and then lain under an equipment array. For twenty minutes, Huerta had asked questions that were, by turns, insensitive, intrusive, and offensive. Now, wearing a gown and perched on the examination table, she wished desperately that he would give her back her clothes and let her go home.

"I didn't know that a liver scan was part of the process," was all she said. "I don't remember having one last time."

Huerta shook his head. "You wouldn't. We did them differently then," he said. He checked her file, displayed on a nearby console. "You were younger, and so was the process. When they adjusted you to accommodate long-term low-G, they didn't know some of the things we do now."

Enola didn't think she liked the sound of that.

He looked at her and smiled. "There's no need to panic," he said. "But that doesn't mean there's no cause for concern, either. You exercise regularly, right?" He spoke as if he knew the answer to that, too.

Enola nodded. "Every day," she said.

"You know why?" he asked.

She nodded again. "Muscle density and bone mass retention," she said. "Mineral retention."

"Astronauts in the last century complained about loss of muscle tone when they returned from all but the shortest trips," Huerta said. White-haired and courtly, he spoke with what Enola suspected was a deliberately cultivated air of authority. "The body is lazy," he continued. "It adjusts quickly to a reduced load. Longer stays in zero-G led to the loss of bone mass, too, as minerals leached out. The early stages of osteoporosis set in, for some. It takes longer in low-G than in zero, but it happens here, too."

"I know that," Enola said. She shivered, uncomfortable. It was cool in the examination room, and the gown she wore was a light disposable. She wasn't eager to hear a lecture she still remembered from twelve years before, even if Huerta was clearly eager to deliver it. "I've been through the therapy before."

He shook his head. "No," he said. "You haven't. You've had the initial protocol, but not regression sequence. That's not as easy. Or as consistently reliable."

"I—I don't understand," Enola said slowly. It had never occurred to her that there could be complications. Everything was so easy now. "Just do it again, but in reverse."

Huerta frowned slightly. He settled into the chair opposite the examination table and paused a moment, considering his next words. He glanced again at his display, read something that Enola could not see, and nodded. "You're an engineer, I believe?" he asked. "You should understand manufacturing processes."

"No," Enola replied. "Not an engineer, but I know a little bit about it. I specialize in modeling presentations." Her job—her *former* job—entailed knowing a little bit about a lot of things. She worked with specialists and marketers to create three-dimensional mirages and animations, to demonstrate what Duckworth could do and how.

"That's close enough. You should have enough of a technical background," Huerta said. He smiled again, sure at last of how to proceed. "The body is a highly refined instrument," he said. "Billions of years of research and development shaped it." He paused. "*Your* factory settings are written very deeply. We can change some, but not all of them."

"I know about that," Enola said. Still nervous, she tapped with delicate fingertips on the table's padded surface. She very much wanted to leave. The cool air of the physician's office held a faint chemical scent she associated with illness and death. She didn't like it. The lighting was harsh and bright and made her eyes hurt. "I've heard it all before, twelve years ago," she said. "The first time. Can't you just—"

"But if you're returning to Earth for long term, we have to undo those changes," he interrupted. "That isn't as easy, for a variety of reasons."

Now, Enola was certain that she didn't like the sound of what he was saying.

"The first time, technicians made small adjustments to hormone production, and metabolism, and other factors," he said. "Maybe not as small as they should have been. They used programmed viral sequences, especially bred for the process. Hormone doses sped things along. You were a teenager, which made it easier. You were already changing, and all they had to do was add to that change."

Enola could remember pills and injections, and a nose that had run for a week and ears that had rung for longer, all in an Earthside hospital. She could remember the anxious bedside watch by two of her mothers as their only remaining daughter lay sick with the symptoms of transition.

The worst part had been the expressions on her mothers' faces. She remembered the sorrow that they had shown at losing another daughter so soon after their first, no matter how different a form that loss took.

Then, Enola had not cared. Now, sometimes, she did.

"They said it would be easy to backtrack," Enola said. "They promised."

"But it's been a long time, and that was the old technique," Huerta said. "We don't use it anymore. We've learned a lot in fifteen years. You're an old-timer by modern gene therapy standards."

Enola had heard that kind of rhetoric before. Too often in her experience, saying that a process had been improved was a tactful way of admitting that there were problems in the old method. She bit her lip but didn't say anything.

"If we•were doing it now, the revisions themselves would be less extensive, for one thing," Huerta said. "We're more careful, and we try not to make any changes we don't have to. These are the fundamental elements of life we're rearranging, after all, and evolution spent billions of years putting them in place. Now, we have to be sure that we put things back exactly the way they were. Otherwise—"

"What do you mean?" Enola asked. Her eyes widened. "You said this was going to be easier! Do I have go back to the hospital?" Unless matters changed, only eight weeks remained for her on the Moon, and the idea of spending one of them under a physician's constant care wasn't attractive.

"No, no, no. The new technique is fast and relatively safe," Huerta reassured her. "To change you back, we'll reference a file copy of your own DNA, conditioned for slow-dose administration via retrovirus. Rejection won't—*shouldn't* be a problem. But the resequencing required in your case is extensive, and there might be some issues along the way. We'll need to monitor things closely."

Panic touched her. "Will I get sick again? Could I die?" Enola asked. She had never intended to go back to Earth except perhaps for a visit. Now that permanent relocation loomed, the idea that it brought hazards with it frightened her.

He laughed, but it sounded hollow. "No, no," Huerta said. "You might have some rough nights, but you're not going to die!" Abruptly, he turned serious again. "But after fifteen years, regression will be a challenge. You're not a teenager now, and your body is more set in its ways. It can still change, but it doesn't want to. Look at it this way: There is only limited play in your factory specifications, and the adjustments get more difficult each time."

"But I'll be all right?" Enola asked anxiously.

"You should be," Huerta said. "Insomnia is likely, though. You might experience some weight gain, no matter how much you exercise, but I think we can compensate for that."

The image of Lyle Chesney, fat almost beyond the scope of humanity, flashed through Enola's mind. The big man had said something about gene patches not working for him anymore. Huerta had said that the adjustments got progressively more difficult, and that meant it became progressively easier for things to go wrong. She shuddered.

If Huerta noticed, he didn't comment. "Minimize your alcohol intake," he continued. "The same goes for other euphoriants. Between your liver and overall metabolic shift, you'll have difficulty processing them. You'll be uncomfortable. You may experience kinesthetic hallucinations."

She looked at him blankly.

"*Kinesthesia* is the sense that tells your body where it is, how much it weighs, and where it's moving," he explained. "It's how you can tell where your hand is, without looking to see. You may have some difficulties as you transition. They may present as lightheadedness, or impaired reflexes."

"Will I be in danger?" Enola asked. Even with half a bottle of the blue stuff still inside her, she still felt queasy.

It was as if she had not spoken. Huerta made no reply, but leaned close, dabbed something cool on her forearm, and pressed a small square of translucent film into place. He nodded in approval. "There," he said. "Now let it work."

Enola eyed the gene patch warily. Already, the wisp of gossamer membrane had begun to fade. It was submerging into her skin and fusing with the flesh beneath. As she watched, the last of the patch disappeared, but she knew the agents it carried were with her still.

Huerta presented her with a small case, no larger than an appliance compact. He opened it, revealing more of the gene patches and pretreated chemical swabs. After she nodded in acknowledgment, he closed the case and thumbed the lid display to life. Lines of instructions scrolled by, too fast for her to read. "These patches are for you, made *from* you," he said. "Apply one, once a day, at about this time. Follow my example. Drink plenty of fluids and get lots of rest, and see me again next week. Call the service if you have any difficulties—any at all. And don't be late next time, or you'll forfeit your appointment."

She didn't say much to that. Her attention was drawn by a tingling sensation in her forearm. She was certain that it was psychosomatic, prompted by mental suggestion, but it seemed real. Genuine or not, it commanded her attention.

Within her body, she knew, her cells were being rewritten, one at a time. In a very real sense, she was already on her way back to Earth.

"BE *careful, Erik,"* Wendy Scheer said.

The feed ended. The wallpaper display reverted to its default settings, canned images captured in the depths of the Marianas Trench. Pale and luminescent, exotic fish drifted lazily through prerecorded darkness.

Erik leaned back in his easy chair as he considered Scheer's recorded words. The placid murk of the Earth's deepest place helped him order his thoughts, never a very easy thing to do when dealing with the chief administrator of Armstrong Base. For the moment, at least, the lingering pleasure of hearing her voice far outweighed the import of her words. A reassuring sense of tranquility had taken the edges off of the world. It was always like this when Wendy called, and it made communicating with her difficult.

The manual remote was still where he had left it, on the end table. He raised it now and placed the ball of one thumb on its spring-loaded switch. He rocked it back and forth, testing it. Everything seemed in order.

"Replay that," he said in his command voice, and took a deep breath. "I'll take it from here."

"Hello, Erik," Wendy Scheer said, as she sprang into focus on the wall. She was an attractive woman, but not

beautiful. She had the same kind of practical good looks possessed by Sarrah Chrysler, good bones and good skin, and expressive eyes that obviated the need for most cosmetic appliances. His heart sped a bit as he saw her. *"I was really hoping to talk to you in real time."* She paused. *"For a change."*

Erik almost laughed at that. Scheer knew that they weren't likely to speak in real time at any point in the near future—at least, not with his consent. She knew that he was one of the few who knew her secret, and certainly understood the impact that his awareness had to have on their communications.

Wendy Scheer had what a researcher in the previous century had termed a "wild talent." People liked her. The underlying mechanism was unknown and did not really matter. A chance encounter with her cheered, and made a man see the world as a brighter place. A directed smile, a few kind words, a brush of her fingertips—those were enough to create a permanent attraction and desire to please. The effect was not overwhelming and didn't seem to be particularly sexual in nature. It could be worked against consciously, but most did not even realize that it existed. That was how much of the Scheer network had been built, by exploiting casual meetings and random encounters. Many of those who met her ended up working for her, directly or indirectly.

Erik had met Wendy Scheer. He had eaten with her and drank with her. They had even waltzed in a trompe l'oeil forest to the strains of Strauss, the same evening he had danced with Enola Hasbro. He liked Wendy, very much. But he was the one who had identified the Scheer effect, and he knew how to resist it.

The prerecorded Wendy got down to business. *"First, I wish you'd quit getting rid of people,"* she said, clearly irritated. *"Or at least, get rid of fewer of them. You're casting your net too wide and ruining too many lives. Poor Souphanousinphone doesn't even know how to speak Laotian; he won't do well at all. And Aelita Hanover—"*

Erik thumbed the remote control. Wendy went silent, and the picture sped forward. He liked listening to her voice, but he knew better than to overindulge. Initial, in-person contact activated the Scheer effect. Subsequent Mesh communications could reinforce it. Time-shifting the messages reduced the effect further, but didn't eliminate it. Being safe was better than being sorry.

Besides, he'd already watched the message at normal speed twice. This was where she went down an abbreviated version of Kowalski's list, demonstrating her intimate knowledge of what were supposed to be confidential details.

"—worth proposal shop," Scheer concluded as he released the switch. *"It hardly seems fair."*

Erik thumbed the control again. This time, the image froze. "I'm sorry, Wendy," he said, speaking clearly so that his words would record well. "I had nothing to do with any of those personnel." He didn't like lying, but it really wasn't very hard, at least not under these circumstances.

"I'm sure you'll deny any influence on these actions," Wendy resumed. *"But my objections are on the record. You're being unnecessarily disruptive to the workforces of several federal procurements."*

Again, he almost laughed, this time as much at the odd turn their relationship had taken as at what she said. In a very different way than seven years before, he was still dancing with Wendy Scheer. As her designated liaison within ALC Over-Management, he communicated with her on a regular basis. As someone who was subject to and aware of her allure, he took pains to keep those conversations insulated by time and space. They were rival authorities on the Ad Astra Project, so each kept track of the other's activities, and each made certain that the other knew of the surveillance.

He didn't suppose she cared about Souphanousinphone or Hanover or even Enola Hasbro. She was concerned only with letting him know that she knew more than he would have preferred.

He used his remote again. "Thank you for the advice,

Wendy," he said, careful to look mildly puzzled as he faced the phone camera. "But I don't even know who most of those people are. I think you overestimate my influence. Certainly, you seem to think I have more authority than I do. I can't terminate anyone. Most of my work is in public relations now."

More lies.

"Now, here's the real reason I called," Scheer said, as the recorded feed resumed. *"Do you recognize him?"*

She brought something into the phone's field of view and presented it to Erik. It was a hardprint image. Erik paused the feed again. He murmured a few commands to isolate the picture and enlarge it.

A face that he had never seen before gazed out at him from the phone display. It was the face of a younger man, at least twenty years his junior, with blonde hair and features that bordered on the pretty. Even in the single still image, he looked reserved, even slightly condescending. He wore data-lenses in circular that Erik supposed were intended to look old-fashioned. It was an affectation he had seen before.

Erik left the isolated image frozen but released the rest of the feed. He didn't bother to record a response.

"This is the unfortunate Erik Morrison," Wendy Scheer said. She smiled. Even prerecorded, the effect was startling. *"He worked for EnTek. He just returned to Earth after a stay on the Moon."*

She managed perhaps half a laugh before the feed froze again, in obedient response to a thumbed switch. Erik stared at the twin images frozen on his wallpaper, choosing his words carefully. The contrast between Scheer's amused expression and his namesake's cool one didn't help matters. Neither did Scheer's use of *unfortunate* and *worked,* words that carried ominous implications.

"It's a common name," he finally replied, for no good reason. "I'm not familiar with him, however."

Scheer's laugh faded almost instantly as her feed resumed. *"I'm sorry,"* she said. *"But I wish I could see your expression."*

Erik was rather happy that she couldn't.

"But I really shouldn't laugh," she continued. *"It's really not very funny. He's dead, Erik. And we don't think it's a coincidence."*

She recited the basic data-points in tones that were cool and matter-of-fact, and Erik listened again. The other Erik Morrison had been twenty years younger than Erik, a seven-year veteran of EnTek Europe. Following a honeymoon in Villanueva, he had returned to Earth a month before, to a new billet in France, where he had joined a brainware research team. A week later, he had died on the job, when a demonstration by an anti-Ad Astra group, the Gondwanalanders, had collapsed into a riot. The other Erik's broken, bloody body had been found at the bottom of an airshaft.

"The local authorities think that he was trying to escape the scrambler gas bombs, but we think different," Scheer continued. She didn't bother say who "we" were. *"We think it was a case of deliberate murder and mistaken identity,"* she said. *"Someone thought they saw an opportunity to hurt the Ad Astra Project and got him instead. These people aren't particularly intelligent, after all."*

Erik thought again about the French developmental facility. A moment's research had confirmed for him that the place was reasonably secure and that the people who ran it knew what they were doing. But the anti-Ad Astra movement manifested most of what strength it had on the continent, and those who belonged to that movement had never struck him as being particularly competent. "Just because they don't share your—*our*—vision for the Ad Astra Project," he said, activating the record function again, "doesn't mean they aren't intelligent. I'll include some background on EnTek France with this."

"It might even have been a warning, an indirect one," Scheer continued. *"I hope you'll treat it that way, Erik. I like working with you. I don't want to see anything bad happen."*

He nodded reflexively. He knew that she could not see

him, but he felt the need to make some response to what
seemed to be sincere concern.

That was the maddening part of dealing with her. The
attraction that she projected made her true motives and priorities much harder to assess and balance. For the entire
course of his association with Wendy Scheer, he had always been conscious of something like affection, or at
least real respect, on her part. It seeped out sometimes
from behind the masking effect of her allure, at once startling and distracting. Conferences like this would be much
easier if he discounted such comments completely, but he
couldn't.

"I know," he said, but didn't record it.

"I'll send you a backgrounder," Scheer continued, all
business again. *"Be careful, Erik."*

CHAPTER 5

THE following days flowed one into another, desperately hectic and yet passing with paradoxical slowness. In the mornings, the hours when she did her best creative work, Enola labored on her portfolio. She knew all too well that her only chance of staying on the Moon was to find a new position with another company. That knowledge and that chance, however small, were all that drove her from her bed in the morning and forced her to meet the day.

Every minute she spent at her personal apartment workstation seemed wasted. She had long opted out of working at home, having graduated to the synergy of colleagues and an office setting. Now that her circumstances had changed so dramatically, she found that her modeling system had not. Time had been cruel to it. The modular hardware was hopelessly out of date, its built-in Gummis generations old. They would have been unable to comprehend, let alone run, current brainware releases, even if Enola had been able to afford them. If only she had taken advantage of Duckworth's generous upgrade policies.

Again and again, she told herself that the tools did not matter. Again and again, reality proved the tools wrong.

Enola's fingers flowed across the touchpad, stroking here, pressing there as they traced elaborate contours. In response, light bent above the modeler display bank, looping and bending back to touch itself. Gossamer strands seemed to materialize in midair, then take on form and structure and even stolidity. A few more finger-strokes and their boundaries became cleaner, and the illusionary surfaces glistened. Enola murmured a few command words and tapped recessed keys, and the elaborate, three-dimensional image of a construction lattice shifted slightly, as the Gummi processed engineering data and made appropriate accommodations.

Titanium steel was funny stuff; it had its own idiosyncrasies and preferences. A crossbeam of X meters' thickness could support only Y tons of load if shaped in such and such an arc. Curve that same steel a few more degrees, however, and it could bear up under Z tons quite readily.

Unfortunately, the human eye didn't like the new arc and preferred the old one. That was where a good designer would adjust the next buttress to create a complementary, balancing line and produce visual harmony again. Unfortunately, each concession to aesthetics presented new engineering challenges of its own, and the requirement revisions rippled anew across the entire project.

Temperature ranges, projected load, environmental and operational factors—one by one, she accessed the appropriate data points and fed them to the modeler. Each time, she adjusted and worried and worked, trying to tease the modeler into recreating the image in her mind's eye. The results didn't need to be perfect, but they needed to be good enough to show that she knew how to model.

Mesh databases, consumer-level quality and available to everyone, provided passably accurate data. Enola told the modeler what to do with that data. The modeler's brainware was supposed to bridge the gaps between conceptual framing and reality, to create a realistic illusion. The best models were almost palpable demonstrations of how the final versions would look and sound and even smell.

Enola closed the Mesh links, locking out the dataflow. She pressed keys and murmured more command words. The color of her holographic construct shifted as the hypothetical light source moved. The caws of gulls and the sibilant susurrus of river water sounded from the ceiling speakers. The rich, organic scent of a living, working river filled the air. Enola leaned back in her chair.

A miniature of the Huang-Lu "Catfish" Hawkins Memorial Mississippi River Bridge stretched from one end of her workstation to the other. It seemed to glow beneath the rays of a rising sun. The ends of the bridge faded, as if into fog banks, and its pylons' illusory bases vanished into the equally illusory dirty gray depths of the once-mighty Mississippi River. To a casual, untrained and educated eye, the image seemed perfect.

Enola knew that it was not, and the knowledge gnawed at her. She opened a new view and reviewed the underlying data. All seemed to be in order, at least from a technical standpoint. From an aesthetic angle, however, other concerns were evident.

She shook her head. Some quality, ineffable but real, was missing. The model seemed accurate, and perhaps it was, but it did not *convince*. It did not *sell,* neither itself nor Enola.

That was Enola's gift, the ability to take the stuff of reality and make it a promise that would be believed, and to know when it would not. For a proposal model to work, it had to be more than accurate; it had to be *right*.

Enola was only a middling artist. With much study and aggressive reference, she might have made a mediocre engineer. That wasn't what mattered. She understood enough of both disciplines to yoke them together, and had enough adaptability to address the needs of widely varying projects. With appropriate technical data and the right imaging tools, she could make a convincing case for almost any solution. Each year, Villanueva-originated proposals had won Duckworth billions of new-dollars of major-scale construction projects. With the right tools and the right resources, Enola had made substantive contributions to that success.

She didn't have them now, she realized with a sick feeling. Her gift remained, but demonstrating it was impossibly difficult in this context. Standards had risen too much in the years since she had purchased her home kit.

The modeler was hopelessly out of date, the data she could access on the Mesh was insufficiently refined, and from her recent tenure, she knew that standards had risen exponentially since her home system's last update. To find new work, she would need to demonstrate brilliance or absolute competence, and she couldn't do either. Brilliance was beyond her, and the outdated modeler lent the sheen of the nearly primitive to her work, at least by professional standards. The model was good, but it wasn't good enough.

She was good, for that matter, but she wasn't good enough.

She moaned very softly, then filed the draft model and started a new one. It was silly to try such a large-scale project, anyway, especially one that already existed. Duckworth proper certainly wasn't going to hire her back, not on the Moon. But there were many subsidiaries and subcontractors producing environmental systems and incidentals. Enola could adapt. Something smaller and more intimate might work for her.

The engineering specs for most Villanueva residential units were reasonably consistent, and reasonably detailed files were readily available. She had some small experience in marketing interior design services. If she could offer some company a convincing habitat presentation that embodied existing elements—

"Noon," Donelle's voice said, breaking the hours of silence that had stretched since a quick, casual breakfast. Enola worked better in the presence of others, but when alone, she needed quiet.

"File," Enola said, relieved. The morning hours were her best for creative work, but these particular morning hours hadn't been very good at all.

The first sketchy lines of a bilevel apartment faded as the modeler shut itself down. She stood and stretched, twisting herself just enough to tease the tension from her back muscles. She placed one hand in the other and squeezed. Knuckles popped. Despite herself, Enola made a slight smile, suddenly very hungry.

"What's for lunch?" she asked in her command voice.

The housekeeper recited a list of readymeal options as Enola drifted slowly toward the eating nook. The faintest hint of vertigo went with her. Now that she was up and moving around, the world seemed suddenly a bit less solid, as if ready to give way beneath her. She had experienced this before. It was either a generalized anxiety or one of the kinesthetic illusions Huerta had mentioned. Either way, food would help.

"Soy-elves," she told the system. "And mushrooms. Tea."

"You have fourteen messages," the housekeeper said. It ran down the list quickly. Eight were from people that Enola had thought friends, declining social invitations. Five were from prospective employers, announcing that they had reviewed her applications and found her qualifications to be a poor match for their needs.

One was from Crag Fortinbras.

Her meal was ready. She took it from the autostove and leaned against the counter. One by one, she speared soy-elves from the multicompartment dish and popped the little creatures into her mouth. They giggled as she ate them. Each was a trademarked intellectual property creation, co-branded by Zonix Lifesystems and Biome Consumables. They were good but easy and inexpensive, which suited her current mood and budget.

Enola didn't particularly like hand-cooking or dining alone at home. She liked eating out. She liked being with other people. Her current days, spent almost entirely at home, wore. But ever since that terrible ride home from Chesney's office, she had felt the world pulling away from her. Old friends and lovers had responded to social invitations with polite rebuffs. Business associates had made excuses not to see her, or to review her portfolio. Her list of contacts had dwindled with disturbing speed. She felt like something unclean.

She remembered the look of pity Narçissa had given her on the commuter train. They all looked at her like that now, Enola realized sadly. And she was terribly lonely.

She finished the elves and moved on to the thick slices of mushroom. Quick, small sips of pungent black tea from a waiting carafe punctuated her meal.

The one exception to her de facto exile was Fortinbras. After days of mutual silence, and after she had transitioned from shame to irritation to confused desperation, he had begun calling again. The housekeeper had captured a dozen messages from him, ranging from abject apologies to blasé greetings to eager invitations and back again. All of them, she had purged from the system.

"There is a visitor," Donelle's voice announced.

"Show me," she said, suspecting the worst.

The display above the autostove presented feed from the outside corridor. Fortinbras was there, in his work clothes, hair slicked back and teeth gleaming as he smiled.

"Enola?" he said, leaning close to the camera. *"Enola? Are you there? Answer, please! We've been worried."*

She doubted that. Terminations weren't common, but she had seen enough of them in her career to know their aftermath. By now, no one in the old offices was likely even to mention her name, because no one was eager for the uncomfortable silence that would surely follow.

"I brought you a present," Fortinbras said. He held up the box so that the housekeeper camera could see it more clearly. It was big and square and had handles on the side to ease carrying. *"Let me in. It's heavy."*

"What do you want, Crag?" she asked.

She knew what he wanted.

"Oh! You're there! I—I just wanted to see you, Enola. I wanted to make sure that you were well," Fortinbras said.

Enola sighed. She didn't believe him, but she was

lonely, and she liked getting presents. "Wait a moment," she said. "Let me get dressed."

A few minutes later, when the door slid open, she wore a blouse and slacks, neat but casual. She had been careful to select an outfit with nothing suggestive about it. She didn't want to give him any ideas, or remind him of ones he already had.

"Hello, Crag," she said, and gestured for him to enter.

He set the case down on the foyer table and leaned forward to kiss her, but she dodged neatly. "It's good to see you, Enola," he said. "I was worried."

She glanced at him, but said nothing. This was awkward. Things were always awkward when they were outside her control. She had meant it, the previous week when she had told him he didn't interest her. She could say the same thing now, and mean it. But given what had happened between them, when she was desperate and lonely, he was sure to think otherwise.

Fortinbras twisted the handles on the case, and it came apart neatly. It was a smart-box, expensive and trendy. The textured plastic hardshell went limp as he disengaged it, reverting to a membrane that folded easily. "There," he said, the gift revealed.

"Oh, Crag," Enola said, genuinely impressed.

It was beautiful. He had brought her a self-contained aquarium unit. Cubical, perhaps half a meter on each axis, its plastic walls and top were absolutely transparent. It looked like a block of water confined by nothing other than air. Drifting through that six-surfaced space were a dozen fish of various colors, swimming in elaborate patterns shaped both by instinct and by gene-work. Reaching up from the base, which hid mechanisms that fed the fish and cleaned the water, fronds waved in obeisance to unseen currents.

"It must have been very expensive," Enola said, captivated by the living kaleidoscope. A thought struck her, and she sighed. "But I can't take it," she said.

"Of course you can," Fortinbras replied. He was standing

closer to her now, close enough that she could feel the warmth of his body.

She shook her head. "No. No, really, I can't," she said. "I'm going back to Earth, and I can't take it with me."

"Keep it until you leave, then," Fortinbras said. "Besides, maybe you won't have to go. You're looking, aren't you?"

Enola had nothing to say to that.

"How long until you leave?" Fortinbras asked.

"Eight weeks," Enola said sadly. "No. Seven."

"Seven weeks is a long time," Fortinbras said. He sounded surprisingly sincere. He really could be sweet, Enola realized. "Things can change a lot in that amount of time."

Enola thought of the draft presentation, filed away. She thought of the applications and personal calls she intended to place over the course of the afternoon. "I'm trying to change them," she said. She paused. "How is everyone?"

He shrugged, looking at her as she looked at the fish, adrift in their self-enclosed world. "The same. Nothing ever changes at Duckworth," he said. "Not really. You know that."

"I can think of one thing that's different," Enola said dryly. She turned to look at him. "Why didn't you call?" she asked.

"I've called a dozen times," Fortinbras said, raising his hands as if in defense. "I can send you copies."

"Those were later. Why didn't you call the day after?" Enola was surprised at how much she wanted to know.

"I don't know why I didn't," Fortinbras said. He sounded slightly embarrassed.

"I told you I wasn't interested in you that way," Enola said.

Fortinbras smiled. "You changed your mind," he said, with an easy confidence that bordered on the oafish.

Enola rested her fingertips on the aquarium top and felt the almost imperceptible vibrations of hidden mechanisms, of filtering pumps and aerators and food dispensers.

She thought back to that day, to how angry she'd been at him in the morning and how unhappy she'd been when she got back to her home that evening.

"Not really," she said. That was the hell of it. She had made a mistake.

Fortinbras looked unhappy for a moment, then shrugged. "Would you like to go dancing tonight?" he asked.

Enola blinked. "I just told you," she said. "I haven't changed my mind."

He shrugged again. "So?" he asked. He smiled at her, and the smile seemed sincere. "We could have fun. I'm not busy, and I don't think you are, either. You should be with someone when you're this unhappy, Enola. Even if it's not someone you want."

Almost despite herself, Enola smiled, too.

AFTER he'd left, and as Enola lugged the cumbersome aquarium to a more appropriate place of display, the housekeeper spoke again. *"Keith Arreigh is recording a message. He is aware that you were otherwise engaged, but would like very much to speak with you."*

The name was familiar, but it took Enola a moment to remember where she had heard it. As she set the aquarium in a convenient wall niche, the memory came back. Arreigh had called the week before, when she was readying herself for the appointment with Huerta. Other than that, she had no idea who he was.

"Summarize," she commanded.

"It regards a potential employment opportunity," the apartment told her.

"I need information on someone," Erik Morrison said. He leaned back and rested his feet on his desk's faux marble top. "How good are your assets on Earth?"

"Reasonably good," Kowalski replied. He didn't look

directly at Erik but focused instead on a personal handheld. The device had a featureless shell made of brush-finished metal and offered no clue as to its nature. Erik was reasonably certain that it was some kind of toy or game, but it could have been something more utilitarian. Kowalski's appetite for gadgets was boundless. "Horvath is still our advocate, so I have reasonable access to EnTek's resources," Kowalski continued. "The other sisters aren't as generous, but we work—technically—for Over-Managment now, so there is some cooperation. Better here, though."

The five ALC sister companies engaged less in full partnership than in an informed alliance. Each had interests in common with the others; each had interests opposed to the others. The pooling of security and intelligence assets had been tentative since the coalition's earliest days.

"Find out what you can about Erik Morrison, then," Erik said.

He didn't have to wait long for a reaction. Almost instantly, Kowalski fixed him with a glance that flowed quickly from the quizzical to the studiously neutral as he concealed his surprise. Then he did something to the handheld, nodded, and laughed softly. "Over the years, I've found out quite a bit," he said. "But I think you already know most of it."

"I'm talking about a different Erik Morrison," Erik said, and handed the other man the hardprint that he had made by isolating part of Scheer's recorded feed. "Here," he said. "This one."

Kowalski examined the image carefully, then tucked it away with his free hand. Though his choice of wardrobe styles ran the full gamut from undistinguished to nondescript, most of Kowalski's clothing these days included multiple pockets, to hide his toys and the various tools of his trade. One of them now became the home of the unfortunate younger Morrison.

In quick, matter-of-fact tones, Erik summarized the subject of Scheer's call, along with the results of his own, tentative research. He could have accomplished the same download by mail or via Mesh, but since relocating to the Moon, he had manifested a new fondness for face-to-face. There was so much more that a good observer could learn, especially if he made an effort to look past the surface.

That was only part of the reason, though, and a bit of rationalization. More to do with fundamental human nature and inherited social instincts. One of his first acquaintances in Villanueva had explained that. Living some four hundred thousand kilometers from the world of Mankind's birth tended to make people huddle, just a bit, no matter how much therapies had changed them.

"It sounds to me like someone was unlucky," Kowalski said. "But I'll learn what I can. Was he working on anything important?"

"Nothing that hundreds of others weren't working on, too," Erik said. "And in more prominent roles. They're still alive."

"You don't think it's a coincidence?"

"Wendy doesn't," Erik said.

Kowalski snorted. He had made it a point never to meet Wendy Scheer in person, but he had researched her thoroughly and didn't like her. Even though he recognized the utility of Erik's ongoing liaisons with her, he didn't approve of them. "She's only trying to keep you distracted," he said. "She saw the name on a list and saw her chance, too. Or she had it done herself."

"You might be right," Erik said. He didn't particularly mind when Kowalski disagreed with him, as long as his instructions got followed. "But look into it."

"It sounds to me like what you need more is information on opposition groups," Kowalski said. He had returned his attention to the handheld, eyeing the small display and moving one thumb along the thing's control surface.

"You can help with that, too, then," Erik said. An ample number of organizations were bitterly opposed to the Ad Astra Project, cadres convinced that the credit would be better spent on food or housing or any of a score of other priorities. He could understand that. A mere ten years before, he had been skeptical about the value of Villanueva itself, let alone trans-Plutonian exploration. The *Voyager* find had changed his mind about such things, but others had not been so easily convinced. Already, he received weekly reports on the anti-Ad Astra movements, but there was no harm in getting more data.

"I'm fairly heavily tasked at the moment," Kowalski said. The handheld made a low *ping!,* and he hastily shifted his thumb. The device fell silent, and Kowalski's features became a study in innocence.

Mock innocence, Erik decided. The slip had been deliberate, but he knew better than to bother reacting. Kowalski liked his games entirely too much. "Find time," he said instead. "It was your suggestion, after all. Get me a report by the end of the week."

Kowalski nodded. The device disappeared into one of his various pockets. "I can do that," he said. "But there is another matter of concern."

Erik glanced at him.

"I think I've identified another three members of the Scheer network," Kowalski said. He spoke with utter casualness, as if he attached no particular importance to the words he had said.

Erik did. He didn't like them, and he didn't like their implications. "You told me that last group was the end of it," he said sharply. He took his feet off the desk and twisted in his chair to face Kowalski directly.

The security chief's shoulders went up and came back down in a dismissive gesture. "I told you I thought that those last twenty-three were to be the end of it."

Still blasé, Kowalski continued. "I told you I *thought* they were the end of it," he said. "There's no way to be certain. These may only recently have become active. They may even have been new recruits."

"That's not possible," Erik said. Contact between site residents and Armstrong staff was aggressively monitored and strictly controlled. Wendy Scheer had made no new acquaintances among Villanueva's numbers during the previous five years, at least. That was Over-Management policy, strictly enforced, even if most staff didn't know why.

Kowalski seemed to read his mind. "Of course it's possible," he said. "Villanueva personnel work with federal experts at mining strikes, in study groups, at design reviews. Any of those experts could be your friend."

Again, Erik ignored the veiled accusation, if that were how Kowalski had meant it. "I want an ending," he said. "Deal with them, but put an end to it."

"I can't promise you that," Kowalski said. "These three were probably sleepers. There may be more."

"Make it happen," Erik said, with a sudden weariness. He was tired of destroying careers. "No more. Draw a line and don't go past it."

"It's very difficult to be certain," Kowalski said. "Scheer had the run of this place for years, and she spent half her time here in disguise and under assumed names."

That was true. Among the reasons for Scheer's success had been the diligent use of her unexplained gift, at once subtle and aggressive. He had first encountered her in a crowded restaurant, in a "chance" incident that had played out like a slapstick comedy. A waitress had tripped, food had gone flying, and the woman he only later identified as Wendy Scheer had plucked his entrée from midair. That, and a smile, had been enough. A week later, and a live Mesh call had found him curiously predisposed toward protecting the government woman's interests.

How many other flying pork chops had she caught? How many other men and women had she smiled at, or hooked thumbs with, or nodded toward? Was there, really, any way ever to know?

"I'd rather err on the side of caution," Kowalski continued.

"There's a point where caution becomes madness," Erik said. Not for the first time, an alternate possibility occurred to him, one he did not like. "I hope you're not doing this because you enjoy it," he said.

"There are other reasons," Kowalski said.

"Ones that are reasonable," Erik replied. He fidgeted a bit, something unusual for him, and toyed idly with the computer. He liked to think of himself as both tolerant and reasonable, willing to make the hard decisions but unwilling to take pleasure in them.

Kowalski, he sometimes suspected, looked at things a bit differently.

"We'll need to trim the ranks sooner or later," Kowalski continued. He seemed to think that he was offering an explanation. "The resident population has been kept at inflated levels, to help justify the ALC's case in the courts. With Ad Astra, that's changing."

There was carefully shaded truth in his words. A large resident population counted for something when what remained of the United Nations argued against Villanueva's special status before the World Court. Now, however, with the various Ad Astra contracts in place, the Earth authorities were more interested in working with the ALC infrastructure rather than against it. The hearings hadn't ended, but they had lost much of their urgency.

"Maybe so, but the process won't be for anyone's amusement, I promise you that," Erik said. "What about the others? The last run? Have they made their transitions?"

"They're in process," Kowalski said. The remote quality of his words had increased by some microscopic increment. "I don't expect many difficulties."

"Many?" Erik asked. Options were available to displaced staff, but few and far between. Social pressures made many of them unacceptable to even the most desperate. Kowalski's words were a surprise.

"Enola Hasbro will interview for a potential employment contract at Zonix Infotainment later today," Kowalski said. For the first time in Erik's recent memory, the ordinarily unflappable security chief appeared slightly disconcerted. The effect was subtle enough that it was difficult to perceive, let alone recognize.

"Zonix isn't supposed to hire anyone who has been terminated by one of the other sisters," Erik said. His words were calm, but he was surprised. He knew a little bit about Enola. Even setting aside the issue of her termination, she simply didn't have the skills that would make her an especially desirable candidate for one of the sisters. There were other people who could do the same work better, more cheaply.

"Zonix isn't supposed to even *interview* anyone terminated by one of the sisters," Kowalski said. "That's policy. But they're doing it."

"See what you can find out about that, too," Erik said.

Kowalski nodded again. He paused. "Should I bring anything to your dinner party?" he asked.

"I wasn't aware that you were invited," Erik said.

Kowalski merely smiled.

Erik capitulated. "Just bring yourself," he said dryly. "And a friend, if you have one."

He hadn't told Kowalski about the event, much less invited him. He hadn't seen any point. One way or another, he knew, if Kowalski wanted to attend, he would.

"AH! Enola! Come in, come in," Keith Arreigh said. He smiled. He took her hand in one of his, not to hook thumbs, but to guide her through the open door and into the office foyer. He was taller than she was, perhaps a meter and three quarters, but he moved with such energy that he seemed larger as he whisked the door shut. He said, "I'd offer to take your jacket, but you're not wearing one. Not much need for outer garments in a controlled environment, is there? Silly me! This is the Moon! Would you like something to drink?"

The entire interaction took perhaps seven seconds. It wasn't so much that he spoke rapidly as with enormous energy and enthusiasm. The syllables were precise and cleanly formed, but carried great gusto.

"Thank you, but—" Enola started to say.

"Here, follow," Arreigh said, over his shoulder. He had already taken the lead and was moving fast. He had longish hair, reddish-brown, and he moved rapidly enough to make it flutter a bit. "All we have is imported new-coffee and local alcohol. I wish it were the other way around."

"I—" Enola said, almost tripping as she hurried to keep up. She followed him through the foyer, down a short hallway and into the main office.

Arreigh's sanctum was like none that Enola had ever seen before. If anything, it reminded her almost of a miniature of the Mall, Villanueva's main commercial district. Like the Mall common areas, the office's walls were made up almost entirely of display boards. These, however, did not advertise shops or galleries or restaurants or sexual services, but focused instead on the wares of Zonix Infotainment.

Confronting Enola now were countless images from those programs. Mesh comedies set on the Moon. Mesh dramas about corporate detectives solving crimes on the Moon. Mesh historical dramas featuring unlikely images of the colony's founders. Mesh science fiction thrillers featuring stalwart Villanueva residents tackling outlandish monsters. Mesh concert programs with melancholy chanteuses singing beneath the benign rays of a full Earth. The images flowed, and feed clips flowed across the walls, each giving way to another before encountering its own successor. Shaped acoustic fields brought sound bites to her ears, and even the faintest hints of scent seemed to hang in the air. Almost involuntarily, she paused, basking in media overload.

Villanueva was an enormous, ongoing investment for Zonix and the other four sisters. The colony had been generous in return, providing near-endless subject matter for the lifestyle conglomerate's entertainment divisions. But to experience so much at once . . .

Arreigh paused, too. He turned, looked in her direction, and shrugged. "I know," he said. "It's all terribly déclassé. I told them that I wanted an office, but they gave me an advertising kiosk, instead. And not a one of these feed clips is my work, damn it!" But he smiled as he said it.

He had been smiling ever since opening the door. He probably always smiled.

"I'm certain—" Enola started to say.

"You never did tell me what you wanted to drink," Arreigh said, hurtling toward a refreshment nook. Before Enola could reply, he had plucked a bottle of lavender fluid from somewhere, then placed it and three crystalline flutes on a small silver-finish tray. A moment later, the energetic man was on the move again. "Take a seat, please," he said. "Your choice, but that's the only one that's available." He gestured at the center of the room, and at three low, upholstered chairs and the even lower table between them.

Enola paused, started. So preoccupied had she been with Arreigh's nonstop pleasantries and so impressed by the elaborate display walls that she had not realized that a third person was also in the room. Composed neatly on one of the chairs was a strikingly attractive, vaguely exotic woman with hair that was even blacker than Enola's. She had almost translucently fair skin that seemed never to have encountered even a single ultraviolet ray, and broad, strong features that marked her as of Eastern European descent.

Her host noticed Enola's reaction. "Oh," he said. "I forgot. That's Katalin. Say hello, Katalin." As he spoke, Keith Arreigh decanted the wine.

"Hallo," the woman said. She spoke with a slightly guttural accent. She did not rise and offered only a reserved smile in response to Enola's offered hand.

"You'll like Katalin," Arreigh said. "Katalin Cassidy. She's my—"

"Associate," Cassidy interrupted, stressing the syllables with slight but undeniable wrongness. She reached forward in a liquid motion, appropriated one of the flutes, and leaned back again. She moved with the easy elegance of a natural athlete.

"Associate," Arreigh said, positively beaming. "That's very good. I like that." He sat down, took the second glass, and passed the third to Enola, who had taken a seat next to Cassidy. "I'm Keith Arreigh," he said. "But you already know that. I produce Mesh programming in a strategic alliance with Zonix Infotainment. I have my own little company, of course, but I've always found it makes the most sense to let the prime movers spend the credit."

"I see," said Enola, who really didn't. She still held her glass, its contents untasted.

"Drink up," Arreigh said. "It's plum," he said, and waggled his finger at her. "You'll like it."

Enola looked at the beverage hesitantly. The faint, astringent aroma of alcohol found her, and Huerta's words came back to her. She said, "I'm really not supposed to—"

"Drink!" Arreigh said. "To success!" He brought his glass forward for a toast, and Cassidy followed suit.

Enola did, too, if only to avoid being rude. She raised her glass and took a tentative sip. The wine was sweet and intense. Even the slightest bit warmed her.

They were both watching. Arreigh smiled and nodded. "It's plum!" he said again, as if imparting some great discovery or urgent news. He seemed delighted when she drank more and smiled. "I knew you'd like it!" he said. He turned toward Cassidy, and the phone he wore on one earlobe glinted. The thing was shaped like a dragon, Enola realized, like the ones her mothers had collected.

She hated dragons.

"Didn't I tell you she'd like it?" Arreigh continued. "Everyone likes it. It's the only acceptable choice that this miserable facility has to offer."

Cassidy smiled indulgently, but said nothing. The expression looked practiced. She seemed as much an exhibit as an attendee.

"It's very good," Enola said, if only to please. As if of its own accord, the glass moved from her left hand to her right, then back again. She tried to choose her next words carefully. Nervously, she said, "But—"

"Now, you must be wondering why I asked you here," Arreigh said. He set his drink down on the low table and leaned back in his chair, utterly at ease. Once again, he impressed Enola as a man completely delighted with life in general and with himself in particular. He glanced again at Cassidy. "Isn't she lovely?" he asked.

Enola wasn't certain what to say to that. She must have blushed, though, because Arreigh started laughing and even Cassidy's reserved features took on an impish cast.

"No, silly," Arreigh said to Enola. "I was asking *her* about *you*." He grinned. "But don't worry, Katalin, you're pretty, too."

Enola blushed some more.

"She's very attractive," Katalin said. Her voice was low. "I think you have chosen well."

Arreigh nodded. "I think so, too," he said. "I thought so, too, the moment I opened the door." He beamed. "Tell me, Enola, have you ever considered working on camera, on the Mesh? Would you like to be famous? Very, very famous?"

Enola blinked, but could think of nothing to say. She stared at him in something like shock.

"Hah!" Arreigh said. He grinned and pointed at her. "You must have thought about it," he said.

When she was a little girl, Enola had dreamed of being an actress. Every little girl did, she supposed. She laughed, softly, self-consciously, but said nothing.

"I knew it," Arreigh said. He kicked his feet in delight. "The pretty ones always do."

"I think you have the wrong impression," Enola said carefully. "I'm really not qualified for—"

"That's precisely the point!" Arreigh said. "My audience doesn't *want* people who are qualified!"

"That is not very nice," Katalin said coolly. Her dark eyes gazed out at both of them from beneath half-closed lids.

"It's true, though," Arreigh said. He used his hands a great deal as he spoke, Enola realized. He waved and pointed and gestured to emphasize points. "They want reality, or something they *think* is real. Next year it will change, but right now, they don't want packaged newsheads like Chrysler or the others. They want the people who do the work." Again, he beamed. "I think they want *you*, Enola!"

"But I've never—" Enola started to say.

"That's the point!" Array said. He laughed again, a short, sharp, bark. "But you can do it! According to your backgrounder—"

This time, Enola interrupted "I didn't apply to Zonix," she said. "How did you—"

Arreigh would not be deterred. "—you have the right disposition. You're comely, and I'm *sure* you're photogenic. If you aren't, we can make you. You've marketed, and that's the biggest part of it, after all. Your basic technical knowledge—"

Enola looked in Katalin Cassidy's direction, hoping for an explanation. What came was a wisp of a smile. "He will not stop for a while," the other woman said.

She was right. Arreigh didn't. He had stood and now paced energetically on the carpeted floor, holding forth on audience expectations and demographic trends and subliminal enhancement. When he wasn't talking about himself, or about work he had done, or about famous people he had met, he demonstrated an understanding of his target audience that was at once impressively comprehensive and vaguely dismissive. Enola was impressed, by his spiel and by his physical demeanor.

Arreigh moved very nearly as fast as a man could move in low gravity and remain grounded. He moved with reasonable grace and great energy. Midway through a discourse on intellectual property rights and the perception of novelty, however, he made one move that was just a little bit too swift. The force of one stride, some fractional increment too powerful, lofted his entire body a few centimeters.

"Gah!" Arreigh said.

Arreigh didn't compensate in time. When he came back down, he lurched and stumbled. An ankle twisted, and he toppled. As he fell, he reached out instinctively with both hands. One groped spastically toward the table, and toward the bottle and glasses it held.

"Oof!" Arreigh gasped.

Cassidy did something remarkable then, something that Enola had seen before only in animations and mirages, never in real life. She moved faster than any human being should, faster and differently than anyone else in Enola's experience. Cassidy did not so much lunge as *surge*. Her buttocks and hips shifted only slightly, but the upper part of her body moved like rushing water. Arms, shoulders, neck, head, all moved as one fluid whole. Her hands raced toward the table, fingers reaching and straining.

As he tumbled, Arreigh's knee struck his empty seat, hard. His outstretched hand hit the table harder. The hard plastic shattered with a noise like a small explosion. Arreigh's fall, unimpeded by the table's demise, concluded as he struck the floor. The silver tray that had held the wine bottle flipped free and spun upward, arcing over the supine Mesh producer.

It was unburdened as it took flight, however, and so was the broken tabletop. Cassidy had been just in time. Her left hand held the half-empty bottle, and her right held the three glasses, their stems intertwined between her fingers. Their drinks were well out of harm's way and not a drop had spilled.

Enola blinked. She would not have believed that anyone could move that quickly, or with such instant reflexes. Cassidy's total body control had seemed as reflexive and effortless as it was impressive. She made a sound of astonishment. "That was amazing," she said.

Cassidy smiled. She glanced at Enola and dipped her head in a mock mini-curtsy as she passed the appropriate wineglass to her. Still holding the other two, and the bottle, she looked in Arreigh's direction. She murmured something in a language that Enola did not recognize.

"No, no, I'm fine," Arreigh said. Still on the floor, he rocked from side to side, gripping one knee. "Don't worry about me. It just stings," he said. He looked surprisingly boyish.

"Three tables, now," Cassidy said, speaking for Enola's benefit. She looked amused and very mildly disgusted.

"Um," Enola said, taken aback. She knew how difficult it could be to adapt to low G. "Smartshoes will help."

"I know, I know," Arreigh said, buoyant again as he pulled himself easily to his feet. He dusted himself off. Cassidy offered him his drink, and he took it. Entirely businesslike now, he turned to face Enola. "I hope you're interested in the role," he said.

"I am," Enola said, still a bit dumbfounded by the opportunity, so utterly unanticipated. Confusion made her honest. "But I'm really not certain that I qualify."

"Oh, piffle," Arreigh said. He made a dismissive gesture. "That's my decision. Oh, and Bainbridge's. Now, we'll need some of your time over the next week. I do hope your schedule's open." He raised his glass again, and said, "To success!"

"To success," Enola said, too, and drank.

CHAPTER 6

"I'D like a British accent," Erik said. He gazed into the mirror and ran dampened hands very gently along the outermost boundaries of his graying mane. Obediently, the outermost stray hairs fell into place with their fellows and stayed there. There were countless ways to impose control that were more effective and more permanent, but sometimes, Erik liked the oldest ways best.

"Veddy good, sir," his apartment replied. *"Will this do?"*

Erik shook his head, confident that the mirror's receptors would recognize the motion. He drew the tips of his thumbs along the sides of his face, to trace the narrow sideburns that he had affected in recent months. He still wasn't certain that he liked them.

"Like this, sir?" the housekeeper system enquired, in slightly different tones.

"You sound like Sherlock Holmes," Erik said. He scowled at the mirror. "Too condescending. Try again, and mirage out the sideburns."

The imaged sideburns faded away. Erik's scowl remained. Even without the whiskers, his face definitely looked wider, fleshier than it should have been. He had a definite mental image of what he looked like, and this wasn't it. Only the narrow line of scar looked right. Even his eyes looked old.

"And this?" the system asked, speaking now in a pleasant baritone with a less patrician accent. It was the kind of voice he might have heard in a middle-class, business district pub.

"Fine," Erik said. He stared at the mirror some more, wondering why he hadn't noticed the change before. "How much do I weigh?" he asked, and then shook his head at the housekeeper's response.

It wasn't just a matter of weight gain, of course. He was getting older, and his body knew it. On a cellular level, the human body had its difficulties with lunar gravity, but on a larger scale, there were blessings. Muscles strained less, joints wore out slowly, and skin didn't have to work as hard. Despite all of that, flesh sagged with age. It was inevitable. Time moved on, and there was nothing to be done about it. He pushed the issue from his mind.

"Status?" he asked in his command voice, then turned from the mirror to pad out into the main apartment. "Are we ready?"

The housekeeper responded, working its way down a preconfigured checklist. Erik followed suit, confirming some items even as he checked a few of his own.

The refreshment nook was fully stocked, with stemware and beverages alike, less the prized bottle of imported bourbon. That, and some other breakables and personal treasures, rested now in his bedroom, which was locked. There was no sense in tempting fate, after all. The autobar was loaded and primed, available for anyone incapable of mixing his own drink. In the kitchen apse, hors d'oeuvres warmed in the autostove, with additional stock in queue. The two buffet tables were full and equipped, and the cleanup crew had been alerted and scheduled. Carpet and furniture alike were spotless, and extra chairs, stools, and slings had been strategically arrayed.

"Davros Harlington and Helena Liebman have ar-
rived," the apartment announced.

That was no surprise. Those two were always the first to
arrive, whether at meetings or reviews or social occasions.
More than once, Erik had wondered if they had been born
together, and prematurely.

"I'll greet them personally," he said. He patted his various pockets until he found his house phone and clipped it
to one ear. "Ready?" he asked.

"Ready, sir," the very proper, yet hospitable British
tones came, voiced along his private channel now. *"Should
I commence the musical selections?"*

"Start with the Ellington," he said, and immediately, the
quirky improvisations of "Money Jungle" found their way
around the room. Erik had a fondness for classic jazz.
"Stay with jazz, but nothing obtrusive," he continued, as he
moved toward the door. "No requests from guests."

"No requests," the housekeeper agreed.

He drifted to the door. As he moved, wall displays came
to life. By the time Harlington and Liebman had taken
their first steps over the threshold, they were walking into a
high-resolution art gallery and stood amid a collection that
focused on the American southwest. Decorative masks and
blankets seemed to hang from the walls, interspersed with
historical photographs of forgotten conquerors. It was the
art of the frontier, and it amused Erik on some level.

"Davros," he said, hooking thumbs in turn with each of
the distinguished couple. "Helena. I'm so happy to see you
both."

Helena, elegant and lean, smiled in acknowledgment.
"Thank you for the invitation. I know you remodeled recently, and I've been eager to see the results."

"Feel free to explore," Erik said. "It's mostly open
space now, though. Can I get either of you a beverage or
something to eat? First here, first served." He smiled.

"Oh?" Davros asked. He managed to sound surprised.
"We're the first?"

"You're always first," Erik said, with a wry smile.

"Well, it's not deliberate," Davros said, but Erik knew that he was lying. "But, as long as we've a moment of privacy, I'd like to ask you about next quarter's—"

Erik shook his head in polite refusal. "This is social," he said. He gestured, leading them to the refreshment nook. "We can speak about business during business hours." He smiled again. "Now. Drinks? If I recall, Helena, you like herbal. I have something new that you might enjoy." His big hands found a bottle and glass. He poured, as he had so many times before.

There were times when the familiar was good, and the beginning of the evening went familiarly, indeed. In ones and twos and threes, the guests arrived at Erik's door, friends and acquaintances from Over-Management and the five sisters. All were welcomed and admitted, whether by himself or by the housekeeper. Erik moved among them, making introductions and offering refreshment, and generally making his presence known.

As the numbers increased, he found himself correspondingly more occupied, but the housekeeper kept him informed and ahead of the curve. He was always able to meet or greet, or at least to make a murmured pleasantry. Before very long, his receiving room was half-filled with guests, their orbits intersecting as they sipped and nibbled and chatted. The air grew warmer, and the aromas of food and drink mingled, as did half-heard snatches of conversation.

Erik had no doubt that strategic information was being exchanged and deals were being made. Not by him, however. That was his personal rule. Instead, he focused on making everyone welcome. Later would be time enough to reap the professional benefits of being a gracious host.

More than an hour had gone by before Sarrah Chrysler arrived. He was discussing the benefits of new-generation durum wheat in pasta with the director of research from Biome Consumables when the housekeeper announced her. To his mild surprise, she was not alone, but brought with her an entourage of two—a man and a woman Erik did not recognize as they followed her through the entrance.

"Sarrah Chrysler," came the housekeeper's reserved tones at his ear. *"Accompanying her are Keith Arreigh of Zonix, and guest."*

"Excuse me," Erik told the research director, clapping him on the shoulder. "I hope we can continue this later." He slid through the throng and made his way to the foyer area, smiling. "Sarrah," he said. "I was beginning to wonder."

"Professional obligations," she said. The two words, along with her familiar smile, were explanation enough. "I'd like you to meet someone," she said. "More business, but a friend, too. This is Keith. We were meeting."

"Sarrah has mentioned you," Erik said, reaching to hook the other man's thumb.

"Only in a good way, I hope," Arreigh said. He was a bit shorter than Erik and much younger, and had a playful quality about him. A chortle seemed to lurk just below the threshold of his voice, threatening to bubble up into conversation. He shifted his grip quickly, turning the thumb-hook into and old-fashioned handshake that was firm and strong. "She's spoken of you, too. I hope you'll reconsider granting us the interview."

Erik's teeth grated momentarily. "We can talk about that later," he said, making himself sound pleasant. "This evening is not for business, but pleasure." He glanced past Arreigh, at his companion.

Sarrah noticed. "This is Katalin Cassidy," she said.

It seemed to be the evening for old-fashioned gestures. The Cassidy woman did something that Erik had seen only in ancient movies. She extended her right hand, wrist cocked and palm down, presenting it to him. Erik, with a smile, executed a perfect half-bow, accepted her fingers, and pressed his lips to them.

Sarrah giggled softly, but Cassidy turned to Arreigh and favored him with an imperious smile. "I told you," she said. For a woman, she had a deep voice and a trace of accent that made it seem even huskier. "Some know their manners." She smiled, showing teeth that were small, sharp and white, and closely set.

"I try," Erik said, still smiling. "I'm pleased to meet you, and pleased to welcome you to my home."

He was sincere. Whatever her role was, whatever place she had with Arreigh, the Cassidy woman possessed an ethereal charm that enchanted. Black-haired and dark-eyed, she was lean elegance made form, and even the slightest movement was an exercise in animal grace. He knew without checking that more than a few of his guests had turned to look in her direction.

"And so, I lose another wager," Arreigh said. For a single, transitory instant, he looked glum. "But, say, is that a refresher I see in the corner?" he asked. He pointed. He grinned.

"Yes, of course," Erik said, attention commanded. His manners resurged. "Can I get any of you something to eat or drink?"

"No, no, no," Arreigh said, with the cheerful enthusiasm that seemed to be his default setting. "C'mon, Kat," he said.

"Katalin," she corrected him, shaping the *K* sound deep in the back of her mouth in a way that gave it a husky, earthy quality. Arreigh didn't hear the correction, though; he was already gone. She nodded at Erik and moved to follow him into the depths of the not-quite-a-crowd.

"Quite the pair," Erik said. He offered his arm to Sarrah, but she declined it with a slight roll of her eyes. She wasn't old-fashioned at all.

"I hope you don't mind," she said. "We were in a planning session, and I mentioned your name. He wanted to meet you. That's why I'm late, too. He can be very tenacious."

"Not late at all," Erik said gallantly. "The party begins now." He paused. "And who is his associate?" Belatedly, he realized that Cassidy had said nothing to him directly.

"That's the word he uses, too," Sarrah said. She fell into place beside him as he led her into the party. "Associate. The visitor logs at Zonix just list her as 'guest.' That's all that I know about her."

"You checked?" Erik was mildly surprised.

"Purely professional interest," Sarrah said. She had found a buffet and was assembling a plate-load of wassabi peas, chicken gels, and pigs-in-blankets. "That woman was born camera-ready."

Erik had to agree, but he didn't think it would be wise to say so. "Try the fruit loops," he said, instead. Something caught his eye. "And I don't think that I was the only one Arreigh wanted to meet."

The Mesh producer was working the house. As Erik watched, Arreigh and his charge moved methodically from one cluster of partygoers to another group. Harlington, Leibman, Seven, Curry, almost everyone—one by one, he introduced himself to each. He hooked thumbs, conversed, then moved on. To some, he handed briefing chips from his pocket, tiny data modules that doubtless held information on himself and his various endeavors. He held a drink, sipped from it only rarely, and never seemed to lower the level in the glass. He behaved like a politician running for office, or like an executive angling for a new billet. Katalin Cassidy was never more than two meters away from him, her hands unburdened by food or drink.

"He's very social," Sarrah said, gazing in the same direction.

"And she's not," Erik said, as Cassidy slithered out of Davros Harlington's abrupt half-embrace.

"Maybe I should have found a way to leave them behind after all," Sarrah said. "Erik, when I suggested an evening, this wasn't quite what I meant."

"I didn't think it was," he said easily. "But my schedule has been very busy of late, and I did want to see you." He paused. "Would you like something to drink? I have the same white they served at Kim's." When she agreed, he smiled and said, "Let's go, then." Together, they plunged into the throng.

This time, Erik didn't bother playing the host, at least, not to anyone but Sarrah. He threaded their way through the gathering, careful to avoid eye contact with the other partygoers, and to miss any conversational gambits. He didn't even pause at the refreshment nook, instead slowing just enough to scoop up a bottle of wine and two glasses, and then kept going.

"Very neatly executed," Sarrah said, mere footsteps behind him.

"It comes with practice," he replied. "Now, let's find somewhere. Watch this."

As with most parties, the crowded part of the room was where the food and drink were. People tended to move away from the entryway as soon as possible. Erik led Sarrah toward it, instead. He glanced over his shoulder. No one seemed to be paying much attention. "Here," he said, and turned around the corner of an adjoining partition and into the space beyond. Sarrah followed.

Now, they stood together in a half-hidden alcove, small enough to be intimate but far from cramped. It was as if they had gone into some other residence entirely. Rather than the gentle curves of the kitchen and other apses, this nook had walls that were straight-lined and square. They were clad not in display paper but in plastic paneling that looked, felt, and even smelled like natural oak. Positioned between them was a couch and a low table.

"Sit," he said.

"A snuggery?" Sarrah asked, using a word that he didn't recognize. She smiled. "Or the old foyer?"

"That's right," Erik said, honestly delighted at her perceptiveness. He knuckled one sidewall. "This is structural," he said. "I had to leave it in place when I combined the spaces. Rather than open up the other side, I kept them both and sealed off the old door."

"Very intimate," Sarrah said, settling onto the sofa. She rested her plate on the small shelf that extended to take it.

Erik nodded. "I meditate here sometimes." He sat, too, and poured wine.

"That surprises me," Sarrah said.

"The meditation?" Erik asked, handing her the first glass. When she nodded, he continued. "I had never planned on relocating to the Moon."

"I'd heard that," Sarrah said.

"The transition wasn't an easy one. I couldn't sleep." Erik sipped his own wine and waved his free hand in a random gesture, vaguely nervous. This was not quite the way he had intended to address the issue. "Low gravity usually helps sleep, but not for me. I had nightmares."

"That was after the Alaska incident, wasn't?" Sarrah asked.

Erik didn't bother answering. Instead, he asked, "How are you adjusting?"

"Fine," Sarrah said. "I took a preliminary round of gene therapy on Earth. I can finalize if I stay. I haven't had any problems."

"I did," Erik told her again. He managed to make the words sound matter-of-fact, but even now, he didn't like thinking of those nights and days.

"But medication—"

Erik shook his head. "Didn't help. The problem wasn't the gravity, or the change in foodstuffs, or atmosphere mix." He paused. In the distance, he could hear the background chatter from the party he had abandoned. Sooner or later, his guests would come looking for him. "It wasn't that mechanical—that physical," he continued. "It was *me*. That's why the meditation helped, when medication didn't."

Sarrah didn't say anything, but watched attentively as he spoke.

"I had taken a bad turn," Erik said. He looked at her with sudden intensity as he remembered how thoroughly his career had been in disarray. "You've been doing your research, you know that."

She nodded. She seemed to have forgotten her food. The still-mounded plate rested on the sofa shelf, unattended. "It's my job, Erik," she said.

"It was *me*," Erik said again, still speaking as if she had not. "Who I was, where I was, how I had come to be here."

"They wanted you out of the way," Sarrah said.

"They gave me a new beginning," Erik said. "They

didn't mean to, but they did. I'm part of something very important now."

"I know there are opportunities," Sarrah began.

He interrupted. "Ad Astra is important in a different way," Erik said. "Transcendentally important. Once I realized that, I knew my place, and I knew that I had found it. Earth is just somewhere I go on vacation now." He sipped more wine. "I like you, Sarrah, and you're very attractive, but you have to recognize that Ad Astra is more important. This is a watershed event in the existence of the human race."

His own zealousness surprised him sometimes.

Sarrah rolled her eyes. "Erik," she said. "All I asked for was dinner and an evening."

He laughed politely. "You've asked for more than that," he said. "And you're still asking. If you want to spend time together, we can. But if you want to make that part of your job . . ."

His words trailed off.

"I heard you tell Keith that tonight wasn't for business," Sarrah said.

"No nights with me are for business," Erik said gently. "I can't allow it. If we see each other socially—and I'd like to—it can't color any professional relationship." He felt strange saying something so personal in such clinical tones, but his experience had proven it was absolutely necessary.

"That's why you invited me? Because you wanted to tell me that?" Sarrah asked.

"I invited you because I wanted to see you," Erik said. He was being honest and hoped she recognized it. "And I think I'd like to see you again."

"Nothing's going to make me give up my career," Sarrah said. She wasn't smiling.

Erik nodded. "I would never act to impede anyone's career," he said. He thought fleetingly of Enola Hasbro and the other alleged members of the Scheer network, and he winced. "Except, maybe, for the well-being of my own."

"I go where the news is," she persisted. "And you're still a story."

"Or part of one," he agreed. He sipped from his glass. The wine had lost its chill, and the flavor seemed more complex now, less muted. "What I can't be is a source."

"You're the director of communications, Erik," Sarrah said dryly. "You're a source."

"Beyond that, I mean," he said. "I'm serious."

She grinned, the elfin quality he had noted earlier returning to her face. Something about her eyes was familiar, too; whatever they reminded him of was of older vintage. "I think that's reasonable," she said, and leaned against him, taking his hand in hers. "If there's a relationship, I won't trade on it. I promise. So? Dinner? And an evening?"

"That much, at least," he said. He was abruptly aware of how close she was to him. "But first, I'd better see to my guests. I wonder how many your friend has driven away."

"You mean Arreigh?" someone said.

Startled, both Erik and Sarrah turned, away from each other and toward the alcove's entrance. They were just in time to see Hector Kowalski step into view. In one hand, he held a corked bottle of wine; in the other was one of his ubiquitous and anonymous gadgets.

"There you are," the security chief said impassively.

"Kowalski," Erik said, in acid acknowledgment. He was irritated, uncomfortable at having such a personal moment and place invaded. He turned to Sarrah. "This is—"

"Over-Management Security operative Hector Kowalski," Sarrah said. She dimpled, unembarrassed. "Formerly of EnTek." She looked smug as she extended one hand. "I'm Sarrah Chrysler."

Kowalski favored her with a half-bow of acknowledgment. "And I'm not the celebrity you are, ma'am," he said, as he hooked her thumb. His words were polite but cool as he glanced at the jewelry she wore. "You've done your research. Or are the pearls dataphones?"

"We were having a private conversation, Hector," Erik said.

Somewhere deep within himself, he felt the faintest echo of amusement, too mild to undercut his irritation or even self-consciousness. Sarrah's work was finding and publishing secrets; so much of Kowalski's consisted of hiding them. Under other circumstances, seeing such fundamentally opposed drives clash would have been interesting.

Kowalski passed him the bottle. It was cool to the touch, old-style glass. "Here," he said. "For you."

Erik looked at the label and nodded in surprised appreciation. It was an Argentine shiraz, the import seal still in place. "This is very considerate," he said, a bit taken aback. "An excellent choice."

Kowalski smiled. "I do my research, too," he said.

"What were you saying about Keith?" Sarrah asked.

"He left a few minutes ago. He offered his thanks and apologies, but I think he had spoken with everyone he wanted to," Kowalski said. He glanced again at Erik. "I thought your policy was that there was no business talk at these gatherings."

"ENTER," roared the voice that was not a voice. "ENTER THE SPLINTER!" The words came in a rolling thunder that was felt rather than heard, a rushing, rolling spill of sound that shook the teeth and rattled the bones. It did not so much cut through the background music as smash through it, leaving sonic debris in its wake. "ENTER THE SPLINTER!" the roar repeated itself, an iota less loudly this time.

Directional suppressors had cut in as they moved through the entranceway, Enola supposed. Either that, or they were going deaf. "Isn't this great?" she shrieked. Despite herself, she hugged herself to Crag Fortinbras. "Isn't it the *best*?"

She waved her hands as she spoke, moving them through one band after another of the brilliant colors that painted the air surrounding them. They painted her digits, too, in hues that were as electric and precise as a spectrograph display. Red, green, blue, orange—the colors rippled over her hands like flowing liquids. Among the other attendees streaming through the entrance were some who wore body makeup or appliances that fluoresced brightly, to even more brilliant effect. Enola, however, was content with what glamour she had.

The bustle of the crowd, the molten hues, and the growling subsonics all had their effect on her. The frets and worries of the last week were swept aside, along with the curious apprehension she felt about the surprising Zonix offer. For what seemed like the first time in a very long time, Enola felt truly happy.

"It's great," Fortinbras said back to her. She could hear him clearly in her personal phone, clearly enough that she didn't believe him. His enthusiasm sounded entirely too deliberate. At the moment, she didn't care.

They moved forward, deeper into the Splinter's confines. The hammering of the greeter faded a bit, and the background clatter resolved itself back into music. It was at least partly live, neo-Cajun, and even from here, she could tell that the band was very good. The syncopated beat was less thunderous than the greeting subroutine, but more commanding. Strings and drumbeats and washboard-strikers collaborated to create a heady mélange of multi-layered music that was at least as expressive as the sliding ululations of the lead singer.

Enola could hear the lyrics and almost understand them. Dialect-inflected English, French, and Spanish syllables jostled with one another, often in the same stanza. Someone had lost his love and would dance all night with the devil to get her back. Either that, or someone's family had been destroyed by "the battlefish," and war would surely follow. Their souls demanded redeeming. Enola wasn't sure which, but she was confident that it was one or the other.

"I thought you wanted to go dancing?" she demanded of Crag, still speaking along her personal channel.

"Dancing would be fun," he said, still not sounding very enthusiastic. Enola wondered if the crowds or the sensory overload were too much for him, or if he simply didn't like the music.

"We need the inner galley, then," she said, leading along. "This way, Crag."

They had entered the Splinter through its Mall entrance, a cast-stone gateway on a lower level of the vast restaurant and retail complex. The gate's frame had been formed and stressed to look like naked rock, and the motif continued inside the club proper. The Splinter was a curved, ragged cavity in the lunar crust, with extensions that let to a half-dozen other passageways. The official story was that the Splinter was one of the leftover spaces, an odd remnant of construction that plucky entrepreneurs had found, leased, and outfitted, but Enola knew that the official story was a lie.

Before the place was the Splinter, it had been the Oubliette. Before it was the Oubliette, it had been the Rift. Before it was the Rift, it had been Lysenko's Maze. Before it was the Maze, it had been nothing but an indeterminate volume of native lunar rock, a set of coordinates and engineering specifications. That had been before it had been gouged out and shaped and sold as a "found space," then marketed properly. The target clientele was tourists and locals who weren't satisfied with merely *knowing* that they were on a world that was alien to their species. They had to experience something that told them they were far from home.

A Zonix subcompany had designed the place and partnered with a rapid succession of management companies to make it an exotic haven for people who had credit to spend. It was a Duckworth subcompany that had actually built the place, however, and Enola had helped create the models.

"We're lucky," she said. "In six weeks, this place will be packed." It was a life cycle that the Splinter and its predecessors had all followed, from obscure to novel to trendy to passé. That was why the place wasn't Lysenko's Maze anymore.

"Lucky," Crag said, barely keeping up with her as she moved quickly along the corridor.

They had been very lucky, Enola realized as she rounded one corner to the main dance floor. The lines for this round were just forming, two serpentine queues that snaked along the black plastic dance floor. Each was mostly sex-specific. Men and women faced one another, mostly paired, across a distance of perhaps two meters. "Hurry, hurry," she said. "Here." She took her place at the end of one line and gestured for him to do the same.

"Enola, I wanted to go *dancing*. I'm not sure that this—"

"Hush!" she commanded. "Just follow the directions!"

One musical movement came to an end and another began. On the platform stage above the dance floor, the first, demanding strains of a well-played para-fiddle sounded. Someone began to sing, high and sweet.

> *Faire face à votre partenaire,*
> *votre amour, votre allumette*
> *L'étreinte et le baiser alors*
> *danse et danse dans une pirouette*

Enola began to dance, and her neighbors did the same. She loved Cajun music, and loved zydeco line dancing even more. The air in the Splinter, thick and muggy and scented by scores of human bodies, was as intoxicating as wine as she stepped and danced and spun. Soon, she was moving very nearly as fast and as forcefully as the human body could move in low gravity, at least without smartshoes. The sound of footfalls around her was a thunder only slightly less thundering than the greeter. Even the floor seemed to shake, which should have been impossible, given the construction techniques involved.

In seconds, she had lost sight of Crag, but that was how line dancing worked. The two queues moved past one another in opposite directions, and she danced with what seemed like countless men in rapid succession. Bands of lightshow color slashed across their features and forms, alternately obscuring and illuminating. At random intervals iridescent bubbles drifted lazily through the air. One by one, each burst in response to some clandestine prompt, to release a gasp of salt sea spray, or sharp pine, or arid desert. Overlaying all of it were the mismatched beats of the music and of her heart.

> *La balançoire votre partenaire,*
> *Votre rond et votre rond . . .*

A hundred hands, one after another, found Enola's. Partner after partner tried to download personal data into her phones, but she rejected them all with murmured commands. Fifty faces, anonymous to begin with and made more anonymous by strobing hues, moved past her as she stepped, dipped, and whirled. She danced with fifty men whom she did not know.

And then she danced with one woman whom she did.

Enola almost missed a step when Katalin Cassidy's strong hands found hers. She was in the mostly men line, which only made her presence that much more unexpected. Cassidy grinned and winked one dark, deep-set eye, even as she moved her body in an easy match to the music. She was a very good dancer and matched Enola's steps perfectly, as if they had practiced together for years. Step forward, step back, then spin and reverse—Enola moved as if she had been born to it, and her partner moved with her. Rainbow bands of brightness rippled along Cassidy's alabaster features, and Enola realized with some surprise that the she and the other woman were precisely the same height. Then Cassidy released and spun away, and new hands reached for Enola.

"Hello!" Keith Arreigh bellowed amiably, speaking loudly enough that she could hear his actual voice over the music rather than via her phone. "It's a coincidence, I promise you!" He seemed happy enough, but he sweated and breathed heavily as he moved through the steps of the relatively simple dance. Clearly, he was not as physically fit as his "associate." A few months on the Moon, and the strongly encouraged program of exercise that was part of most peoples' lives, would change that. "Let's chat after this is done!" he said.

Before Enola could respond, he was swept away and it was a total stranger who smiled at her. But the music was the same.

"GETS the blood pumping," Arreigh said, afterward. He drank dark beer and ate cheesecake. Though his breathing was more regular and less labored than it had been, he still glowed from exertion. Perspiration glued strands of his longish hair to his forehead, and it was all Enola could do to keep from reaching across the table and pushing them back into place.

"The band was very good," Enola agreed. "There's something about live music that makes things different. More exciting."

After several more rounds on the dance floor, the four of them had adjourned to DiNuvio's, a pseudo-Italian Mall restaurant. DiNuvio's had found new popularity in the preceding year or two. Enola liked the place's decor, unchanged since her last visit and thoroughly retrograde by most standards. The high ceilings and airy openness reminded her of Duckworth's work environment. With Crag sitting overly close to her, making his presence known much too aggressively, she could almost have been back at the office.

Almost, but for Arreigh and Cassidy's presence. They were seated across the table from her. The exotic-looking woman had restricted herself to mineral water and sat in near silence, but Arreigh had devoured two portions of blueberry cheesecake and was working on a third. "Well, I *am* exhausted," he said. "That really burns the calories."

"Not that many calories, friend," Crag said, watching him eat. Under the table, his hand found Enola's thigh. She removed it.

"It's good for me," Arreigh said. He lifted another fork-ful. He seemed very pleased with himself. "I do well by indulging."

"That's right," Enola said, prompting a subtly startled expression from Cassidy. "Do you plan to stay here long? Either of you?"

Both shook their heads. "On the Moon, you mean, right?" Arreigh asked.

"Don't like it?" Crag asked. He offered Enola a morsel of blancmange from his plate, and did it in the most objec-tionable way possible, raising a spoon to within an inch of her lips. She shook her head and had to do it a second time before he took the hint.

Katalin Cassidy's sculpted features formed a faint, brief moue of displeasure. Now that Enola had spent some time in the other woman's presence, she realized just how im-passively Katalin Cassidy typically presented herself to the world. For all the elegant grace of her body language, her facial expressions were almost always subtle and re-strained. Her more effusive moments startled and some-times seemed deliberate. When they happened, Enola felt like a member of a select, target audience.

She liked feeling that way.

"I like it perfectly well, but we're here entirely on busi-ness," Keith said. He drank more beer and muffled a small belch. "Not that we won't have fun, too. Right, Kat?" He grinned, more boyish than ever.

Another woman might have rolled her eyes, but all Cas-sidy did was correct him with a murmured, "Katalin."

"How did you find the Splinter?" Enola asked, shrug-ging off Crag's long arm, which had draped itself across her shoulders.

"We have a hospitality suite in the studio hotel," Arreigh said. He ate another bite, and this time, Enola could detect the sharp aroma of blueberries. "The concierge had recom-mendations. The Splinter for dancing, DiNuvio's for cheesecake."

"Well, the cheesecake *can* be good for you," Enola

soldiered on. "It's high in calcium, and unless you take the gene therapy—"

"This is good for you, too, Enola," Crag said, offering blancmange again. The fluffy dessert tempted, but she brushed him aside.

"You're not eating," Arreigh pointed out. "Cheesecake or anything else."

Enola shook her head. She wasn't feeling particularly well. She saw no reason to mention that to a potential employer, but now that the burn of exercise had faded, a hint of nausea was making itself known. "I've had the therapy," she said. She still hadn't told him that she was taking regression patches now. "Mostly, exercise is all I need now."

"Well, at least have some more wine," Crag said.

Enola shook her head again. The last of her second rosé lingered before her, and she was reasonably sure that a refill would not be a good idea. She wished she had ordered new-coffee instead. She said, "Well, how long will you be here?"

"Ah! That's the high-credit question!" Arreigh said. For emphasis, he slapped the table with one open palm. The table took its support from a central stalk that reached down from the ceiling, and Arreigh's blow was enough to make the plastic slab vibrate faintly. "I'm here to start things, Enola. I'm here to put legs on this new Mesh initiative, and then I'm here to go back home. I'll stay as long as the work keeps me." He pushed his plate, empty now, aside and looked at her seriously. He pointed at her. "And you are part of that work."

He didn't look very comfortable being serious, Enola decided. She supposed that could be a problem for the Mesh producer, but maybe his overall, infectious enthusiasm made up for it.

He paused, then smiled again. "At least, I hope you'll be. That will depend on the tests. But I have a trained eye, and now that we've spent some time together, I'm sure you'll do fine."

"I hope so, too," Enola said. She meant it. The very idea

of making such a radical career shift brought with it considerable cause for worry. Despite the uncertainty, however, she desperately wanted to stay on the Moon.

Arreigh glanced at the watch tattooed on his wrist. "It's late," he said. He looked at her meaningfully. "And you don't want to miss your camera test," he said.

"We'd best be going, then," Crag said. He stood, his fingers suddenly entwined with Enola's. She pulled her hand free as she stood, too.

"I can *manage,* Crag," she said. She hoped that he would take the hint, but wasn't surprised when he didn't.

CHAPTER 7

ERIK Morrison apparently went through life very nearly alone, which was both understandable and a bit of a mystery.

It was much later in the evening that the thought presented itself to Sarrah. It came after the party, after the surprisingly impressive kiss, after she had made her way through the winding corridors and public shuttles of Villanueva and back to her company-sponsored quarters. It came when she was seated at her vanity, removing the minimal cosmetics she had worn to the party. The realization came not as the conclusion of any deliberate thought process, but had arisen instead, as if of its own accord, from the simmering ferment of observations and remembered conversations.

She sponged her brow clean of the light dusting of makeup with a mint-scented pad that made her skin tingle pleasantly. She peeled away the minute extensions that reshaped her eyebrows. By making and carefully watching a very specific gesture with the fingertips of her left hand, she reset her prosthetic lenses to her eyes' natural color. The tiny clips that hid behind her ears served as discreet relays for the dataphones in her jewelry. She removed those, too, and returned them to their cases. They were consumer-class product, inexpensive and inferior to what she wore on the job, but she liked them, and they were worth salvaging.

As she worked, she considered the thought that had bubbled up from her subconscious. In retrospect, the likely reasons for Erik's status were obvious, but they puzzled, nonetheless. She had never expected him to be such a mystery.

He was handsome enough, with good bone structure and slightly weathered good looks that seemed not to be the result of any enhancement, but only of living. He dressed with a casual elegance that he probably considered purely functional, but which comported remarkably well with current fashion trends.

He was clearly heterosexual and socially adept. He had ample credit and authority, more of each than he had possessed five years before, and trended to have even more five years hence. Women liked him, to judge from the two marriages and multiple affairs Sarrah's reading of his biography revealed.

Sarrah liked him, for that matter, and he seemed to like her.

Despite all of that, he seemed utterly unsure of how to deal with a woman who was attracted to him and said so. His formal demeanor, his scrupulous restraint even before Kowalski's interruption, the awkward pauses in their conversation, none of those tracked with what she knew of his life on Earth.

Something had happened to him. Something, or someone.

Sarrah's own face stared back out at her now from the mirror, unadorned and unenhanced. It was the product of good genes and the most minor of surgeries. Looking at herself reminded her. She had seen Erik looking at her more than once this evening, taking sidelong glances when he thought she wasn't looking. He had worn the expression of a man tantalized by a half-memory. Sarrah prided herself on reading body language and facial expressions well. She had seen that look before. The memory nibbled persistently at her.

Abruptly, realization dawned. The flash of insight bubbled up in a gift from her subconscious, and brought everything else into sharp, coherent focus.

"Open my private notebook," Sarrah said. She massaged lotion into her fingertips. "Secure protocol."

"Notebook open," the housekeeper said in its drab, neutral voice. *"Secure protocol."*

"Notes to self," Sarrah said. "I seem to remind Erik of someone, at least on a subtle level. Find out whom. I think it's a physical resemblance, and probably not very pronounced. It's probably someone he met since coming here, probably someone important. He's having difficulty dealing with me. Run a match with lovers, known and presumed, and prominent business associates." She paused, thinking, and then her thoughts were interrupted.

"Incoming message," the housekeeper said. *"Priority One."*

She accepted it, and recognized Bainbridge's fussy tones instantly. "Sarrah," he said. "Go to Mesh. Something terrible has happened! Terrible!"

MEMORIES of her childhood on Earth seemed to come to Wendy Scheer only when she dreamed, but they came more often of late. Since her exile from Villanueva, her schedule had been far less hectic, and her sleep far less refreshing. Now, adrift in restless slumber in her Project Halo quarters, memories and dreams came to her in force.

Wendy had been born in New Sacramento and raised there, in one of the few Earthly regions remaining with a night sky that was clear, at least on occasion. Wendy's father had been a professor of biology and an amateur astronomer. In the summer, on weekends, the little girl whom Wendy had so long ago been would take the shuttle bus to the outskirts of the city, then rent a personal vehicle and secure a permit, and venture out into the desert's arid plains.

In her dreams, Wendy was there now. In her dreams, she was not enduring fitful sleep alone on an inexpensive, government-issue mattress. In her dreams, she was with her father, all slippered feet and coveralls, peering through the eyepiece of a portable telescope that he had anchored for stability to the recreational vehicle bumper. It held a forty-centimeter reflector and state-of-the-art image enhancement brainware, sufficient to resolve coherent images through the haze of light pollution overhead, too great and too extensive to escape completely. In the desert night, coated in perspiration and nibbled by insects, Wendy accepted his guidance and peered through the eyepiece.

Her father had been a kind and gentle man, a man who had chosen a useful career and a useless hobby. The day when Earthbound amateurs could make meaningful contributions to astronomy had been long gone, even then.

"There," she could hear him saying. "See? That's Betelgeuse. That's Vega. See? That's Mars, and there's Jupiter. There is the Moon. *Mare Crisium, Mare Tranquilliatis.*" The memories of a hundred juvenile evenings flitted through her mind in a chaotic jumble, each blending into all the others. Again and again, she peered and squinted, obediently acknowledging each fleck of colored light against blackness or blotch of shadow on Luna's bone-white face.

Awake, Wendy never thought of those nights. Asleep, she thought of little else. She could recall bits of each, bright shards of memories broken by the years, and reassembled into new, incomplete patterns.

"See?" her father said again, pointing.

"I see, I see!" said the little girl that Wendy had been.

"Do you know what that is?" he asked her.

An electronic chime sounded, needle-sharp and demanding.

"I'll go there someday," Wendy muttered aloud, awake enough to speak, but not enough to recognize the irony of her words. She had never considered that the Moon would be her place of exile, as well.

The chime sounded again. It was the monitor room alarm. She heard it in the sleeping world, but knew that it had sounded in the waking one, so Wendy woke, too. She sat bolt upright in bed, throwing back the sheets that covered her trim form. She was instantly awake, her dream forgotten. In response to her sudden, convulsive movement, the liquid filling of her mattress shifted and sloshed, and the sheets drifted slowly floorward. She ignored both events.

"What is it?" she asked. The question was an order. Wendy's voice was clear and bright, not thickened by sleep, and her words were precisely formed.

"Our friends in Villanueva are reporting a disturbance in the Mall," came the answer. *"Something big."*

IT took the better part of an hour to get home, and almost half that long to get rid of Crag, who had become vastly more aggressive. With each hint and grope and physical innuendo, he reminded her that she had made a mistake with him the previous week.

"I could be good for you," he said, his words scented with whisky and blancmange. "I was good for you once." He grinned. "I remember, even if you don't."

. He spoke standing entirely too close to her, but she couldn't move away. They were in the corridor outside her apartment, and her back was against the display-paneled wall. It was very late, and the advertisements that scrolled there were in subdued mode, but the tension in their voices made the Zonix cat prick up its ears and take notice. Absurdly, Enola felt very self-conscious repelling Crag's advances under the cartoon mascot's animated, attentive gaze.

"No, you weren't," she said, twisting her face aside so he couldn't kiss her. "I was lonely, and I was wrong. You were just there." Regret drove her words, regret not for their content, but for her actions that had made them necessary. "I shouldn't have had sex with you then, and I shouldn't have gone out with you this evening. I shouldn't see you again, ever." Ordinarily, she would have said something more gracious and politic, but she had consumed just enough alcohol to be blunt. "I don't *want* to," she said.

The lazy, drunken grin on Crag's face shattered. He showed his age. It was as if he had peeled away whatever appliances he wore and undone half a dozen minor surgeries. He paused, as if in shock, and Enola took advantage of the moment to squirm away from him and through her apartment portal. As it whisked shut, she turned and said, "Don't call me again, Crag. I'll block you. And I'll file complaints."

SHE thought about that threat the next morning, as she tottered into the kitchen to nibble at a readymeal soufflé. She thought about it some more as she checked her accounts and defined the first, tentative lines of a new presentation piece.

The threat had been a bluff, or nearly a bluff. Now that she was no longer a full employee of Duckworth, the measures available to her were limited. Certainly, she had no advocates in Company Court.

The thought weighed on her well into mid-morning, heavily enough that it affected her concentration and her work. Even after the judicious use of relaxant medicines and deep breathing exercises, she felt as if heavy machinery were at work in her stomach, and her vision drifted in and out of focus. Finally, disgusted and frustrated, she shut down the modeler.

The housekeeper took that as a cue. *"Narçissa Peron Alejandra Esposito would like to speak with you,"* dead Donelle's voice said. *"If it is not an interruption. She seems very nice."*

Enola blinked with more than one kind of surprise. The housekeeper wasn't supposed to make that kind of observation.

"Narçissa?" she said, accepting the call eagerly. The older woman's familiar features condensed into being on the wall above Enola's workstation. "It's so good to hear from you!

"Hello, Enola!" Narçissa said. She beamed. "I have thought so often about you. Are you well?"

Enola smiled wanly. She had taken a moment to comb her hair and adjust her robe before taking the call, but now she wished that she had gone to mirage mode. "I'm fine," she said. "I was out late last night, and I am a little tired."

"Oh. Yes. Crag told me that you had gone to the Splinter," Narçissa said. She sounded less than impressed.

It was as if the room's temperature had dropped multiple degrees, but at the same time, Enola's face felt curiously warm. She wondered if she were blushing. "And did Crag also tell you that we won't be socializing any further?" she asked.

A moment passed, stretched to the point of awkwardness and beyond.

"Are you well, Enola?" Narçissa finally asked again.

Enola leaned back in her chair. She took stock of the previous days. She thought about the awful interview with Lyle Chesney and the long ride home, about Huerta and his treatments and warnings. The grinding in her stomach worsened.

"I don't know," she said honestly. She thought about Arreigh and Cassidy, and the interview at Zonix. "But there is some sunshine."

"I am pleased," Narçissa said. Her concern was still surprising. After her termination, Enola had never expected any contact from any of the company bones. "We all miss you so much. It is terrible, all of these terminations."

The smile Enola made this time was even more faint and wan than the one before.

Narçissa licked her lips nervously. As far as Enola could tell, she had applied no image enhancement for this call. The middle-aged woman from Accounting seemed genuinely concerned. "Did you get the aqua-bouquet?" she asked.

"The aquarium?" Enola asked. She was suddenly very conscious of the softly lit alcove to her left, and the bright flashes of color that lived there now.

"We—the office—we put some credit together and bought it for you. To cheer you," Narçissa said. Her voice trembled. "It—it was my idea."

Enola stared at her. She felt a sense of conclusion, as if she had finally identified the last stroke needed to complete a model. It did not make her happy. "And did Crag contribute?" she asked.

"Not in credit," Narçissa said. "But he said he would deliver it."

"He did," Enola said. She exercised every fragment of self-control she still had and forced warmth into the words. She liked Narçissa, and there was really no need to wound her with knowledge of Crag's shabbiness. "Yes, he did, Narçissa. Thank you very much. Thank everyone for me. I should have thanked you earlier, but—well, things have been difficult."

Narçissa must have known that something was wrong, however, because after another awkward pause, she changed the subject.

"Enola," she said. "Have you heard about the terrible explosion last night? In the Mall?"

THE Mall was at the heart of Villanueva, dead center and running from top to bottom. It was a well, a cylindrical shaft that included some of the earliest architecture and engineering within the lunar colony's boundaries. Decades before, the same space had held the original spaceport serving the facility. That was in the earliest, least populous days of the colony, before the ALC had reconsidered the wisdom of landing and launching spacecraft in the heart of what amounted to a small city. Now, visitors to Villanueva came and went from a facility some eighty kilometers lunar west, and the Mall was home to commerce.

The Mall was a pit filled with ordered chaos, thirteen

levels of shops and theaters and restaurants and galleries and brothels. The Zonix casino, operated over decades and under a dozen different trade names, stretched, zigzag fashion, over three levels and ninety degrees of the great shaft's circumference. Service industries, specialty shops, and wholesale distribution centers rubbed shoulders there, all operated by or under license from the five ALC sisters and catering to locals and tourists alike. More than 70 percent of consumer-level commercial transactions took place in or were serviced from the Mall, and when groundhogs talked about Villanueva, they usually meant the Mall.

Even as the Mall ran from top to bottom of Villanueva, four banks of elevators ran from the Mall's tiered floor to its vaulted ceiling. Bubble-cars drifted lazily up and down those banks, encased in shafts so transparent as to be effectively invisible. Cantilevered balconies and parapets projected from rock walls that were alternately naked and raw, and clad display panes. More display panels hung in the vast space between those walls, and swaying suspension-bridge walkways shared the space with them, held in place by gossamer-fine tungsten spring cables. Most of the arbitrary day, the Mall was a very busy place, in every sense of the word.

In the small hours of the night, however, the tides of commerce ebbed. That was when most tourists, their credit and energy spent, returned to expensive hotel rooms to talk about how badly they missed Earth and wanted to go home. That was when most of the indentured casino attendants and paid companions and restaurant wait staff, exhausted after long days of work, returned home to rest muscles that had found fatigue even in low G, to talk with loved ones about how greatly they hated tourists.

And it was in the smallest hours of the night that an explosive device of moderate force and unknown origins detonated, with a sound like the thunderstorms of far-off Earth.

The blast ripped though the third bubble-car, mercifully unoccupied, of the northeast elevator bank, and through the harder-than-steel shaft that surrounded it. Air shook with the explosion's reverberations and shrieked as shrapnel split it. Flying chunks of sundered elevator car sliced through tungsten-steel cables as if they did not exist, and three footbridges fell. They snapped and cracked like whips, one stabbing through the largest of the signboards and snuffing the life from the famous Zonix cartoon cat. Other display panels merely shattered, their wafer-thin mechanisms pulverized by the shock wave. The bits and pieces fell like bitter rain, mixed with fragments of windows and facades.

People screamed. They screamed in confusion as their safe, solid world abruptly proved fragile, and they screamed in panic as they and their fellows competed desperately to reach the nearest exits. They screamed as shrapnel and debris found them, cutting and hammering and stabbing.

Not very many people frequented the Mall in the night's smallest hours, but not so few that their screams could remain individual and distinct. They merged into a wailing wall of sound, a cacophony of tortured larynxes, punctuated by shrieking alarms and the blast's last echoes.

"THAT'S how it happened," Hector Kowalski told his audience as the screens went dark on the carnage. "Or rather, that's *what* happened. I stress that the damages were not as great as they seem to the untrained eye. The device does not seem to have been placed to cause maximum damage."

He stood at the front of the presentation room, the manual remote neatly concealed inside one hand. Confronting him were twenty quiet men and women, corporate delegates of the five ALC sisters, and of the Over-Management committee that coordinated them all. Alone on a raised stage in front of some of the most powerful people he was ever likely to meet, he felt utterly at ease. He was completely in his element, trading in information for the benefit of others.

"How accurate was that?" Douglas Seven asked. He was

the first to speak, a burly black man, in attendance on behalf of Biome. His voice was smooth, like smoke, but the flesh of his face had turned the color of ash and was dotted with perspiration. He hadn't liked what he had seen.

"Reasonably," Hector said, still calm. Part of that was self-confidence, pure and simple, but part of it was the discreetly placed medical patch he wore, a heady cocktail of physical stimulants and mental tranquilizers. Forced wakefulness and demanding, detailed work were not good partners. Kowalski had been awake for many hours and could not afford to pay fatigue its toll just now. Without one kind of drug, he would have been nearly comatose with fatigue; without the other, he would have been made nearly as useless by a lack of focus and excess of irritability. "I spent sixteen hours with Zonix Media imagineers editing it together. We were able to get 83-percent coverage from security cameras, advertising feed-pickups and even a few tourist recordings. The rest is interpolated miraging and sound enhancement."

He didn't like telling them that, but he had to. Sooner or later, one or more of them would have noticed. The human eye, especially the trained human eye, was a remarkably subtle instrument, and less forgiving than people realized. All the miraging and Gummi-rendered images in the world couldn't change that.

"So it's not entirely accurate," said Bonnie Gibbons. She worked for Over-Management directly, but made no secret that her true loyalties lay with her original employer, Zonix. "You spun it."

Hector shook his head. Under other circumstances, he might have made a sarcastic retort, but these were serious times. Even through the slight haze of chemical equanimity, that thought was foremost in his mind. "No," he said. "It's as objectively accurate as we could make it. It's tailored, but not to any one viewpoint's benefit. It's a re-creation, not a dramatization."

He almost smiled at his own words. There was no way that such a composite could be objective. The simple act of assembling it entailed choices, and choices were defined by agendas, articulated or not.

He was talking too much, he knew.

"Then why the mirages?" Gibbons prodded.

"We recovered as many images as we could from ambient sources," Hector said. "We miraged to fill the gaps."

"What about the security cameras?" Bonnie demanded. "Weren't they running?"

"They were," Hector said. "But the coverage wasn't complete, and the Mall is a riot of visual noise."

"Still, it seems to me that a comprehensive system of well-placed pickups, properly maintained and deployed—"

The words stung. Hector liked to watch people. He had argued for precisely such a system in the public areas on more than one occasion, only to have display boards or wallpaper or trompe l'oeil holograms take priority in the limited shared space. Now, he opened his mouth to snarl a reply, only to be cut off.

"We're learning from our mistakes, Bonnie," Erik Morrison said, cool and authoritative. He was at the back of the briefing room, in the shadows. He spoke without amplification, but his measured tones carried well. "When the Mall reopens, things will be different. Management didn't anticipate any need for end-to-end coverage, and perceived privacy remains an issue for some tourists."

That was accurate. Candidate Villanueva residents were selected to conform to specific psychiatric profiles, but tourists were a slightly different matter. Most tourists wanted a peculiar mixture of anonymity and special treatment that would enable them to indulge in vices and practices unthinkable at home. That was the reason that, despite the urgings of Hector and people like him, some privacy prevailed in even the most public places.

That would change, Hector knew. It would have to.

"Specifics?" That was Seven again. Most of the others were still silent, staring either at Hector or at the blank panorama wall behind him, but Seven was proving to be entirely too attentive.

What they looked at wasn't what they were seeing, Hector knew. What they were seeing was the impact the incident would have on their individual employers' profit projections, and on their own positions within those companies.

"I've provided tailored backgrounders with the details," he said aloud. "You're to receive them in your personal accounts."

"Tailored?" someone said.

"Tailored," Hector said. "Base information is the same, but certain items, I'm not authorized to share. They're of a competitive nature." One of the factors that made the ALC possible was that the five sister companies were largely noncompetitive. Because they *were* superconglomerates, however, inevitably, certain conflicts of interest remained. They were simply too large not to have subcompanies and allies that contended. "I'm here to answer general questions and offer insight, but there are limits to the detail I can provide in this context. Please remember also that we have blind attendees."

Irritation flared again, however briefly, burning through his chemical calm. He wanted to spit, but refrained. In addition to the men and women in his physical presence, unidirectional links allowed a select few more to audit the session. They could participate, but only passively. Wendy Scheer was among them, despite his emphatic protests. Morrison had insisted, maintaining that the federal authorities had a valid need to receive at least an overview. Ad Astra, Villanueva's largest single present initiative, was a federal project, after all.

"Focused, if you prefer," Hector continued. "If you think they're lacking, let me know and we can discuss it. If you don't trust me, appeal to my boss. It's policy."

"Please, Hector," Erik said. "Just continue."

"The specifics I can provide here are basic. Physical damage looks worse than it is; we already have it almost entirely cleared up," Hector said.

That was yet another source of irritation. Representatives

from Halo had also participated in the physical investigation and assessment. Hector was as eager as anyone to determine the specifics of the explosive incident, but he also had as a priority the cleanup and reopening of the Mall. Project Halo wanted the place locked down and examined centimeter by centimeter, no matter what the expense, or impact on business. The difference of opinion had prompted some heated discussions.

Villanueva's viewpoint had won, of course. Credit always won. Other than pride in doing a job well, Hector had no problem with that.

"Reconstruction and Restock are already at work," he said. "We should be able to reopen in another nine hours."

Members of his audience turned to look at one other and whispered into neighbors' ears or closely held phones. Another nine hours would mean that the Mall had been shut down for more than a day and a half. More mathematically oriented minds than his were hastily assessing the financial impact. He knew it had to be bad. There were other places in Villanueva to eat and drink and spend and have sex, but the Mall was 90 percent of the show. Shutting it down had impact that couldn't be ignored.

"I'll remind you that there is to be no recording of this session," Hector continued. He knew that the reminder would go unnoted, but he didn't want any complaints later, after participants had discovered how well his privacy fields had done their work. Blank recorders had a way of enraging.

"Anything I give you now that isn't in your back-grounders will be in the follow-up report." He glanced specifically at the front row of his audience, and at the Zonix executives who sat there. "Remember, I work for all of you. Putting me all over the Mesh is the best way to keep me from being able to do my job well."

No one said anything.

Hector squeezed his remote. Using voice commands in a group situation was always a bit of a risk, especially on a multiple-use system, so he had zeroed out the office manager's capability even before the session had begun. The silence of his command made it no less effective, however. Diagrams, tables, and animated histograms played across the panorama wall.

"Thirty-three injured; five dead," he said. "Most were night workers, but all five casualties were tourists." He paused. "Drunk tourists, seeing the night out."

Softly and indistinctly, stray syllables of murmured comments from the audience reached his ears. He took no note of them.

"The injuries were simple stuff, broken limbs and cuts, electrical burns. Nothing worse than Class Two. The medical teams are growing new eyes and fixing teeth as we speak. Most of the injured were residents, which makes things easier," he said. "We have procedures, and no one who wants to keep working is going to complain. There should be no great impact on productivity."

He smiled faintly. It had been a very long time since Hector had met anyone who didn't want to keep working.

"The tourists," Morrison prompted.

"The tourists are another matter," Hector said in acknowledgment.

"They're insured, all of them. And waivered. We're not responsible. We can't be indemnified."

That was the Gibbons woman again.

"They're insured and waivered," Hector continued, as if she had not spoken. "But not against terrorist activities."

There was a sharp hissing sound, like a gas leak, as twenty men and women inhaled sharply and simultaneously.

"I object to the use of the word *terrorist*," Gibbons said.

Hector shrugged. "It's not for the record, so I can afford to be accurate. And the courts *will* use it." He squeezed the remote control again. A few square meters of display wall blanked before them, filling again with an ornate logo.

These days, it seemed that everyone had a logo, some of them surprisingly elaborate. This particular one was an image of the Earth, as it might have looked from lunar orbit in the days of the dinosaurs. It was more than a map and less than a mirage, with land and ocean rendered in detail, but bereft of the atmosphere's obscuring haze. It followed the visual coding universal to the human eye, blue for water and brown-green for landmass, but the topography was one that no human eye had ever witnessed. Australasia, Africa, South America, and Antarctica. They huddled together, shoulder to shoulder, subsuming their familiar contents into a single gigantic clot of a continent. Except that, and a scattered few dots of island, everything else was ocean.

"This is a map of Gondwanaland," Hector said. His tongue no longer stumbled over the clumsy name that he had spoken so many times in the preceding hours. "There is on Earth an organization that calls itself 'The Children of Gondwanaland.' This is their trademark."

Now, he smiled. At last, he had reached the substance of the meeting.

Twenty men and women stared at the logo. Most had no idea what it meant, much less what it represented.

"Gondwanaland?" the Gibbons woman said, tentatively.

"Gondwanaland," Morrison said, again from the back of the room, again in tones that were cool and authoritative. The baleful look in his eyes, however, suggested that Hector might do well to suppress the smile. "An ancient supercontinent, one of two that used to comprise most of the Earth's land mass. That's the southern hemisphere, Earth, two-hundred-some million years ago. There was another in the North. They broke up and dispersed over millennia."

"I've compared feeds with our friends in the civil sector," Hector said, moving to take control of the presentation before Morrison could proceed with a lecture on plate tectonics. He managed not to sneer. "According to anonymous feeds uploaded to Earth Mesh, the Revolutionary Army of Gondwanaland claims responsibility for this incident." He paused again, to correct himself. "Is claiming credit, rather," he amended. "There's no prior record of the Revolutionary Army, but it's hard to believe that the two aren't associated."

That did it. Private phones and business etiquette forgotten, his audience fell to chattering among themselves.

"Credit? Who would want credit?"

"Then we know who did it. Good!"

"Well, Great Edison, of *course* they're related! With a name like that—"

"Gondwanaland. What silly kind of name is that?"

"And it makes sense. One continent, one world."

"What about here? What about the Lunar Mesh?"

The last was a good observation, sharper than Hector would have expected from Bonnie Gibbons. He would need to track her activities more carefully, he decided.

"As yet, nothing equivalent has been provided directly to the Lunar Mesh," Hector said. He was suddenly very thirsty. The drugs were reaching their limits. "A few relayed reports made it through before we clamped down on Earth-Moon message traffic."

"Why?" Seven demanded.

"Because I'd like to keep some control of the situation," Hector said, testy now. He reached casually into one of the pockets that hemmed his tunic. Two small bottles were there, neither larger than two fingers. He passed them over and kept looking.

From the audience, Seven continued, "The people of Villanueva deserve—"

"The good people of Villanueva deserve to know that they're reasonably safe. They do," Hector said. "I don't suppose they deserve to be lied to, either, and I don't propose to do that just yet. But we don't have any clear-cut linkage between this incident and the G-landers, and the lack of upload suggests that there isn't one."

Seven fell silent again. He sat down, clearly fuming.

"Why not tell them a bit about Gondwanaland, Hector?" Morrison asked. He was showing surprising depths today, too. Hector would have a made a mental note to monitor his activities more carefully, too, but that really wasn't possible.

He already studied Morrison more than he watched anyone.

· "I'll be happy to," he said. "If you'll give me a moment to refresh myself."

His questing fingers had found what they wanted. One thumb had hooked through the eyelet of the plastic Lethe water sac at his waist. He took it out, popped the seal, and waited for it to chill before sipping with elaborate nonchalance. A chemical taste bathed his mouth, and almost immediately, the world felt better. Voices become gentler, the air become fresher, and his skin seemed to have loosened.

"I'm sorry for the interruption," he said, and took another sip. "This is thirsty work."

That was the secret. No stigma attached to psychotropics use, only to *obvious* psychotropics use. As far as anyone else knew, he was enjoying mineral water and not a supplement.

"Thank you," he said, to no response.

They were waiting.

This time, they let him speak. In short, precise sentences that he had carefully memorized, Hector outlined the strategy he had suggested and that Over-Management's decision makers had accepted. In nine hours—eight and a half now—the Mall would reopen for business, all scars and damage corrected, new cameras and microphones discreetly installed. In fourteen hours, ALC grief counselors on the Earth and the Moon alike would meet with the victims' families, loved ones, and business associates, to discuss settlements and considerations. In twenty-three hours, the last of the wounded would transition from Biome HealthCare Concepts and back into their respective workforces, all damages to them repaired at no cost. In thirty-two hours, the censors and content guides so newly imposed on Earth-Moon message traffic would be partially lifted. By then, carefully spun newshead presentations would have gently guided the Villanueva populace away from perceiving a fearful, terror-filled reality and toward a gentler, less distressing one.

"So we're going to lie to them," Gibbons said. She didn't sound displeased.

"The truth is plastic," Hector said. He shook his head and the world shook, too. His eyes seemed slightly loose in their sockets. "But outright lies almost never work. We'll condition the truth, and push people to prefer our version. We'll put the events in a favorable context."

"A favorable context." That was Seven again, his voice flat and skeptical.

"Hundreds of thousands of people have gone to the Mall, but only five have ever died in an incident like this. Why dwell on bad data, especially when it's so negligible?"

"Five lives aren't negligible," Seven said. "If they'd been dignitaries, or executives—"

"To Earth at large, Villanueva is a synonym for the Moon," Hector interjected. "And Villanueva means the Mall. They *have* to believe that it's a safe, secure place to spend credit, eat food, and have low-G sex. When most men and women say they've gone to the Moon, they mean they've gone to the Mall. We're going to keep things that way."

"What about these Children of Gondwanaland?" Morrison prompted.

"I've provided backgrounders, but there's not much to tell," Hector said. "It's an obscure reactionary organization, headquartered in Northern Europe."

"They're all obscure, until they aren't," Gibbons said sourly.

Hector continued. "Until less than two months ago, their name wasn't associated with anything but broadsides and Mesh pirate-casts. No bite, all words, and not very many of them. Again, your backgrounders—"

"What's the objection to Ad Astra?" someone asked.

"The objection that a chicken has to being eaten," Hector said sharply. As muffled gasps and muttered comments sounded among his audience, he regretted the words. Fatigue had brought glibness with it.

"I'm sorry," he said. "In the broadest possible terms, the Children of Gondwanaland believe that the sending of the *Voyager* plaque was a crime against humanity, a promise of easy pickings to anything smart enough to track it back. If they could figure out a way to do it, they'd try the descendants of the old NASA scientists for that crime and execute them."

"They are the very exemplar of the lunatic fringe," Morrison said. He was still trying to steer the presentation.

"That comment would offend them deeply," Hector continued, without even glancing in his direction. "But not for the reasons you might expect. Do you know what 'lunatic' meant?"

"It means crazy," Gibbons said.

"It used to mean, subject to the influence of the Moon," Hector said. He laughed softly, but not softly enough. He realized that, even as he realized they were staring at him.

"I'm sorry," he said. For perhaps the first time that day, he spoke the absolute truth. "I'm very tired."

"What about the Gondwanaland movement?" Morrison asked again. "Is there any hard evidence pointing to their involvement?"

"No," Hector said. He sipped the water. He knew that the question was for the audience's benefit; Morrison's briefing had been separate and thorough. "There's very little hard evidence, at all, really. What we have is primarily circumstantial. They knew about the incident in advance, far enough in advance to take credit. That's the only direct link."

"What about the bomb? Forensic data?" someone said. It was a new voice, someone who hadn't spoken before.

Hector didn't care. "Straightforward chemical explosive, using processes and components commonly available at consumer level. Adhesives, cleaners, medications, that sort of thing."

His entire audience stared at him, horrified by the implication of his words. Even, he was pleased to note, Erik Morrison.

"Building a low- to moderate-yield explosive devise really isn't very difficult," Hector said, in answer to the unspoken question. "In the last century, you could buy books that told how to do things like this. You could find them in lending libraries. You can find them now, from antique vendors, if you look hard enough. It's just kitchen chemistry. A chef could do it."

There was more to it than that, of course. He saw no point in releasing specifics without a reason.

"The difficult part is placing such a thing," he continued. "Whoever placed this one knew what he was doing. Destroying the elevator shaft ensured collateral damage, and doing it at night kept outright casualties low. Panic is what they want, not slaughter."

"And the culprit?" Gibbons asked.

"We're working on that, too," Hector said. "But there simply isn't very much evidence. This was an explosive device planted in a highly trafficked area, even if it detonated during low-traffic hours. It will be very difficult to identify any specific genetic evidence. Our most likely prospect is continued review of what surveillance records we have, and that's going very slowly."

"Is this the kind of thing that they're likely to do?" Morrison prodded. "Can we screen the tourist backgrounds?"

Yet again, Kowalski shook his head. "I don't know," he said. "I don't think so. This was a real working-class bomb, something used by revolutionaries. They used bombs like this back during the Czech Challenge. It's not a good fit for a band of cranky fanzine publishers." He shrugged. "We're working on it, though," he said.

CHAPTER 8

KEITH Arreigh gripped the segmented plastic cube loosely in his slightly pudgy hand and studied it, rotating it idly this way and that. Each of the block's six square faces was an abstract mosaic of nine equal-sized segments, and each of the segments was one of six colors. The cube was segmented in layers of three across major axes, so that the segments could rotate. Arreigh was trying to arrange them so that each face would be a single hue.

So far, he had failed.

"Debris," he said, and tossed the cube from one hand to the other, pouting. He was sprawled in a low, shapeless piece of furniture that was half chair, half cushion, tucked away in an out-of-the-way corner of the Mesh program production area. His legs stretched out before him, and he slumped deeply enough that his chin was lower than his shoulders.

He looked the worse for wear. His hair was stringy and unwashed, and his eyelids hung heavily behind the data lenses he wore. As he worked the cube, he seemed deliberate to avoid making any eye contact with Katalin Cassidy, balanced atop a high, backless stool some two meters to his left. Her lean form was clad in a simple, cream-colored shift that clung close. Her trim legs were folded beneath her, and her hands rested in the well they made. Her posture was perfect.

Her posture was always perfect, Enola had noticed. As always in her admittedly minimal experience, the Cassidy woman seemed utterly in command of herself. Cool and quiet, she said nothing in response to the other man's ramblings.

"Be careful with that," Bainbridge said. The command seemed vaguely incongruous coming from him, especially directed at a figure of authority such as Arreigh. "It's an antique."

"Then it shouldn't be where people can play with it," Arreigh said. He twisted the cube again, wrenching it this time. He cursed very softly. Clearly, the results weren't what he had wanted.

"It's an *antique* toy," Bainbridge said, speaking to him but standing entirely too close to Enola. Ensconced well within her personal space, he was close enough that she could smell his perspiration. Most of the fussiness had left his voice, and he sounded very matter-of-fact as took readings with a handheld. "It's to look at, not to play with. It's mine," he said. "Be careful."

They were in Bainbridge's personal production facility, a blunt, blocky chunk of space that he sublet from Zonix. The floor footprint was roughly rectangular, with a small stage at one end and a control booth looking down from above. In honor of his guests, Bainbridge had excavated a wheeled console from its storage space. He worked at it intermittently, fussing with one group of settings after another. Enola stood nervously on the stage, lights and cameras strung on whisper-fine filaments to confront her from various angles. A faint scent of electricity hung in the air.

Now, Enola glanced at Arreigh, who still held the cube but no longer worked it. His brow was knit with thought, and he remained studiously unmindful of Katalin.

Something had changed, Enola realized. There had

been some shift in his relationship with his "associate." In his office, in DiNuvio's, he had favored the other woman with frequent, sidelong glances, but now he seemed determined to ignore her existence.

"No, dear," Bainbridge said to her, in a tone of easy authority. He leaned closer, and she could feel his warm breath splash against the skin of her face. Curiously, she didn't mind. She was barely aware of his presence. "Not like that. Look at me."

Enola looked. Away from Sarrah Chrysler, in his place of authority, Bainbridge had become remarkably self-assured. Even his pursed lips had relaxed.

"Now look from my eyes, to this," he said, raising his instrument. He sounded a bit like Doctor Huerta.

She obeyed. A light flashed, and Bainbridge grunted softly. "Now here," he said. "No, like this."

He took her chin between finger and thumb. His touch was as casual as hers might have been on the modeler's controls, but she could feel strength in his hand as he reangled her face, so that she had to adjust the angle of her neck, too. His touch was intimate but impersonal.

Bainbridge gave a grunt of satisfaction and let go. Now, she was facing Katalin directly. "And like *this*," he continued. The hand moved to her waist, then slid with casual familiarity upward to pause just beneath her breast. Again, there was contact, but no real connection as he gently guided her into a new posture. "Keep looking there, but stand up straight. There. Smile."

Katalin raised one perfect hand and wiggled delicate-looking fingers in a rippling wave of encouragement.

Enola stood up straight. She smiled. Again, the light flashed, and again, Bainbridge made a sound of pleasure.

"You're doing it wrong," he said suddenly.

"But I—"

"Not you," he told her and turned to face Arreigh. "You. That's not just an exercise in hand-eye, it's a test of spatial relationship skills." As he spoke, he stepped away from Enola and back to the nearby console.

Arreigh was twisting the cube again, harder this time. The old plastic squeaked as he worked it. Clearly, he lacked either well-developed spatial relationship skills or patience.

"Gently!" Bainbridge said again.

Rather than make any direct response, Arreigh asked, "Do you have a verdict for me?"

Bainbridge ignored him, intent on his console's readings.

"May I move now?" Enola asked. The session of structured posing had made her stiff and sore. She knew full well that she was quite physically fit; her Villanueva-mandated regimen kept her in better shape than many groundhog athletes. Even so, an hour-plus of putting her body in unfamiliar positions and holding them while Bainbridge did his nebulous work had taken its toll. The hard studio floor felt plastic beneath her feet, and objects at the edges of her field of view had taken on a quivering quality.

Worse, the slight nausea that had been her almost constant companion of late had returned. She was hungry, but the thought of eating made her feel worse, not better.

"Please?" she asked again.

"Go ahead," Bainbridge said, then looked up from his work. "Tell me something. Do you think you're easy to work with, Enola?"

She wasn't certain how to answer that, and only smiled tentatively.

He sighed. "What's your Thurlinger index, then?" he asked. When she didn't answer immediately, he continued, "I can access it without too much difficulty."

"Eight-four," Enola said meekly. Thurlinger's Quotient was a social adaptability score, part of the psychiatric profiling that Villanueva personnel underwent at regular intervals. Eight-four really wasn't a very good score.

Bainbridge nodded, smiled. He glanced at Arreigh. "Sarrah's is only three over two," he said. "Prima donna rating."

"Sarrah has other qualifications," Keith said. He crossed his legs and made a great show of turning his attention away from the variegated cube, as if he had been distracted from a matter of vital importance. "And Hasbro here was tested for an office environment. Mesh work is different. You can't draw a line from one to the other."

He sounded newly unenthusiastic. Enola had to wonder if she had somehow offended him. Before she could gather the courage to ask, Bainbridge laughed.

"I don't care if she was tested at a companion agency," he said. "Eight-four is very good. I'd take a salary cut if you promised me I'd only ever work with values of over seven-oh. A big cut."

Enola beamed. Her heart raced. The implications of Bainbridge's words were obvious.

"Never mind that," Arreigh said. He pulled himself together a bit, enough that he no longer seemed in danger of being swallowed by the chair. "Can she fill the role?"

"I haven't tested her voice, but visually, there's a good match," Bainbridge said.

He did something at the console to throw ten enlarged images on the studio wall. They were pictures of Enola, or at least of parts of her, taken from various angles. It seemed very strange to see herself like that, segmented.

"I can work with this," Bainbridge continued. "I've already started color and light modeling. With the right mirage overlays—"

"With a bare minimum of miraging," Arreigh said, from his corner. "The absolute minimum." He emphasized each syllable of all three words, took a breath, and continued with both energy and hauteur. "We want authenticity, remember? We want something that's real."

"She's real," Bainbridge said. He picked up a laser pointer and began indicating elements of the projected images. "No substantive enhancement needed, at least not for newshead work. She'll never go to Holo-wood without a major overhaul, but there's an info-Mesh audience waiting for her." He smiled again. "You won't have to dress her down, either. She's real-world enough. Sarrah's likely to feel threatened."

"We can worry about Sarrah some other time," Arreigh said coolly.

Bainbridge sounded even more like a doctor as he launched into a discussion of facial symmetry, eye-to-nose proportions, skin coloration, skin/hair contrast, and something he called "specific Bertillon standards." The pointer's red dot moved from image to image. The lecture was clearly more for Enola's benefit than for Arreigh or Cassidy's, and Bainbridge tried to keep it clear of specialty jargon, but in a matter of minutes, she was utterly lost. After a few more minutes, she said so.

"He means you're pretty," Arreigh explained. Despite his grudging enthusiasm, he still seemed tired and edgy. He continued to play with the cube.

"I think Enola knows that," Katalin said, from her perch. They were the first words she had spoken since they had come to this place.

Enola blushed.

"He means that the cameras think you're pretty," Arreigh amended. He continued not looking in Katalin's direction. "At least, you're prettier than most people who can speak easily about large-scale, heavy metal construction processes. You know enough—you *will* know enough to impress, and you're attractive enough to make that knowledge accessible."

"I don't think we'll do any better locally," Katalin said. It was one of her longer sentences, but Arreigh seemed to take no note of what she had said.

"Photo-congeniality is a subtle quality," Bainbridge said. "People have studied it for as long as there have been cameras, and they've studied it more since miraging began. It's a quality separate and distinct from comeliness, even though the two generally go hand in hand." He smiled. "You've got them both, Enola. You'll make a fine spokesperson."

"Subject matter expert," Keith said. "That's what we call them this cycle." He turned hazel eyes in Enola's direction. "And don't worry about expertise. If you have working knowledge, we can manage the rest."

"Subject matter expert," Bainbridge agreed. "And just in time, too. Especially after the Mall incident."

"I worked on parts of the Mall, though," she volunteered. "The newer parts, at least. And the Splinter. I worked on the prop models for them, I mean."

Arreigh fixed Enola with a speculative gaze. "I don't suppose you're represented?" he asked.

She shook her head. Nearly two decades before, an employment broker in Syracuse, New York, had arranged her contract with Duckworth, but that professional relationship had long since ended. She had no one to negotiate for her.

"Hmph." Arreigh grinned. It took years from his already youthful features. "Well, now. I think I'd better start by taking a look at your present compensation schedule," he said. "Then we can talk about expectations."

Bainbridge looked as if he wanted to say something, but refrained.

"I'm not currently employed," Enola reminded him, embarrassed by her status. "I'm on severance."

Arreigh nodded again. "That makes things even easier," he said. "Your severance package, then. Let's go."

"There will be legalities," Bainbridge said. "And Guild standards, and—"

· "Credit can take care of that," Keith said. He stood, tossing the cube aside. Bainbridge yelped in dismay as the antique hurtled toward the nearby wall.

It never made impact. Katalin Cassidy had dismounted her seat with fluid grace. Now, her nimble fingers plucked the toy from the air, mid-trajectory. Her hands twisted the cube once, twice, three times, in a blur of motion. When she set it down on her so recently vacated stool, each of the cube's six faces presented only a single color. She smiled at Keith, but said nothing.

Neither did he, so she stuck out her tongue.

ERIK had composed his body in a modified lotus, his legs folded and looped beneath him, his hands resting, palms up, on his knees. Up-pointed fingers waved like fronds in a subsea current. He barely noticed.

But for him and the aids he required, his apartment alcove was effectively empty. The couch he had shared with Sarrah Chrysler had returned to its storage niche, and the long, low table was gone, too. In its place, squarely before him, was an ergonomic keyboard, presenting itself to him on jointed, spider-like legs. Attached to the keyboard was a polymer film computer and display screen. The housekeeper enunciator emitted the steady click, click, click of a metronome, and the air was heavy with the soothing incense aroma from a scent-thesizer. All of these things, Erik was aware of, but only on some level that commanded no conscious thought.

Erik breathed deeply, steadily, pulling the air as far into his body as he could. The loose clothing that he wore rustled against his skin, but he paid it no mind. Instead, he listened to the rhythms of his body and worked first with them, then *past* them. The last bits of doubt and indecision fell away, like forgotten dreams, as Erik found his center.

This was the only part of the process that required effort, and even that need had become vastly less with practice. Here, in familiar seclusion and quiet, the transition was an exercise in ease.

Years had passed since Erik had meditated on a daily basis, but his mind and body remembered. In moments, he had achieved an autohypnotic state, a kind of lucid dreaming. His mind settled into a light trance that closely resembled sleep, but where conscious thought and self-control lingered. Parts of his mind that were hidden to most were obvious and evident now, as his tranquil thoughts moved in orderly formations. The petty concerns and anxieties that were the business of workaday life remained, but with discreet and clear-cut boundaries that he knew how to avoid.

He was ready, he half-realized. He was ready, and it was time. The link that he had arranged would be open by now.

His hands moved without conscious command. They

drifted forward and up, leading his wrists and arms with them. Erik's spine remained in a comfortable curve, however, and the rest of his body stationary. His eyes remained only half-open as his fingers found the keyboard's tessellated contours.

"Hello, Wendy," he typed.

It only took the least, most glancing strokes of his fingertips on the keys to enter the words. The physical action was so effortless that, again, he was scarcely aware of it. The words seemed to flow from him.

"Hello, Erik," the words appeared, crisp black on low-glare gray. *"Thank you for agreeing to this."*

"It's my pleasure," he typed back. It was not quite a lie. All that Erik felt in his current state was a kind of deliberate tranquility. "And it seemed worth a try." For a while now, he had been trying to find a way to expedite communication. He was the designated ALC liaison for Scheer, in part because he was already subject to her glamour, but willing to work against it. The relayed recordings were one approach, effective but cumbersome.

"I do think that you're being overly cautious," Wendy responded. It was unlikely that she typed the words; typing was no longer a particularly common skill. She was almost certainly using a brainware transcriber, rather than entering the text herself. The brainware crutch was much easier, but riskier, too. Unguarded words could be transcribed, transmitted, and received before the speaker thought to cancel.

"How is life at Hello, Wendy?" Erik asked. Without any intent on his part, the words carried a double meaning. Years had passed since Wendy's feet had set down in Villanueva. It would have been easy for her to take the question as a reminder of her exile.

She didn't. *"Halo,"* she corrected, citing the official name. He was certain that she spoke the word in a way that put an edge on the paired syllables.

"Halo," Erik acknowledged. He began to feel a muted optimism. The challenge at hand was to focus past Wendy and respond to her words, instead—and only her words. The insulation provided by the keyboard/display relay helped, and his meditative state helped more, but he could not be certain that the goal had been reached.

He could never be certain.

"I'm not interested in posing a threat, Erik," Wendy said.

"I know that," he replied. Being in a half-trance aligned him with his emotions and gave him some perspective on those feelings, but did not banish them. He could still feel irritation. "We compete, but you're not an active threat. If I thought you were, we wouldn't be speaking in real-time, not even like this. We might not be speaking at all. I wouldn't take the risk."

After a moment's thought, he typed more. "And it is a risk."

That had been the subject of much discussion with the various specialists hired by Over-Management and cleared for full briefings on Wendy Scheer. The exact nature of her gift was unknown and perhaps unknowable. Everyone agreed, however, that it included aspects of reflex conditioning. Everyone liked Wendy Scheer, and the more they knew her, the more they liked her.

All that was known about the process's specific workings was that they required initial personal contact, and found reinforcement in subsequent, real-time encounters. Meet Wendy once, in person, and like her. Each subsequent exposure, via Mesh link or phone-feed, prompted the contacted party to like her more. It had to be real-time, however; record-delayed interactions didn't have the same impact.

And neither, Erik hoped, did transactions such as this.

"I hope this works for you," Wendy replied. *"We lose too much with the delay, without the give and take of conversation."*

Erik typed nothing. He retreated a bit more deeply into himself and thought of chrysanthemums blooming beneath a summer sun. Peace received him.

"I want to offer Project Halo and Armstrong Base's full

cooperation in the investigation of the Mall incident," Wendy typed after a too-long lag.

"I'm not sure that Halo has anything to offer that we don't already possess," Erik typed. "But thank you. I'll raise the issue with Over-Management."

"I've already tendered a formal proposal under official seal," Wendy replied. *"But they won't accept the offer if you don't endorse it."*

"You overestimate." Erik's fingers moved again as if of their own volition. "It's not my decision."

"No, I don't think I overestimate at all." Again, the scrolling letters paused. *"I have my sources, Erik. Perhaps you can't make things happen, but you can make things not happen. Your judgment is very highly regarded."*

The flattery had no effect on him, but its preamble did. Hector had been right, Erik realized. Pique poked through the haze of tranquility. He examined the errant emotion carefully and almost smiled. For some reason, he was less troubled by Wendy's apparent activities than he was by the possibility that Hector had been correct all along.

"The network is still in place, then?" he asked. His breaths still came in steady, measured rhythms.

"I have my sources," the words came again. His mind's eye could see her smile. *"Here, and on Earth. I work for the government, after all."*

"Hector is confident that he can deal with the situation," Erik typed.

Click, click, click went the metronome.

"Hector is confident that he can bury the incident, make it a footnote. I don't want that to happen. We have specialized analytical equipment and human resources that could be helpful," Wendy persisted. *"We have specialists Earthside who could be here in days."*

"You have a priority requirement to achieve greater input in the day-to-day operation of Villanueva," Erik typed. "The ALC has a policy of resisting such overtures."

A long pause followed. The metronome's steady beat continued, relentless.

"I'm not your enemy, Erik," Wendy repeated.

"We're rivals," Erik typed.

"Rivals with common interests."

"We're rivals," he told her again. "That's probably to the good, too." He was a firm believer in competition.

"We're rivals working together on something very important," Wendy replied. *"Something vital to the future of the human race."*

"And because we're rivals working toward a common goal, there will be conflict," Erik typed. "That can't be avoided." This time, he paused. "The ALC built this establishment, Wendy. The private sector made commercial space travel a reality after the governments of the world had abandoned it. We're not going to cede control of Villanueva just because we've accepted federal contracts."

The rhetoric was old and familiar. It flowed from his fingertips like water.

"We can help," read Wendy's words. *"Let us."*

He had no doubts about her sincerity, or at least, lack of enmity. Wendy Scheer was one of the very few truly idealistic people Erik had ever met, committed to a goal and effective in her pursuit of it, without letting the process of pursuit become an end unto itself. There was something of the evangelist or missionary about her, but she was no fanatic. That was good. He could never have worked with her otherwise.

She believed in something bigger than herself, however. And even though she had convinced him of the fundamental correctness of her goals, their respective preferred paths for reaching those goals would always have points of opposition.

"I'm quite confident in the ability of our own people to resolve the incident successfully," Erik typed.

"Erik, I am not making this request—this offer solely on my own authority," Wendy's response finally came. *"I've been directed to."*

"The ALC has judicial autonomy and investigative authority within the constraints of the Villaneuva charter,"

Erik typed rapidly. The words were engrained deeply in his mind.

"Within those constraints," Wendy agreed. What she said was what her superiors were no doubt saying, too. Already, ALC Legal was fielding a firestorm of queries, letters of concern, legal instruments, and general complaints from old Earth.

"When Kowalski's investigation is complete, any personnel determined to be responsible by Company Court will be shipped back to Earth for appropriate disposition," Erik typed. The words came easily. He had already drafted them for a Mesh release.

"And what if the investigation is never complete?" Wendy asked. *"What if the ALC never quite manages to come to a conclusion?"*

Erik paused. Even in near-trance the direction the conversation had suddenly taken was enough to unsettle him. Wendy was entirely too perceptive, and she understood people like Hector Kowalski entirely too well. The metronome's clicks no longer soothed, but chipped away instead at his composure.

"Speaking strictly in a back-channel capacity, I've been asked to remind you that the World Court, which has jurisdiction over Villanueva's charter, resumes session next month," Wendy's words marched across the screen. *"The justices have agreed to entertain several new motions."*

"And the government has decided to enter the same," Erik typed. "That's understandable, I suppose." He could certainly see their point of view.

"Five tourists, Erik. Five citizens, none of them covered by resident work contracts."

"But covered by releases and waivers," he parroted back the words he had heard at the briefing.

"That have been untested by circumstances such as these," Wendy continued. *"Five people, five productive, taxpaying citizens have died. It's appropriate that the federal government take an interest."*

Another pause stretched for too-long seconds, and Erik

tranquilly considered her words. They seemed fundamentally correct, even undeniable.

"There are also funding issues," Wendy continued. *"No one is eager to contract with a facility that isn't at least reasonably safe. They have their own priorities."*

"That seems reasonable," he typed. It did. "If we can balance—"

Erik drew himself up short as his fingers moved to complete the words. He sat bolt upright and pulled his hands back from the keyboard, as if from fire. Sweat erupted on his forehead, and a wave of chills swept through him.

"My God," he said softly, fully awake now, and fully aware, even if not totally in command of himself. The panicked words sounded very small and remote in the small room's close confines.

His very thoughts and viewpoints had been seeping away, eroded by a senseless desire to please the woman who sat at the other end of the Mesh link. He hugged himself, almost trembling. He had forgotten how insidious Scheer's effect could be. For now, that wish to do her well was expressing itself along the only avenue available to it, business-managerial. Under other circumstances, it might play out very differently.

Under other circumstances, years before, it nearly had.

Had her allure somehow become more powerful? Or had he become particularly susceptible? Or was it simply a matter of conditioned reflex, triggered now even by sterile type? Erik couldn't tell, and worried that he would never be able to.

"Erik?"

"I'm going to have to end the session, now, Wendy," he typed. He could work against her, but it was an effort. "You're doing it again."

"No."

The single word popped into existence even before his had finished forming.

"Yes," he typed.

"I'm doing nothing to you," Wendy insisted. The words

flowed like electricity. Despite the distance between them, despite the strictly informational mode of their communications, there was no mistaking her urgency. *"I can't. Believe me, I have some idea how this works. It doesn't work like this."*

He didn't think she was lying, but he was reasonably sure that she was wrong. Either that, or her rhetoric had made entirely too much sense.

"I'm ending the session," he typed again. He didn't want to. It was all he could do to enter the words.

"We can try again." A pause. *"Please."*

"Maybe," he said aloud as the screen blanked, but he knew that she could not hear him.

"I want you to wear this," Huerta told Enola. He sounded very serious. "I want you to wear it at all times."

What he handed her looked like another gene patch, but several times thicker. She flexed it tentatively and was surprised that it resisted, however slightly.

"This is the skin side," he said, indicating. "Use the same solution I gave you with your kit to make it cling. Make sure you wear it on your torso, somewhere that it can't be dislodged. I recommend the base of your spine, right above the buttocks. You can get a good reading there."

She looked at him, worried. "What is this?" she said. She flexed it again. It felt like skin.

"Outboard diagnostic relay," he said. He paused. "I don't like some of your readings, Enola."

She flinched. Those were words she never wanted to hear from a physician. No one did, she supposed.

"It's probably nothing to worry about," he continued.

"Probably?" she said. That wasn't something she liked hearing, either. The good news of her earlier session with Bainbridge and Arreigh suddenly faded into the back of her mind.

After the audition and tests, she had enjoyed a quick and casual lunch with the others before returning to her apartment for a change of clothes. Waiting for her had been four messages from Crag Fortinbras, rubbing shoulders with the other ten or so she had rejected in recent days, and one from Huerta, with instructions to call him. That, in turn, had led to this follow-up session.

And the bad news.

"The numbers are wrong," Huerta said. "The regression therapy seems to have gone slightly off course."

She looked at him, horrified. She thought of Lyle Chesney, the terribly fat man in Personnel, of his wheezing breath and oily skin. "You said it was safe!" she nearly yelped.

"It is safe," Huerta said. He actually raised his hands as if to ward off a blow. "Usually, it's very safe. But no process is perfect."

Enola rolled the skin-colored patch he had given her. It was woven plastic, and she could tell that it was multiple layers thick. A very slight springy quality suggested that there was a metallic aspect to it, too.

"What's going to happen?" she asked.

"There are some enzyme levels I want to track. Your liver chemistry is suboptimal. Bone density is off, too, but not seriously. None of it's very serious, but taken together, it's a situation I want to monitor."

"What's going to happen?" she asked again, more sharply this time.

Huerta managed a smile. "You're going home," he said. "Almost certainly, your body will adjust properly, and you'll go back to Earth and a new life. That is, if you follow instructions."

Enola shuddered, very slightly. Another wave of nausea swept over her. She hadn't mentioned that symptom to the doctor, and now she wondered if she should.

Probably not. It could only bring more bad news.

"What if I'm not going home?" she asked instead.

Now it was his turn to look as if he'd heard unwelcome news. "I don't understand," he said. He flipped his personal computer in her direction, so that she could see that her own file was on display, and then turned it back again. "You're going home," he said. "Therapy is to be completed within six weeks. Your passage is already booked. It's all in your severance."

"I may have found other employment," Enola said slowly.

He looked at her with something like disgust. It was the first time she had seen that reaction, but she knew that it would not be the last. Even for displaced staff, job-hopping was generally considered the very trademark of the unprofessional.

"Term work? I don't think that would be a good idea, Enola," he said slowly.

Again, she looked at him without speaking.

"You've been here many years. The treatment you required now is a very specific protocol, and very expensive," he said. "It's Duckworth's expense, however. Interrupt it now, and you'll need to pay for it yourself if you resume it. Your basic plan won't. If you interrupt it, if you want to resume it, you'll have to pay for it yourself. I don't think you can afford to do that."

"And what if I have to go back without the therapy?" she asked.

His only reply was to shake his head.

"What about—about this?" she asked, indicating the flexible little patch, but certain that he would know what she really meant.

"I can adjust your patch dosage," Huerta said, clearly happy to be on safer ground. "All we're seeing now is warning signs, and not very severe ones. If we monitor you properly, things should work out." He paused. "Have you experienced any other symptoms?" he asked.

Enola thought about the nausea again. "No," she said.

"Good," Huerta replied. "Now, have you been drinking alcohol? Or ingesting any other psychotropes?"

CHAPTER 9

"—AND my guest, Enola Hasbro," Sarrah Chrysler said. She swiveled in her chair and smiled not so much at Enola as in her general direction. The soft studio lighting did little to soften the strong lines of her face, lines that had been made stronger with discreet cosmetics. "Shall we talk?" she asked.

"Of course," Enola replied. Her voice was steady and sure as she parroted the words she had rehearsed so many times, but the smile was nervous and strained. Chrysler's subtle disdain had begun to wear.

They were seated behind a low, shared desk that stretched in a graceful curve before a smartwall screen. This was very nearly the archetypal venue for newshead Meshcasts, common to nearly every news or information or discussion program. Some things never changed, Enola realized. She had seen setups like this on feeds for as long as she could remember, and in archival programming that she recalled from school. Now, for some reason, she wondered how many men's and women's bottoms had rested in this very chair in this particular studio's lifetime. She wondered how many of those men and women were remembered and

how many had been completely, absolutely forgotten, sub-
sumed again by anonymity.

As a child, on Earth, Enola had fantasized about fame.
She was surprised to realize that she had not forgotten
those dreams.

Chrysler turned now to face the primary camera; she was
too much of a professional, too experienced, to be unmindful of the others. Smaller than the main unit and less capable but vastly more maneuverable, the secondaries roamed
the production space like slave satellites. They rode fine cables that were translucent to the human eye and that the
Mesh brainware had been told to ignore, and were able to
capture images from countless finely calibrated angles.
Enola found them distracting and worrisome, additional un-
wanted peripheral visual noise in a working environment to
which she was unaccustomed. Monitor panels on the opposite walls offered further distraction, but Enola didn't dare
even consider them. She had enough to worry about.

Enola hoped that her fretfulness wouldn't show. The
possibility of saying something foolish or wrong while thousands watched and listened worried her. Bainbridge had
promised that this would be a local Meshcast only and that
he personally would edit out any egregious missteps before
relay to Earth, but embarrassing herself locally would be
quite bad enough.

If the cameras made her nervous, they had the opposite
effect on Chrysler. The older woman seemed utterly at ease
in the spotlight, focusing on the cameras as they focused
on her. If she felt even the slightest hint of ill ease or nerv-
ousness, it did not show. The skin of her face was smooth
and dry.

"Enola is with us from Duckworth, the ALC founder
that also conceptualized and constructed the Mall,"
Chrysler continued. She glanced at Enola again and made
another perfunctory smile, then returned her attention to
the camera array before Enola could smile back.

Chrysler didn't seem to like her, Enola had begun to
realize.

"No," Keith Arreigh's voice said in her left ear, emphatically.

"Excuse me, Sarrah," Enola said, interrupting the other woman. Instantly, several of the smaller cameras trained their lenses on her again. "That's not entirely correct. I'm not here from Duckworth." That was a lie, in all but the most technical sense. Keith had told her to phrase it that way. Most of the likely audience were term staff and would think she was the same. "I'm here as a private resident, one who knows a little bit about the Mall. I'm not a spokesperson, not officially."

"Oh," Sarrah said. "Thank you for the clarification, but that's what I intended to say, of course." But she smiled in a way that suggested she didn't regret the error at all.

It was a misstatement that could have caused problems for Enola. Arreigh had explained that to them both again and again during preparatory discussions, and the words they should use when addressing her status.

Technically, Enola was still a Duckworth employee. Even creating the impression that she spoke on behalf of the company would cause serious problems with her severance package. Technically, appearing as a paid Zonix consultant could do the same. Those were the reasons for the carefully worded disclaimer.

"You're a guest," Arreigh had told her. "Sarrah's guest. If we resolve things properly, I'll make sure you get paid. Until then, think of it as another audition. Sarrah, you can think of it as a bystander interview, in-studio instead of in the street." He had grinned then. "They don't have streets here, do they?"

"I'm here as a private resident," Enola told the world beyond the Mesh. The words came easily now. Perversely, Chrysler's misstep reassured her.

This really didn't seem to be very difficult.

"Very good," Keith's relayed voice murmured.

"Of course you are," Sarrah said, with an air of disdain so faint that Enola wondered if the cameras and microphones had detected it. Refocusing herself, Chrysler continued. "Earlier this week, the heart of Villanueva was rocked by—"

Enola listened without listening as Sarrah Chrysler briefly recapped the mysterious explosion—she referred to it as "the incident"—at the Mall, and the long hours of confusion that had followed. She spoke in easy, relaxed sentences that used entirely too many words to say very little, but that left a vague good feeling in their wake. To hear Chrysler's telling, no one had been frightened or worried by the mysterious blast, and for those on the scene at the time, injuries had been few and minor and easily resolved. She could have been talking about something long ago and far away, likely to have only the slightest impact on day-to-day life.

Enola glanced at one of the monitor displays, eager to see how she looked. What she saw pleased her. The composite image showed both women, matted against a backdrop of images from inside the Mall. They were archival pictures, of course; Over-Management had cleared nothing new for Meshcast. But Enola herself looked very nice, petite and trim and very professionally attired. With no twinge of ego, she realized that she looked much nicer than Chrysler.

Perhaps that was the problem.

"—more than 80 percent of the Mall has reopened for business," the other woman concluded. "And that's why my guest is here, to talk about what's been done and what's still needed."

"*No,*" Keith's voice said again. Now, he spoke with blunt authority.

Enola didn't need the reminder. She shook her head and turned to face Sarrah, but not directly. She was vaguely aware of activity in the periphery of her vision as cameras slid up and back to track her movement. She smiled. "Well," she said smoothly. "I can't speak with any authority. But I can tell you about what's probably being done, and how we did it years ago."

"We?" Sarrah stressed the single word. Her smile became brittle.

"Duckworth," she amended. "I can't take any real personal responsibility for the work, though. I was on the team that modeled the Mall's most recent renovation, about six years ago."

"So you speak from personal experience?" Sarrah prodded.

"Well, from personal *knowledge,* at least," Enola said. Now that the waiting was over, much of her tension had receded and she could speak more easily, but her next words, she uttered with care. "Or perspective. But, obviously, I can't share any proprietary background data that hasn't been previously released."

"Very good," Keith said, making Enola smile..She felt as if she had an angel looking over her shoulder, guiding her.

For a split second, Sarrah Chrysler's expression seemed to ask just why Enola was there at all, but the skepticism was hidden from view when she smiled. It was a very professional-looking smile, however.

"Let me show you," Enola said. The words came even more easily now as she moved her hands just above the small control station that was on her side of the studio desk, hidden from the cameras' probing eyes. The controls here were more modern, and more sensitive, responding to induction signals sent by the rings Enola wore, but the underlying methodology was the same. The system's response was instant. From the floor between and before them, with the desk's gentle curve, sterile whiteness lanced upward. So clear and distinct were the beam's boundaries that it could have been a physical thing. The studio lights did nothing to dilute or obscure it.

"Very nice," Keith said. During the production process, away from the dance floor or cheesecake trolley, he was entirely business. *"Very clean."*

That was good. Enola had worried that the unfamiliar modeling system provided by Zonix InfoMesh would malfunction, or that the holographic image it generated wouldn't register properly on the Mesh cameras. Her doubts had been unfounded, however. Arreigh had explained patiently that the images she created were also being echoed within the production system's main Gummi. "The studio image is there to make things easier for you," he had explained. "Let the slave system keep the audience entertained."

The on-set modeler hadn't made things any easier for Sarrah, Enola realized, and almost giggled. The Mesh newshead had recoiled noticeably and was only now concealing her surprise. Enola could sympathize. The beam hadn't been nearly as bright during the single, short rehearsal.

"This is the northeast elevator bank," Enola said, working the controls again. The beam condensed into a reasonable facsimile of the elevator shaft in question, augmented by Enola with contour highlights for the sake of clarity. "The real version is nearly invisible, of course," she continued. "But think of this as a diagram." Enola moved her hands some more and one, two, three bubble-cars appeared within the modeled vertical tunnel as she summoned up their images from Zonix archives. "The Mall is the single largest volume of enclosed space in Villanueva," she said. "And the human eye likes open space, so the original design team did what it could to avoid subdividing that space."

There were better ways to do this, she knew. With the right brainware and the proper data files, she could have created images vastly more accurate. Arreigh had vetoed that approach, however, insisting that his needs would be better served by a more schematic approach. "When management finally releases the real images, I want them to be new and exciting," he had told her. "Not a shadow of a simulation."

Enola worked her way through the presentation, surprising herself at the ease of the process. Months ago, she might have done much the same thing for her superiors at Duckworth, or for potential customers outside the company. Her part under those circumstances would have been much the same, though the sources of her information would have been quite different.

With simple, quick movements, she holoed into place a representative sampling of the walkway and display panels that would have been in place that night. She didn't illume them all; the visual clutter would have overwhelmed any audience. Despite the official priority management placed on open space, aesthetics only rarely outranked revenue on the ALC's list of priorities in the real world. She traced into place the lighting arrays and walkways with broad, simple strokes, working more quickly as she accustomed herself to the up-scale modeler.

"Here is where the explosion happened," she said, and gestured at a point on the elevator shaft, some three-quarters of the distance from Mall floor to Mall ceiling. "From what your staff has told me."

"Very good," Keith Arreigh phoned into Enola's ear. He had suggested earlier that she be very careful to credit any information she dispensed as coming from public sources, or a least from Zonix's sources. Sarrah's research staff had interviewed survivors and witnesses in the hours since the blast.

"After that, it was all collateral damage," Enola continued. More light-field constructs traced the paths of debris, of broken walkways, of shattered display boards. Many of the shops and galleries along the Mall's tiered walls hid behind physical sound-breaks, intended either to decorate or to supplement suppressor fields. Enola drew some of those, too, enough to illustrate but not so many as to confuse the casual viewer. Then she showed what they would look like, shattered, their fragments falling in slow motion, to shatter further on the floor below. Throughout the modeling process, she acted on guidance from Keith Arreigh and turned aside verbal feints from Sarrah Chrysler.

She didn't bother to indicate the men and women unfortunate enough to intersect the paths of shockwaves or debris. She didn't like thinking about them.

The process itself was easy, putting old skills to a new purpose. Her hands glided as if with lives of their own, and through the general haze of enjoyment and discovery, a momentary pang of nostalgia flared. Enola had liked her job at Duckworth very much, especially in the early days. This experience was surprisingly similar.

"There," she said, after several minutes of modeling that was at once expert and improvised. "That is how it probably happened."

"Probably?" Sarrah asked. "Your reconstruction—"

Enola shook her head. This time, she spoke without any phone prompting. "It's not a reconstruction," she said. "Not it the sense that you mean. It's a model, based on information that your staff provided." She smiled sweetly. "Think of it as a presentation, instead."

Sarrah didn't say anything.

"Now, after investigation, the next phase would be salvage and reconstruction. Duckworth Construction may make some renovations, but I doubt the fundamental architecture will change." Her hands moved again, this time summoning images from Mesh archives, simplifying them for clarity, and then casting them in light. "Now, according to historical records and public databases . . ."

RANK had its privileges. They weren't immeasurable or all encompassing, but they were real.

Erik sat comfortably in a sling-chair behind the custom desk in his private office. It was a slab of black basalt, native rock from *Mare Tranquilliatis*. A small quarry had been discreetly dug there, not too terribly far from the site of the historic Neil Armstrong landing museum and memorial. In the early days of the colony, that quarry had done reasonable business selling lunar fragments back on Earth for sale at exorbitant prices to would-be tourists who couldn't afford to take the trip. Erik, upon his ascendance to Over-Management and in a fit of symbolism, had ordered a block of the stuff carved and polished and generally equipped to serve as his personal workstation. It stood in his office, an inverted, off-center pyramid. The largest face was his working surface; the point, anchored securely somewhere beneath the floor, was its offset base. The over-all effect was precarious but impressive, and Erik liked it.

Another privilege of rank was the expensive, highly specialized brainware that he'd ordered downloaded to his desk. He was running it now, using the more advanced Gummis available to him in his office suite, and tied in to two data files. One was a text file of his conversation with Wendy Scheer.

The other was a detailed download from the outboard diagnostic relay that he had worn during that session, yet another of rank's privileges. He'd secured the device from his contacts at Biome, requisitioning it on his authority as director of communications for Over-Management. The entire time that he'd been online with Wendy Scheer, the wafer-thin piece of diagnostic hardware had clung to the skin at the base of his neck, just above his shoulder blades. Now, on his desktop display, it played back its readings, in synchronicity with his dialog record. He read Wendy's words again, and read how his body had responded to them, neatly correlated by some of the most advanced medical brainware that credit could buy. The sequence of cause-and-effect was explicated and laid bare.

And he had no idea what to make of it.

"Hello, Erik," she had typed. *"Thank you for agreeing to this."* Now, Erik read the words slowly, a syllable at a time. He looked alternately at the isolated text and then at the cor-related biometric readings. The recorded levels all reflected his light trance state—cellular respiration was low, breath-ing regular, pulse steady, brainwave activity was smooth and symmetrical. If he regarded the readings from prior to her greeting as a benchmark, however, each subsequent ex-change saw shifts in his personal readings.

"We lose too much with the delay, without the give and take of conversation," Wendy had typed. In response, Erik's electroencephalograph readings had hiccupped slightly, then settled into a new rhythm. The jagged line that traced his EEG values jerked and twitched, grew new peaks and valleys, then continued in that path. Respiration,

pulse, and other values changed, too, each working toward a new equilibrium. According to the brainware's annotations, these weren't the shifts that came with conversation or other mental activity. These were what his desk's Gummi termed "nonproblematic anomalies."

Erik wished he knew what that meant.

The brainware annotations suggested he consult a medical professional, and helpfully offered a list of Biome-approved specialists. Erik considered the option, then set it aside. Although they had never fully articulated the terms, part of his personal truce with Wendy Scheer was that he would do as little as possible to publicize her special attributes. In return, she tempered her operations with what she termed "the spirit of cooperation."

Erik's concession regarding Wendy's status had been sizeable, requiring a great deal of mutual trust. Under certain circumstances, Scheer's mere presence disrupted the operation of the large-scale Gummis that were Villanueva's Mesh and operational infrastructure. In a very real sense, the fact that Scheer existed made her a threat to the day-to-day safety and health of the people Erik worked with.

He wondered now if he had made that concession with a clear mind.

He scrolled though more of the recorded readings, reviewing data that looked important and feeling frustrated by his own lack of technical understanding. Throughout his conversation, even when his trance state should have been at its deepest, his pulse oxygen had risen steadily. So had his levels of serotonin, which the brainware helpfully identified as a neurotransmitter chemical associated with the pleasure response. Despite that, he didn't recall feeling particularly happy or even pleased during the discussion.

Of course, whatever the mechanics of the process were, they were moot compared with the central question. Had she actually been influencing him at that level, even over a remote, text-only link? Or was it a conditioned response, an ongoing response to something she had imprinted on him during their several physical encounters?

Erik didn't know. He couldn't know. Nothing he had read or researched seemed to hold even a hint of the answer. Since meeting Wendy, he had read extensively on pheromones, hypnotism, even parapsychology and the occult. None of it seemed to track well with his personal experience.

Without even realizing it, he cursed, very softly. Erik liked things he could understand and processes he could follow and recreate. He liked big black basalt desks and comfortable sling-chairs, and he liked numbers that added in neat patterns. He liked the elaborate, artistic chemistry of food preparation. He didn't like mysteries.

"Incoming message," his office manager reported.

"Record it," Erik responded, still preoccupied.

"Delay overridden," the manager replied, and then another voice continued. *"Are you busy, Erik? Are you alone?"*

It was Hector Kowalski.

"I hope this is urgent," was Erik's only response. He continued trying to focus on the correlated data displays.

"I think it is," Kowalski continued. *"Go to Mesh. Chrysler's feed. Now."*

With a sigh, Erik complied. A moment later, the puzzle of Wendy Scheer and its attendant issues had vanished from his mind. Instead, and with some surprise, he pondered a familiar voice, and the image of an attractive, Asiatic woman busily operating an industrial-grade image modeler.

Why was Enola Hasbro a featured speaker on the Mesh?

"YOU were *brilliant!"* Keith Arreigh nearly barked the words, or crowed them, or made them in some way that sounded less like speech than like the sound an excited animal might make. However he voiced them, they were the sounds of triumph. There was something primal about the man's delight, the way he drummed his hands on the table-top, hard enough to make their drinks tremble and slop. "Brilliant, I tell you!" he said again. "You were *born* for this! You should never have worked for anyone else!"

Enola blushed and hoped that no one would notice. Despite his voiced delight in her presentation, almost everyone else at the table seemed more interested in his or her own contribution to the Meshcast. They talked about that, or about the success of the program as a whole. Bainbridge was talking about photogenic readings and other production issues. Sarrah Chrysler not-quite-complained about how she had looked on the feed and said she was certain that something had to be wrong with the feedback system, because all of the viewer comments were about Enola. By turns, Keith held forth on his own genius for discovering Enola, and on Enola's brilliance in delivering on his genius concept.

Only Katalin seemed to care how Enola felt, or appeared to listen to what she said. The other woman was watching with an air that bordered on the studious. Between her own sips of mineral water and two- or three-word comments, Enola could see the other woman watching her face, her hands, even her body. Enola smiled. She liked the attention.

They were seated in a corner booth at one of a chain of moderately priced restaurants popular on Earth and on the Moon. Following the success of the Meshcast, Arreigh had suggested a celebration, and Enola had suggested *Fargos!*, only a short distance from the production facility. Sarrah had suggested the Mall, instead, and DiNuvio's, but a quick Mesh-check had shown that the newly opened facility was hopelessly crowded. People were very happy to be able to visit the Mall again.

"—low resolution imagery," Sarrah Chrysler said. "No texture!" Now that she had removed her facial appliances, she was quite lovely, Enola realized with some small surprise. The older woman's eyes flashed, and her features took on an energetic quality that made her look more youthful than she was. Enola could understand her appeal, if not respond to it—at least, she could appreciate it when Chrysler was speaking to someone else, anyone else. In the sporadic moments that she directed her attention to Enola, the ambient temperature seemed to drop a bit.

Enola was reasonably certain that Sarrah did not like her.

"Low resolution, less detail, high contrast, more clarity," Keith said. The sentiment was a basic principle of concept presentation—as opposed to final modeling—but Arreigh seemed to think that he had made some great discovery. "That's what the numbers say. We may set a new trend here. People seem to like hearing about disasters from you. They see you as one of them. They're better able make sense of what happened, at least from a physical perspective."

"Of what Enola thinks happened," Bainbridge reminded him. The way the senior imagineer spoke and gestured now intrigued Enola. The man had struck a perfect balance between the fussy deference he offered Sarrah and the authoritative professionalism he typically voiced to Keith. Enola had to wonder which demeanor was the sincere one. Probably both, she decided. People were often self-contradictory.

"We'll replace the model with actual footage before replay, of course," Sarrah said. "And certainly before it goes to Earth Mesh. For a more polished package."

"We will *not!*" Keith said. He mock-glowered at her, then beamed at Enola. "Don't listen to her! It was perfect!" He seemed to make every sentence an exclamation and slapped the table again for emphasis. "Besides, people don't seem to *want* polished right now."

A waitperson drifted up to their table, bearing another tray of drinks and hors d'oeuvres. Her *Fargos!* uniform resembled a generic military fatigue, or would have if military fatigues had been designed with sex appeal in mind. The outfit was low-cut and clingy, and at her Web-belt hung ersatz side arms that Enola knew could dispense freshly ground pepper and other garnishes. With quick, practiced moves, the attractive woman set individual tequila bombs before everyone at the table, flanking each round glass with dishes of soy chips and pigs in blankets. She smiled as she worked, and Enola could not tell if the smile was professional or sincere.

"Just mineral water, please," Enola said, eyeing the lethal cocktail that had materialized before her, without order or request. Different liqueurs and tequilas reposed inside the glass, resting one on top of another in gradated strata. Tequila bombs were not easy to create, or to consume, but very pretty to look at.

Arreigh shook his head. "Drink up," he said. He gestured at the snifter-like vessel that held Enola's layered drink, and then waved the waitress away. "We're celebrating!"

"I really can't," Enola said. She bit her lower lip and tasted the last of the makeup she had worn for Meshcast. The cocktail invited, but she thought of Huerta's warning words. "My physician says—"

"Your doctor isn't here!" Both Bainbridge and Arreigh spoke at once. "Drink!"

"—says I'll have problems when I get back to Earth," Enola continued doggedly. "Serious problems."

Katalin did something then that Enola had never seen her do before. She laughed. Her impassive features broke into a blood-red smile and her head tilted back and she laughed. The sound was like silver bells pealing. The reaction was so out of character that everyone else at the table paused in their chatter, startled and amazed.

"Silly," Keith said, when Katalin had fallen silent again. "You're not going back to Earth, not for a long time." He pointed at her with mock-solemnity. "Not unless you want to."

Enola stared at him. Understanding dawned, however slowly, and her heart raced. She couldn't believe what she was hearing.

"Enola," Keith said seriously. The cherubic quality of his features gave way to a more businesslike aspect. "Your numbers are very good, and so is the audience feedback. I can offer you employment with Zonix now. I'd like very much to use you on the special Meshcast next week, and after that, well," he said, "you and Sarrah seem to make a good team."

She stared at him, trying to believe. At the fringes of her field of view, she could see the others, too—Bainbridge, approving; Sarrah, stricken; Cassidy, distantly pleased.

"I can offer you a very generous compensation package," Keith continued. He lifted his tequila bomb with pudgy fingers. "I've enjoyed just enough of these that I urge you, seriously, to get representation, but I promise you, we'll make you happy."

"But, my severance—"

"That's no longer an issue," Keith said. "We'll buy you out." He made a dismissive gesture. "I'll secure an advocate for you, too." He paused. "You are *not* going back to Earth, Enola."

"I—I—" Enola wanted to speak, but she could not find the words. She wanted to sing, but the only rhythm she could find was the pounding of her heart. The entire world seemed to snap into super-sharp focus around her.

Keith raised his glass higher, in a gesture that Enola knew was very old, indeed. Taking his hint, everyone else raised his or her drink, too. When Enola raised hers, her eyes watered, and not just from tears of emotion.

Fargos! served tequila bombs in the traditional vessel, a largish snifter. The glass's curved walls caught the aroma of the spirits and concentrated it.

"To Enola, and a long future with Zonix," Keith said.

"To Enola!"

"To Enola!"

"To Enola!"

They spoke in rounds. One by one each raised a glass and drank, with even Sarrah joining in, accepting at last.

When Enola's turn came, she was crying.

CHAPTER 10

"I can have her severance package revoked in two days," Hector Kowalski said the next morning. "She'll appeal to Company Court and get the revocation suspended, for a day or two, but I can get that undone, too. I can freeze the retirement escrow account, so she won't be able to borrow against it. All she'll have left after that is her fare-home set-aside."

"She doesn't seem to need her severance anymore," Erik said. "And get your feet off my desk."

Kowalski ignored the command. He had slid down and leaned back in the spider-web guest chair into a nearly reclining position. His feet were on Erik's black desk, and his gaze was fixed on the ceiling. He scowled. "I can get her apartment cut in half, within twenty-four hours," he said. "And again, twenty-four hours after that."

"Oh?" Erik asked. This was new.

Kowalski nodded. There was a bowl of soy-chips resting on his stomach, and he nibbled a few of them before sipping from a bottle-pouch of sugar-water. It had been a very long time since Erik had seen the security chief eat cheap snack food, especially so aggressively, let alone so early in the day.

"There's a housing shortage in the Duckworth sector," Kowalski said. He ate some more.

Erik found that hard to believe. Duckworth was responsible for most of Villanueva's heavy construction, and even though the five ALC sisters collaborated closely, each looked after its own. If there were housing shortages, Duckworth employees and contractors would be the last to suffer. He said as much.

"The severance clause of her compensation package says that they can reassign space on a preferential basis in times of shortage," Kowalski continued. He ate some more. "I can get a shortage declared. Those units are modular. She could be sleeping in her kitchen tomorrow."

"I was unaware that you managed Duckworth housing," Erik said, with a patience that was feeling some strain. Kowalski had arrived, unannounced, unwelcome, and incensed, even as Erik started his workday. More than an hour had passed since then, and still the other man showed no sign of intending to leave.

"No, but I can manage the man who does," Kowalski said. "He has some habits he doesn't want his wives to know about." He paused, as if realizing he had said too much. When Erik made no comment, he continued, "I can talk to Huerta. We could expedite her return to Earth for medical reasons."

"Not after this many years," Erik said. "You're more likely to get a ruling in the other direction." The Company Court had been known to hand down hardship stays based on medical reasons.

Kowalski grunted.

"And I don't want you causing her any additional trouble," Erik said. "You're why she's working for Zonix now. You got her terminated."

"She was terminated because she works for Scheer," Kowalski said testily.

"We don't know that," Erik said. "*You* don't know that."

It was as if he had not spoken. "So she's working for Zonix·because she's working for Scheer, too," Kowalski continued.

"We can't be certain," Erik said.

Kowalski grunted again. Now, at last, he swiveled in his seat and swung his long legs so that his feet came clear of Erik's desk. As he changed his posture, he tossed the snack dish upward and then allowed it to plop down where his feet had been. Soy chips threatened to surge up and over the bowl's lip, then subsided.

"I don't mind not being certain," he said calmly. "About anything except security."

The words weren't welcome, but they weren't a surprise, either. When Erik had first met Kowalski, years before, the younger man had been an obsessive player of simulator games, matching wits and skill against brainware routines. That hobby seemed to have fallen by the wayside when he had begun affecting a more professional demeanor. Now, not for the first time, Erik had to wonder if his protégé had found a new outlet for those tendencies.

Was he angry at Enola for job-hopping to Zonix? Or was he angry because she had somehow parried his move?

Erik shook his head. "You're to take no further action against Enola Hasbro," he said.

"I answer to you, but my duty is to Over-Management," Kowalski said, with equal calm. "I have some discretion."

"No action against her," Erik said again. "The last one didn't work out very well, did it?"

Kowalski said nothing.

"You need to know what we're up against, if nothing else," Erik continued. He was hungry, and his stomach growled as he watched Kowalski eat, but he was in no mood for soy-chips. "No one makes this kind of move without substantial backing."

"Her advocate with Zonix is Keith Arreigh. I met him at your dinner party," Kowalski said. "I sent you a backgrounder. I can send it to you again, updated."

"Do that. But tell me about him first."

Kowalski settled back in his chair again, still holding his sugar-water, but it was obvious that the beverage, like the food, was all but forgotten. "He's a golden boy," Kowalski said. "A crown prince. He packages and produces Mesh for the Zonix and subcompany networks. Specialties are conceptualization and start-up. He starts the show, but others run it." He mentioned several titles, some of them very familiar from Mesh productions, or from associated collateral products such as games and clothing lines.

"Huh," Erik said. "Is he company bones or contractor?"

"He goes back and forth," Kowalski said.

"A job-hopper?" Erik asked. The information didn't fit. Within Villanueva, at least, moving between ALC companies was frowned upon. Only someone with considerable authority would sponsor the hiring of a disgraced sister-company employee, and a power base took time to build. Erik did not believe that a job-hopper could do what Arreigh was doing for Hasbro.

"No," Kowalski said. "All of his work has been for Zonix, or a fully owned sub." He paused and shrugged. "He goes back and forth," he repeated.

He seemed as dubious as Erik, and understandably so. What his words suggested was a very atypical career path. Beginners and tyros worked as subcontractors and consultants—them, and losers. Personnel fortunate enough to secure permanent employment status with a good company held on to it aggressively, even desperately. The idea of deliberately shuttling back and forth between the two classes, especially for a premiere company like Zonix, was nearly beyond imagining.

"What about his friend? The woman?" Erik asked.

"His associate," Kowalski replied, lightly mocking.

"His associate," Erik agreed, but without derision. He had liked the Cassidy woman.

Kowalski shrugged again. "Just a plaything, I think. She's a Hungarian national. I can't find anything noteworthy about her. No employment record or résumé file, at least not at first-search levels. There may not be anything to find. Hungary is pretty much a shambles."

During the rapid sequence of European civil wars that had followed the Czech Challenge of thirty years before, Hungary had been broken down almost completely. What remained was a society that didn't place much value on record-keeping or even Mesh archives. People who left it tended to start new lives without looking back on the old.

"A professional?" Erik asked.

"I honestly don't know," Kowalski said, clearly discomfited by his own lack of knowledge. "If she's a sex-worker, she's not certified."

"So she probably isn't one, then," Erik said. He drummed blunt fingertips on the desktop. Certification was easily achieved and carried sufficient legal protections that forgoing the process was foolish. In his one encounter with Katalin Cassidy, however brief, she had not impressed him as being foolish. "What's on her visa?"

"She's a guest of Arreigh's," Kowalski said. He seemed suddenly to remember his drink and sipped it. "Most of this is public record," he said as he set down the bottle-pouch again. It was empty now. "You should be able to access Zonix's visitor logs yourself."

"I've been busy with other things," Erik said.

"The Pour?" Kowalski asked. He knew that Erik was to attend the precasting ceremony.

"That's one," Erik acknowledged easily. The greater part of his schedule was no secret.

"And Chrysler, right?" Kowalski said, probing. He smiled very slightly and inclined his head in Erik's direction.

Erik didn't respond. Instead, he pressed a thumb to his computer screen and began scrolling through his mailbox. If Kowalski were willing to take it, the gesture was a sure indicator that the interview was close to an end.

"What does she think of Hasbro?" Kowalski asked, unwilling to take the hint. He leaned back in his chair again and idly toyed with what remained of the soy chips.

"I haven't asked her," Erik said.

"Will you?" Kowalski asked coolly.

"I haven't decided." Erik felt control of the conversation begin to slip away, but decided to tolerate it, at least for the moment.

"You don't have to," Kowalski said. "I reviewed the Meshcast records several times. I checked vocal stress readings. I isolated the Chrysler images and reviewed them, too." He chewed pseudo-fried soy and swallowed. "Chrysler doesn't like Hasbro. I can guess the reasons."

Erik glanced at him but didn't say anything. The words were a feint.

Kowalski continued easily. "I ran a recording of the live Meshcast against the version that was made available for download seven hours later," he said. "It had been edited. Someone else must have noticed that she was unhappy. Entire sequences were reangled to downplay her, and even her host close-ups had been miraged."

"On Earth, Erik had been a sport fisherman. He knew enough to recognize bait, and he knew that responding to it was a mistake, but he did, anyway. "Why are you so interested?" he asked. "Is that part of your assignment?"

Kowalski grinned, obviously pleased at the reaction. "I'm to keep monitoring developments in the Mall situation and how it plays out in the media," he said. "She's the media, remember. Maybe you have a way to control her."

The brainware mailbox flared as Erik shut it down, and then the computer screen went dark. Kowalski was baiting him again, but this time, he couldn't hide his irritation completely. He fixed Kowalski with a steady gaze. "I'm glad you mentioned the Mall," he said. "Wendy Scheer has offered us the use of a forensics team."

Kowalski's grin transitioned neatly into a grimace as he said, "I don't need any Feds 'helping' me. I've doubled the guards on duty, briefed them on types of suspicious activity, and I'm working with Zonix and Duckworth to reconfigure the recording array."

"She says they're going to claim jurisdiction," Erik said.

"They can't," Kowalski said. He sounded petulant. "Charter."

"She seems to think they can," Erik said. "And she reminded me that our charter is hardly inviolate."

"That was yesterday?" Kowalski asked. "The secure text link?"

Rather than answer, Erik demanded, "What headway have you made on the investigation?"

"It's not a live issue," Kowalski said. "We're working more on prevention."

That was what Over-Management had agreed on, over Erik's protests. The men and women who directed the ALC's lunar operations had taken as their priority to avoid a repetition of the Mall incident. Janos Horvath, back on Earth, and speaking to Erik via remote, secure link, had been remarkably matter-of-fact about it.

"We're not concerned about the deaths and injuries, Erik," he had said. *"We're concerned with the disruption and potential loss of revenues that the deaths and injuries bring. Just get back to business."*

Erik could understand his point. He remembered cities on Earth that had suppressed the news of disease outbreaks and seaside resorts that had done the same for shark attacks. He could understand, even if he disagreed; short-term repairs rarely addressed long-term issues. He had other concerns as well. Scheer's threat to Villanueva's relative autonomy was one.

Clearly still annoyed, Kowalski continued. "You know about the forensics aspect; what we've found there, isn't much. We're reviewing what surveillance tapes and records we have, but the coverage is incomplete, of course. We weren't lucky enough to record any suspicious activity, so we're trying to identify who was there. We know that there was no sign of any kind of explosive device twelve hours before—"

"How?" Erik interrupted.

"Routine maintenance session," Kowalski said. "So we started with the explosion, and my staffers are working their way back to that time-stamp. Traffic was light enough that we're having some success with purchase records. Transaction trails have the most use, and even they're not perfect."

Erik could understand that. There were simply too many ways for a canny Mall-goer—tourist or local—to conceal spending. Fully 40 percent of the credits that changed hands in the Mall did so at the Zonix Casino, and another 10 percent moved through the various sex vendors. Neither institution had any interest in publicizing its patrons' activities, and had ample reason not to.

"What about the revised facial recognition brainware?" he asked, but without much optimism.

"Some success, especially with isolated images, but facial appliances make it less than reliable," Kowalski replied. "I would outlaw them, if I could." He reached in his pocket and withdrew a handheld. "Here," he said. "Link to me."

A moment later, four faces gazed out at Erik from his display screen, summoned up from Kowalski's files. One image, the largest, showed a buck-toothed man with bushy eyebrows and a narrow snake tattooed on his forehead. Of the other three, no two resembled each other any more than any one of them looked like the buck-toothed man. Their resemblances were roughly equal, and equally minimal.

Without prompting, Erik turned the screen so that they both could see it. Kowalski used a finger to indicate the buck-toothed man. "That's Harris Teeter, a maintenance drone from Sector 7-G. He was running diagnostics on the elevator. He's clean."

"And the others?" Erik asked. He suspected he knew what Kowalski's response would be, and his guess proved correct.

"One of them is him, too. Guess which one."

Erik examined the images carefully. They had been taken from different angles and under different lighting, and the comparison wasn't easy. He knew that Kowalski wasn't doing anything to make it easier, either. The four faces were raw feed, unmiraged and unaltered.

He shrugged. "I have no idea," he said. "But that's not my department."

Kowalski laughed softly. He pointed at the second face and tapped the display with enough force that Erik thought he might damage the gossamer-fine plastic membrane. "Here," he said. "Her."

Teeter's other face could have been that of a fashion model or a sex professional. High eyebrows replaced the bristling red lines above his eyes, and the eyes themselves seemed now to be limpid pools of darkness, deep enough that even Erik felt their pull. Teeter's protruding teeth were absent, too, or hiding behind neatly composed and painted lips.

"That's him at his leisure," Kowalski said. "There's a funny story about how this came to may attention."

"I don't need to hear it," Erik said. Kowalski's interest in others' private lives made sense, but it also made Erik uncomfortable. "But what on Earth does he do with the teeth?"

The security chief laughed again. He pointed at Teeter's masculine avatar and at the protruding incisors. "Those are the prosthetics," he said. "The rest of it's just self-indulgence. He's good enough to fool the brainware, though. Facially, at least. We're having better luck with dynamic measurement of body language. That's just as distinctive and much harder to change."

"But why—?"

Yet again, Kowalski shrugged. He closed the link and returned his handheld to some hidden pocket, as Erik's screen blanked again. "I don't know," he said. "Who can?" He paused. "Why does anybody do anything?" He seemed sincere.

Those weren't words that Erik wanted to hear, even if he sympathized with the question. Rather than try to answer, he asked, "Then what *are* you doing?"

"Read the backgrounder I sent," Kowalski said again. "But, to be honest, I don't think we're going to be able to identify the person or persons involved without more evidence."

"Or a repeat performance?" Erik asked.

Kowalski nodded.

"Anything else?"

Erik didn't like the next words, but he knew that he had to say them. "Look into the Enola Hasbro situation," he said. "No reprisals, but find out what she's doing for Zonix. And how she came to their attention."

THAT had been nice, Enola realized as she awoke and stared at the ceiling above her bed. It had been very nice, indeed.

It was a good thought with which to begin the day.

Moving slowly and with considerable consideration, she gently disentangled herself from her bedsheets and from the arms and legs of the still-sleeping Katalin Cassidy. She gathered the coverlet around herself and stood, then paused and looked back on her bedmate.

Katalin lay curled on her side, her head resting on the gray satin pillowcase. She was beautiful. Under the bedroom's subdued lighting, alabaster skin positively lustrous, looking like pearls against the darker sheets. The other woman's midnight-black hair was tousled and confused, making a dark frame for her strong, emphatic features. Small breasts, well-shaped and dark-nippled, rose and fell with her deep, steady breaths. The limpid eyes that Enola had gazed into so deeply the night before were closed now. Even in repose, however, Katalin Cassidy looked poised for action, the contours of dense, well-developed muscle clearly evident under creamy skin.

Let her sleep, Enola thought.

She trudged slowly across the carpeted expanse of her bedroom. She had to move slowly, in part to avoid tripping over the abandoned garments that she and Katalin had left scattered in their wake, in part to maintain tidy control over her various bodily functions. The celebration had continued for long hours, amid much vague planning and goodwill, at Zonix's expense. Realizing that she would soon be free of Huerta's restrictions, Enola had enjoyed many interesting and unusual beverages and psychotropic compounds. Now, her stomach and bladder both eagerly reminded her of her indulgences, and warned that jostling would not be welcome. Neither her body's reminders nor the fibery feeling in her brain were enough to dispel her sense of well-being, however.

It had been a very good night. She had been surprised at first when Katalin had offered to escort her home and even more surprised when the other woman had made it clear that she intended to stay. Her interest had been as welcome as it had been unexpected, and, at last, Enola thought she understood the air of cool study that Katalin had repeatedly manifested in her presence.

The cover still wrapped around her, she continued her odyssey to the bathroom. Her teal new-silk blouse was a splash of color on the floor. Not willing just yet to trust her own sense of balance, Enola tried to lift it with the toes of one foot and was rewarded with a wave of sickening vertigo. Just in time, she caught herself on a side table, interrupting a slow-motion fall.

"Urk!" she said, but the faint smile she wore remained. This time, there were no regrets or self-recriminations. Without even asking herself the question, she knew that there were no regrets. Katalin did not strike her as someone who would likely make more of a night's diversion that it had been. She was no Crag Fortinbras.

She was moving better by the time she passed through the bathroom doorway and shut it behind her. A middling dose of the blue liquid she kept in the cabinet there, some personal business, and a very quiet shower later, she shuffled back out into the kitchen, feeling more or less alive again.

"Donelle," she murmured, using her command voice at its lowest possible volume. "Give me my calendar. And quietly."

She wasn't wearing her phones yet, but she didn't need them. Speaking softly and with the strategic use of acoustic shaping fields, Donelle reminded her of a follow-up appointment with Chesney in Personnel, a scheduled session with her stylist, and something she had quite forgotten about—a brunch date with Narçissa Esposito, casually made during their last conversation. ,

Not even that reminder of her lost role at Duckworth was enough to make the day seem less bright, Enola decided.

"I have a guest," she said.

"Yes," dead Donelle's voice acknowledged. Enola was sure that she was imagining it, but the housekeeper's tones seemed to hold a faint note of approval.

"Let her sleep," Enola continued. "Tell her I had to leave and that I'll call." She smiled. "Tell her I said 'thank you.'"

"Recorded," the housekeeper said.

"No," Enola responded. "Third-person relay. Don't play it back for her. Just do as I said."

"Tell her you said 'thank you,'" the recorded ghost acknowledged.

Moving very quietly, Enola returned to her bedroom and selected fresh garments. She moved back to her workstation area to dress, rather than risk disturbing Katalin. The medicine and the activity were enough to help her finish the job of waking up, and she was bright and aware and very much at peace with herself as she stepped into the corridor outside her quarters.

Her concluding thought as the door whisked shut behind her was to wonder what Katalin Cassidy thought of her.

"THAT job-hopping bitch," Sarrah Chrysler snarled. "How *dare* she?" Her perfectly manicured and maintained fingers twitched, and the breadstick that they held snapped. Crumbs flew in all directions.

Erik reached across the narrow table and took the two larger breadstick pieces from her. Setting them down, he gathered up the crumbs, wrapped the remnants in a disposable napkin, and set them aside. He performed the entire process with casual aplomb, as if accustomed to seeing his handiwork destroyed on a regular basis.

"If you don't like them—" he said.

Instantly contrite, Sarrah smiled. She pressed her left hand to his right cheek, gently, and pretended not to notice when he pulled back slightly. "No," she said. "They're fine. I just don't like being upstaged."

They were in Erik's apartment, halfway through a late lunch. On the table between them were a small roasted chicken that was flanked by hand-carved slices of meat, a woven breadbasket, a bowl of salad, and a small self-cooling tureen of cherrystone soup, all in various stages of demolition. They had met at his office and returned here, officially to discuss Mesh coverage of the Mall disaster and Erik's possible participation in the coverage of the upcoming Pour ceremony. Sarrah's true goal, however, had been simply to spend some time with him. With the review accomplished, he had surprised her by preparing a complete and balanced meal in about the same amount of time that she would have needed to activate a readymeal or assemble a beanloaf sandwich.

When he offered her another breadstick, she accepted and continued. "They're wonderful," she said. "But you shouldn't have gone to so much trouble."

"I like to cook," he reminded her, after a quick head shake. "It gives me something to do with my hands while I think. I roasted the chicken last night, and the soup takes almost no time if you know how to do it properly. Lately, I've been eating too much, and I can't spend the entire day with exercise. It's good to have someone to share with."

Sarrah smiled, both at what he had said and at his obvious sincerity. She wished now that she had not permitted herself to wax quite so wroth regarding Enola Hasbro.

Erik used a small, two-tined serving fork to spear another slice of breast meat and ferry it to his plate. He reached for the condiment caddy, and onto the meat he dabbed pineapple catsup that Sarrah knew was also of his own creation. As he raised the food to his mouth, he said, "Enola is not a job-hopper. She was terminated."

His words, spoken with such casual assurance and authority, gave Sarrah pause. Mid-bite, she blinked and stared at him, struck by the easy familiarity in his voice. "You know Hasbro?" she asked.

He nodded, chewed, and swallowed. "Only slightly," he said. "I haven't spoken to her in years."

He looked vaguely, minutely guilty. Sarrah wondered why.

"How do you know her?" she asked, a little surprised at the sharpness in her own voice.

"Slightly," Erik repeated. "I was quite surprised to see her on your Meshcast."

"That woman's participation was no doing of mine," Sarrah said. "How do you know her?" she asked again.

"We met after my initial relocation," Erik said. He paused, thinking. If the memory brought any emotion with it, it did not show on his face. "I was on a courtesy call to Duckworth. She worked there."

Sarrah rummaged quickly through the memories of her hasty research on both Erik and Enola. Nothing in the files she recalled intersected. Hasbro was some five years younger than Sarrah, which meant that she was nearly fifteen years younger than Erik—but still a bit older than Arreigh. Their career tracks were radically different and had diverged even more since Erik had joined Over-Management. With the lightning speed of a good reporter, Sarrah tried to determine if any greater-than-casual connection between them was likely, and decided that one wasn't.

Then why was Erik so aware of the specifics of the Hasbro woman's status?

As if anticipating her next question, he said, "Sarrah, I work for Over-Management. I'm the director of communications. It's part of my job to track media developments. Of course I'm familiar with Enola's recent activities."

He had spoken her name again, with a casual familiarity. "What else do you know about her?" Sarrah asked.

Erik smiled, amused for some reason. "She dances well," he said. "She's familiar with Strauss. Is that what you wanted to know?"

If her hand had held another breadstick, it would have crumbled, too. Instead, Sarrah's neatly decorated teeth gritted briefly. She felt a confusing barrage of emotions. There was mild jealousy, and less-mild embarrassment at feeling jealous. There was confused disdain for Enola, mixed with territorial anger that an amateur had encroached on her professional territory. Most of all, there was confusion at how easily he had found the kind of question that would annoy her most.

How could she have ever been so skeptical about Erik Morrison's understanding of women?

"I don't like her," she said. She forced herself to speak mildly. "I don't want to work with her. I don't think that she should be on the Mesh at all. She's not trained for it, and she doesn't have the certifications. Hell, sometimes the work is dangerous."

"Talk to Arreigh," Erik said. "He's your sponsor here, isn't he? You told me that he would support you."

"Keith hired her," Sarrah said sourly. She sipped a spoonful of cherrystone soup. It was sweet and cool.

"Oh," Erik said.

"What else do you know about her?" Sarrah asked. "What's her background?"

"You should have access to her bio-file and résumé."

"I think you might know more," Sarrah said. "Why did she leave Duckworth?"

"We discussed this once," Erik reminded her. "There are things I don't think we should talk about. I shouldn't have told you that she was terminated. That was rude. It would be ruder to talk more about it."

"We can talk about how you know that she dances well," Sarrah responded.

He laughed, with such utterly disarming charm that she

realized Hasbro was nothing to him, after all. "There used to be a nightclub in the Mall called the Grotto. I was there, enjoying an evening with another acquaintance. She had to leave, briefly, and I happened to encounter Enola. We danced while waiting for my escort's return."

Sarrah blushed, embarrassment finally winning out among the conflicted emotions. "I'm sorry," she said, honestly. Less honestly, she continued, "I was just curious."

"That's perfectly reasonable," Erik said, still affable. Either he was sincere or remarkably skilled. "Maybe someday I'll ask the questions."

Sarrah giggled. Erik had dwelled in the relatively small, relatively closed community of Villanueva for years. No matter what his files said, there were doubtless other women in his past, and it was entirely possible that she would encounter them. Her own conquests, however, were safely stowed a world away, on Earth.

"Perhaps," she said.

"She's harmless, Sarrah. Really. She's not someone you have to worry about." The words came with a hint of reluctance, as if he were choosing carefully which of her implied questions to answer.

After a moment's thought, she nodded. "Thank you," she said. They were the only words that seemed appropriate.

"Anything else?" he asked, reaching for the breadbasket.

Another name came up from her memory, shaken free by her hasty review of remembered researches. It was a name that had figured with relative prominence in the Mesh coverage of seven years ago, before dropping back into relative obscurity. Now that she thought of it, she realized that the name was in Erik's dossier, too.

"Yes," she asked. "What can you tell me about Wendy Scheer?"

CHAPTER 11

ENOLA'S quarters were reasonably convenient to her offices, but they weren't in the most affluent part of the Duckworth sector. Getting from them to the Mall meant seven minutes on the Bessemer Run commuter train, three minutes of power-walking along a trans-Biome concourse, and then a hasty hand-over-hand ascent along a civilian access shaft. At least, that was what such a trip consisted of for a local; a tourist or visitor might take the easier, all-vehicle route of train, tram, and motorized treadway. That "easier" itinerary would have taken Enola longer, however, and done her less good.

She was acutely aware of that as she grasped the last rung, pulled her body up one last time, bent her limber form, and then dropped onto the padded deck surface below the transit shaft egress. She hit the flooring lightly and bounced just a bit before righting herself. An easy sliding step should have been sufficient to convert her momentum into forward motion, but her left ankle bent just a bit too much, and she half-stumbled. Embarrassingly, she had to grip a safety rail briefly to recover, before making way for the next pedestrian.

She was breathing heavily and felt a mild burning in the muscles of her arms and legs. The sensations, though not severe, were sufficient to give her pause. Exercise was important. The events of the preceding weeks, by turns traumatic and hectic and deliriously optimistic, had done grave damage to her exercise program. If she were going to stay here, if she wanted to stay here and be healthy, then that would have to change.

Her body had evolved for life on Earth, in gravity six times greater than the Moon's. Her bones, blood, and circulatory system all worked differently here—often to their detriment. The earliest space explorers had experienced loss in bone mass after long stays in zero G, and problems with circulatory anomalies and loss of muscle tone. Milder manifestations of the same symptoms had presented themselves in the lunar environment. That was the reason for the gene therapy she had received, a lifetime before. It was also the reason for the exercise regimen that was part of everyday Villanueva life, at least for long-term residents.

If she were going to stay here, she would need to end Huerta's regression treatments and also put an end to the occasional abbreviation of her exercise program. The clumsiness she felt now was a prodding reminder of that.

She half shuffled, half glided to the nearest observation deck and gazed out over the renovated Mall. She had not been here since her night at the Splinter, and she was eager to see just how well her imaged reconstruction tracked with the reality. She realized with some surprise just how good a job she had done, even with only minimal data to draw upon.

What she saw now was an almost perfect match for what she could have seen a week before, or a month or even a year before, at least in the broad strokes. Men and women still drifted along the Mall's crowded concourses and walkways, moving in and out of shops and galleries and restaurants. Some of those places, Enola, even with all her years on the Moon, had never visited. The chatter of Mall patrons mingled with the ambient music and advertising jingles that seeped somehow past the dozen different acoustical suppressers, to emerge as a rich morass of white noise punctuated by stray syllables and exclamations. Bakeries and restaurants vented the aromas of exotic foodstuffs, to mingle in the great open space with the more delicate scent of human bodies.

Far below, on the Mall floor, she could see the famous Clone Sisters as they glided among the milling throngs, smiling and greeting and signing chit-slips. The women were medically created quintuplets, effectively identical. Tourist attractions themselves, they worked at the Zonix Casino as celebrity sex professionals. They moved along in single file, like matched beads on a string. Enola had seen the five matched women many times before, and the familiar sight pleased her on some vague level.

The restoration was impressive, and so thorough that she now found herself doubting the few authorized images of devastation that management had released. The biggest remaining changes since her last visit were almost entirely structural in nature, and presumably visible to educated eyes like her own.

The northeast elevator bank appeared subtly more new than its fellows, the sheen of its replacement surfaces and elements not yet dulled by age. The cables and supports for several walkways hung at very slightly different angles, with hardware fixtures that Enola knew must have come from different production lots. They showed, however subtly, design changes. The biggest difference was the mammoth central display system, now dark, apparently awaiting final repairs. The Zonix cartoon cat danced no more.

Even for a culture that placed so much emphasis on illusion and image, the reclamation work was impressive. Enola realized with some surprise that it had been accomplished in less than three complete days.

She realized yet again that this was where she wanted to live. She did not want to go back to Earth, ever. Villanueva was still shiny and new. It could become *more* new with each day. Enola's childhood had been nearly smothered in antiquities, and she did not want to be choked again by age.

She turned from the observation deck. To her left was the open-front restaurant that she sought. Seated at a table that straddled the tearoom's shadowy confines and a marked-off section of the concourse in front of it, was Narçissa Esposito. The middle-aged woman smiled and waved as Enola joined her.

"I am so happy to see you, Enola," she said, surprising Enola a bit with the emphatic quality of her greeting. Narçissa was sweet and a friendly acquaintance, but Enola had never truly considered her a close friend.

Clearly, Narçissa viewed things differently. Over waffles and mimosas, she chattered with little prompting about the comings and goings at Duckworth, and about who was sleeping with whom. The Proposal unit had been reorganized since Enola's exodus. Accounting had gained two clerks/administrators, one with Gummi-brain implants to enable some new statistical projection techniques. ("I don't like her very much," Narçissa said, as if surrendering a great confidence. Then she giggled, and the years fell away from her.) A new design team had been imported from Earth to work on Ad Astra. Everyone was very excited about the Pour, both as an Ad Astra milestone and as a major Duckworth project, so the big Mesh auditorium had been reserved for a real-time showing, with all staff encouraged to attend it.

Enola only half-listened and made pleasant responses and comments, but even that took an effort. Most of the names that Narçissa recited could have belonged to strangers. Already, not even a full day since Arreigh's celebratory offer, Duckworth seemed to be part of her past. It was strange to realize that, so recently, Narçissa's call had meant so much to Enola, alone in her exile. She wondered now why she was here.

"We all miss you so," Narçissa said. She toyed with her food, digging at the flaky waffle with her fork, dabbing a morsel in syrup but not eating. "What will you do when you return to Earth?"

Those words, too, belonged to Enola's past. Enola smiled. "I don't think I'm going back to Earth, Narçissa," she said. "I can't tell you more, but there may be a way I can stay."

The probing fork became still. It fell from Narçissa's fingers and rang as it struck the plate's edge. "They have *rehired* you?" she asked. Surprise and hope contended for prominence in her voice and on her face. Clearly, she had never heard of such a thing.

Neither had Enola. She shook her head. Her words came slowly, for several reasons. She wanted to boast of her good fortune. She was not eager to announce that she was about to move from the employ of one ALC sister to another. "No," she said. "There is another way."

Narçissa blinked. "I saw you on the Mesh," she said slowly. "You were very good. You looked so *real!*"

She had said things like that more than once, already, in between praising the model that Enola had crafted on-Mesh and asking if Sarrah Chrysler were truly as nice as she seemed. Her prattle had half-convinced Enola that Arriegh was correct. She should have been working as a news-head for her entire career.

"But you said you were a guest," Narçissa continued.

"I *was* a guest," Enola acknowledged cheerfully. "But the next time, at the Pour, things will be different." Her smile widened. "I'm going to be a guest on Sarrah Chrysler's feed, then, too," she said, shading the truth just a bit.

Apparently not enough, however. Once more, conflicting emotions showed in Narçissa's expression. This time, they included a flicker of disgust, however faint. "You are going to job-hop?" she wailed.

Clearly, she had divined the truth that Enola was trying not to present. Equally clearly, she found it unthinkable. There had been a time when Enola would have felt the same, and those remembered, reflexive sentiments flared faintly even now.

Gently, Enola took one of her hands and held it. "I don't work for Duckworth anymore, Narçissa," she said soothingly. The rationale came to her easily, and as she spoke, she reassured herself at least as much as Narçissa. Transitioning directly from one company to another, especially another ALC partner, just wasn't done. "Duckworth is done with me."

Narçissa seemed remarkably close to crying.

Enola patted her hand, then lifted her mimosa and sipped. The orange juice was good, but the champagne was sublime. Hydroponics-based vineyards had made every year vintage.

"You should be happy for me," she said. The immensity of her career shift loomed. "Please, be happy for me."

"I only want the best for you, Enola," Narçissa said. She was clearly still uncomfortable. "All of us do. But, to job-hop—"

Enola ignored the last words and seized on the ones that had come before. She drank some more and smiled. Now that her future seemed secure, Huerta's warnings were nearly forgotten. "Thank you," she said.

"But—what about Crag?" Narçissa asked.

Hearing the name so casually mentioned curdled Enola's blood and made a bitter taste in her mouth. She thought with shame and embarrassment about waking up with that man, and about how he had seemed to regard her as his personal property in the days that had followed. Just now, Crag Fortinbras's was the last name she wanted to hear.

"I would rather not talk about Crag," she said. She would have preferred not to think about him, either. A moment's weakness, when she had been alone and sad, was returning to haunt her. This was not the time for it.

Her life was showing promise of being in order again. No matter how wrenching the transition from Duckworth had been, no matter now Narçissa and the others regarded her for joining Zonix, her situation was improving. Soon, she would be company bones again, and the fact that it would be for a different company didn't really matter.

Did it? Seeing the look that was in Narçissa's eyes as the older woman sipped her mimosa, she had to wonder about that, however lightly.

"He talks about you," Narçissa said. She spoke like a woman who had secret knowledge and took great pleasure in it.

"He likes you very much, Enola," Narçissa said. "He talks of nothing but you. I think you could be very happy together."

Mortified, Enola set down her drink. The world seemed to go away. She had no intent of ever again entering into a long-term relationship, and if she did, it certainly would not be with the smug, preening man from Purchasing. That she had been with him once, however briefly, was more than bad enough.

"He seems to think that you will be very happy together," Narçissa said. Her tone was light and pleasant, but her words had taken on a certain drumbeat quality. Enola hated hearing them. "Crag has been alone for a very long time, you know, and we were all very happy to hear that you had found each other. When you invited him to the Splinter—"

"I did *not* invite him to the Splinter!" Enola said sharply. She spoke loudly enough that she was aware of other restaurant patrons looking in their direction, and blushed furiously. She remembered how awkward and unhappy Crag had been at the dance club, and how disapproving he had been of the music there. The idea that he had told others it was her idea infuriated her.

"You suggested it," Narçissa said implacably. "He says it was your suggestion."

That was true, but only in a technical sense. Crag had been a mistake, but a mistake of her making, and then she had compounded it.

Narçissa murmured a few more inanities about Crag Fortinbras and the happy life he allegedly planned for Enola and himself. With each sentence, Enola's gorge rose a bit more. But as Narçissa spoke, a curious thing happened.

Enola's remembered life at Duckworth seemed to slip away, folding in on itself to become self-contained and apart from her current existence. What the men and women of Duckworth thought of her no longer really mattered, and no matter how sweet Narçissa could be, she didn't matter, either. Soon, no loose ends would remain.

Bit by bit, that realization was becoming real to Enola. Duckworth was the past now, like Earth. Her future was with Zonix Infotainment systems and Keith Arreigh.

"—told him I would see you this morning," Narçissa said.

That brought Enola up short. "You needn't have done that, Narçissa," she said. She tried to say it politely, but now, she wondered just how quickly she could leave the table without seeming rude. She set down her glass and pushed her plate aside. "It was very nice seeing you," she started to say.

"Now, *there* are words I've heard before," a familiar voice said. Familiar hands, heavy and unwelcome, found Enola's shoulders, and the air was scented with cologne that she knew all too well.

"Hello, sweetness," Crag Fortinbras said. He bent and kissed her forehead, then slithered into the empty chair to her left.

"Crag," Enola said in acknowledgment. Her teeth gritted. The memories of her night with Katalin, so fresh and new, presented themselves to her. Then they promptly began to fade, eroded by the less pleasant recollections that Crag's mere presence summoned.

How could she have had anything to do with him? Anything at all?

One of Crag's big hands found the half-emptied mimosa pitcher. He leaned back and hooked an unused glass from a neighboring table, then filled it. He drank and smiled. "It's so good to see you both," he said, then focused on Enola. "It's especially nice to see you, Enola"

Acutely conscious of Narçissa's puzzled but well-meaning presence, Enola forced herself to smile. "Crag," she said. "I was just readying to leave."

"Oh, please don't," Crag said. He looked nice. His hair was newly styled, and he was wearing decorative dental frames that made his smile glint, even in the subdued restaurant light.

He must have spent some time preparing himself for the encounter, Enola realized. Some small part of her felt complimented, but it was a very small part.

Crag leaned close. "I saw you on the Mesh, Enola," he said. "We all did. You were very impressive."

"Thank you," she responded, and didn't decline as he filled her glass anew. She held it but did not drink.

His smile widened. "Will you cover the Pour?" he asked. Already, half of his drink was gone, and there was a moist quality in his eyes as he gazed at her.

Once again, Enola asked herself how she could ever have allowed herself to associate with him.

"I don't know yet," was all that she said aloud. She knew that she almost certainly would, but Arreigh had asked her not to discuss her schedule with others. There were agreements that needed finalizing, first.

"The model was very effective," he continued, earnestly. "Even the gophers should be able to understand what happened."

"They say they do not know what happened yet," Narçissa said. "Not exactly."

Enola made a sound of agreement.

Crag snorted. He filled his glass again, finishing without invitation the pitcher that Narçissa and Enola had paid for. "They know," he said. "They just don't tell the drones." He smiled and leaned closer. The blunt fingers of his left hand traced the line of Enola's chin with easy familiarity.

"Maybe Enola knows," he said. "She's not a drone anymore, is she?" His smile widened. "She's a celebrity."

Under the table, in the concealing shadows, his right hand found Enola's thigh. With remarkable speed and a kind of territorial imperative, it slid beneath the hemline of the skirt she wore.

What happened next happened without Enola's conscious

control. It seemed as if she were no longer in control of her own body, as if some automated subsystem had come to life. Even without her deliberate control, however, the action came with her wholehearted approval.

She wanted to cheer for herself as she threw her drink at him.

Her arm came up, moving quickly along a short, sharp trajectory. Her fingers retained their secure grip on the glass's stem, so that it remained behind when the hand that held it stopped and its contents rushed forward. Orange juice and champagne splattered against Crag Fortinbras's smirk, then fell to the floor, to blossom there in slow-motion splashes.

"I'm finished with you, Crag," Enola snarled, as he gasped at her in dismay. Hearing Narçissa's sharp yelp of woe, she turned then to face the older woman, and made herself smile.

"It was nice to see you, Narçissa, and I do miss Duckworth," she said. "But good-bye."

THE imaging appointment had been set weeks ago, long before the unpleasant Enola Hasbro had entered Sarrah Chrysler's life. In the days that followed, she had received reminders from her personal management system, flagged them as received, and promptly forgotten them. She regretted that, now. The session had originally been intended strictly for maintenance. Now, however, Sarrah was beginning to think that a more assertive approach on her part might be more appropriate. She should have planned ahead, and perhaps brought her own consultant with her.

It was probably too late for that, she realized. The personal attendant overseeing her session now worked directly for Arreigh. Her loyalty was to him, and it was becoming increasingly obvious that Arreigh's loyalty was to Enola.

Sarrah wanted to spit. The very idea of sharing Mesh time with an upstart like Hasbro was an insult to her, to her professionalism, and to Zonix. Arreigh had always presented himself as being something of an iconoclast, but there was such a thing as taking rebellion and innovation too far. Audience ratings and consumer feedback were all well and good, but there was more to reporting than that.

There had to be.

"Don't scowl yet," the attendant said. "You'll abort the scan. Take the expressions in sequence."

"Sorry," Sarrah said, moving her lips as little as possible, to avoid disturbing the gossamer-fine sensory film that had been applied to her features. Gummi modules along the membrane's perimeter read her skin as she half-reclined in the angled chair. Muscle tone, nerve activity, dermal visual indices, even cellular respiration counts were duly recorded, collated, and filed. Those values would form the basis for her next set of cosmetic appliances.

"Keith says that you're testing too well," the attendant said, in matter-of-fact tones. She was a stocky woman without legs, who glided about the imaging parlor on a wheeled chair that responded to softly murmured commands. "Still too young, too attractive. He wants to make that different, for the Pour feed."

"That's preposterous," Sarrah half-snarled, still careful to keep her features composed. She did not want the imagineer to start again.

It *was* preposterous, though. Bad enough that she had to degrade her appearance deliberately, to make herself look slightly older and more severe. Audiences were eternally fickle, essentially perverse, and weirdly demanding, but she knew the need to cater to them. To do so while sharing Mesh time with Enola Hasbro, however, was more than preposterous; it was infuriating.

"There's not enough of a contrast," the attendant murmured. Sarrah hadn't bothered to remember her name. Unattractive herself, she could not possibly understand the thoughts going through Sarrah's mind just now. "Hasbro's skin and hair could be better, but her bone structure is remarkably symmetrical, and her eyes are several percentage points larger in proportion to her other features than the average human adult's. She evokes youth and vitality without looking childish. People respond to it without knowing why." She laughed softly, the first warm sound she had uttered. "She must have an interesting social life."

Sarrah grunted. She kept her gaze locked forward and up, and tried not to flinch as the attendant attached a series of pickups to her neck and collarbone. The other woman's hands were cool and her technique was scrupulously professional, but Sarrah did not like strangers touching her.

Implacably, the woman continued. "Those are qualities that are very difficult to model or simulate effectively." She did something to the masking film that Sarrah wore. "But audiences respond to them on an intuitive, almost subliminal level. Hasbro *engages* very well. Arreigh was fortunate to find her," the attendant said. "Now smile."

Sarrah smiled, pulling the sensor mask into a new configuration. It required conscious effort.

"The human eye is a remarkably subtle instrument," the woman continued. She had rolled completely out of Sarrah's field of view now, and her fingertips made soft tapping noises as they impacted membranous keys. "It likes novelty. That's one reason for the current trend to embrace 'authenticity.' " She snorted. "But there are universal values that the eye likes, too, and those are values that Hasbro has. Now frown."

Sarrah frowned.

"Less," the attendant said.

Obediently, Sarrah made the muscles of her face relax slightly. She maintained the expression carefully as the attendant took another reading.

"I don't know if Hasbro has a career in this work, but she has the foundations for one. With the right backing, she could do very well," the attendant said. "Open your eyes wider."

As Sarrah obeyed, she heard the whine of electric motors. The articulated wheel-base of the attendant's chair was reconfiguring itself, lifting the legless woman higher.

From her new stance, she leaned closer and held an optical scanner close to Sarrah's left eye. "Look in this direction," she said. "At me."

For the first time, Sarrah focused specifically on the attendant's face. She was approximately Sarrah's age, but looked much older. Her hair, an iron-gray color that looked natural, was pulled back in a utilitarian bun and what some called crow's-feet wrinkles framed her eyes.

What were crows? Sarrah wondered, and she wondered how an expert in appearance modeling could permit herself to look so worn.

As if reading her mind, the woman replied. "I used to be beautiful, you know," she said. She spoke in neutral tones, as if speaking about something out of history. "There was a decompression incident. I lost the legs then. After that, everything else seemed trivial."

A probe caught the edge of the modeling mask and tugged. The film of sensor-lined smart plastic peeled away, leaving behind only the faint, medicinal scent of adhesive compound.

Compassion, surprisingly intense, welled up within Sarrah. "There are prosthetics," she said, careful not to disturb the other woman's work. Too late, she wondered if the problem were one of price, and if she had been rude.

The attendant shook her head. "Not for me. I'm a special case. Nerve/brainware incompatibility issues." She dropped out of view again as her chair retreated. "I have a sketch," she said. "Do you want to see it?"

Sarrah nodded. A computer display dropped from the ceiling, like a curtain, coming to a halt a comfortable distance from her eyes. The transparent film became translucent, then opaque, cutting off the view of the wall beyond. A moment later, Sarrah was looking at an image of a woman with sharp features slightly blunted by cosmetics, and thinning hair that was neatly groomed and impeccably styled into a conservative coif. All of her own cosmetic work and self-grooming had been undone by mirage processing, a foreshadowing of cosmetic overlays that would follow. The woman in the altered image was not unattractive, but the impression she gave was less of beauty than of something well preserved.

"Arreigh wanted a greater contrast with Hasbro," the attendant said. " 'Stronger context' is what he said."

"I don't like it," Sarrah said. It was an understatement. Looking at the image was like looking at a picture of her mother.

"You don't have final approval," the attendant said. "And I've already provided him a copy. He's already signed his approval."

Sarrah bit her lip with sudden irritation that such a decision had been made without her participation. "I still don't like it," she said.

"I can have the appliances ready for fitting within an hour," the woman said. She spoke as if Sarrah had not. "Do you want to wait, or come back for them?"

"Can I access my personal Mesh from here?" Sarrah asked. There was work to do. "Can I have some privacy?"

After the other woman had left for her workroom, Sarrah murmured the commands that would open her account and began reviewing the files that had accumulated there.

Most were backgrounders, on current or past events that might be featured on her Mesh program. Those, she favored with only the briefest of glances. Her opinion was likely to be moot, anyway. The remembered image of her new cosmetics suite loomed large in her mind, a reminder that she was almost certainly losing control of her own program.

Two others were of more interest. They were background reports on Enola Hasbro and Wendy Scheer. Neither was particularly substantive, but for differing reasons.

Hasbro's life simply didn't seem to have included much worth reporting. Prior to her Mesh debut, nothing that the attractive Asiatic woman had done with her life had brought her to the attention of the media. Sarrah scanned the text quickly, absorbing the bare-bones biography with practiced ease. Born in Ukraine of displaced foreign nationals,

Hasbro had attended engineering school on the Continent, settling for construction modeling when the more advanced specialties proved beyond her. Duckworth had recruited her for Villanueva soon after the Czech Challenge, and the disruption that the civil uprising had brought to that part of the world. After her relocation, she had settled into a life of effective obscurity, except for the occasional admiring comment that could be found in open social logs. Her only relatives were two mothers and a sister, deceased.

Scheer's file was of more interest, even if equally brief. To Sarrah's practiced consideration, it showed all the signs of a redacted document. It was almost entirely bereft of useful or interesting information. It noted birth and graduation dates, and terms of public service, and covered a very few official appearances she had made in Villanueva, the last of them years before. What little content the file actually held was sufficiently cryptic that Sarrah had to wonder who the other woman actually worked for. The only information that Sarrah found interesting by its presence rather than absence was a single, isolated image, taken from a Mesh release issued upon Scheer's graduation from Project Halo.

It showed an attractive woman with long, reddish hair and lean, well-defined features. She was smiling for the camera, but it was an official smile, formal and posed. It had no warmth in it, and Sarrah looked past it easily. Instead, she focused on the Scheer woman's eyes.

Even in the stored image, the eyes were bright and alive. They seemed to glint with a light that suggested both secret knowledge and a playful spirit. Even if all of Scheer's other facial features were anonymous and unknown to her, Sarrah found something about her eyes familiar.

And then the entire world seemed to stand still as the realization struck her.

When the attendant returned, Sarrah was still seated in the reclining chair, staring at the computer screen suspended before her. On it were two images, cropped and butted together. Half of the composite face belonged to

Wendy Scheer, the other half to Sarrah herself. Nose, cheekbones, lips, chin, hair—none of them matched. No one would ever mistake one woman for the other.

The two eyes, however, were precisely the same. They were so similar that they could have been a matched pair, plucked from the same skull. The irises were the same size and color, an odd hazel that was Sarrah's natural hue. The match in color was hardly significant, however, except when taken in concert with the other matches. Their eyebrows and eyelashes differed dramatically, but the lids, both upper and lower, were perfectly mirrored curves. Even the softly defined contours where eyeball met eyesocket as were perfect matches. But the most striking match was an expression the eyes shared, gazing out separately from such disparate faces. Both seemed electric and alive, with a quality that was vaguely elfin.

The attendant's words came back to her. People responded to things without knowing why. The thought filled her mind and would not go away.

"These are ready for you," the attendant said, returning. She held a tray of cosmetic appliances. "Close that, and I'll show you how to use them."

"The poor fool," was all that Sarrah said. "The poor, stupid fool."

She was crying.

HUERTA'S expression was disapproving. He sat atop a padded stool in the same examination room as before. He frowned slightly as he divided his attention into roughly equal portions. One he gave to Enola, perched again on the table's edge, and the other, to the diagnostic console that stretched between them.

"You've been drinking," Huerta said. "Alcohol."

"I've been drinking," Enola agreed. "Alcohol."

"I don't even need to look at your values," Huerta said. He gestured at the diagnostic console, at numbers and diagrams and signal traces that Enola could not see from her angle. If she had been able to see them, she knew, she wouldn't have been able to understand them.

"I've had something to celebrate," she continued helpfully. "I really haven't been drinking very much. And nothing stronger than alcohol."

"In some ways, there is nothing stronger than alcohol," Huerta said, still reproving. "It's a bad habit as old as the species. In a very real sense, evolution has predisposed us all to alcoholism, to varying degrees." He thumbed the console, paging through multiple display screens. Upon Enola's arrival, he had reclaimed his outboard module, and that was the source of what he reviewed now. He looked concerned.

Enola said nothing.

He continued, sounding some incremental fraction of a percentage point less disapproving, becoming didactic instead. "In the last century, early geneticists and addiction specialists thought that they could change that, Enola. When the first human genome map was complete, they thought that they could identify the part that made people alcoholics and edit it out, like EnTek edits Gummi scripts," he said. He paused, and fixed her with a cool glance. "They were wrong. The drive to intoxication is just too fundamental a trait."

"I'm not an alcoholic," Enola said. Under the light, disposable gown, she felt a sudden, slight chill. Paradoxically, there was a new heat in her voice. The word wasn't one that she heard very often, and she very much didn't like the idea that he might be applying it to her.

"Maybe not," Huerta said. "Probably not. But if you aren't, you don't have any excuse for these readings." He paged through a few more screens before continuing. "You don't *want* to end up like Chesney, do you?" he asked.

"No!" Enola shook her head emphatically, panicked. The very thought of the fat man appalled her. "No! That won't happen, will it?"

"Probably not," Huerta said. "His is a special case, from a different error. But your regression still isn't proceeding as it should. I think that one cause is that you were changed so long ago, and with the old process. But the alcohol is a contributing factor, too." His point made, he sounded soothing now. "You need to understand, your body needs the opportunity to adapt. You've unnecessarily stressed your liver and endocrine system, and they're having a very difficult time responding to the retro-therapy."

"Chesney said that the process was routine," Enola said. Her stomach gurgled and tensed, and she wished desperately that she had forgone breakfast with Narçissa. She wondered how much damage two glasses of diluted champagne could cause.

She decided not to think about the celebration with Arreigh and the others.

"Have you experienced any episodes of lightheadedness?" Huerta asked. "Tell me truthfully."

"None," she responded. "One or two."

"Food cravings? Loss of appetite?" They were the questions that physicians always asked, and always had, since the beginning of time.

Enola shook her head.

"Inappropriate mood swings?" Huerta asked.

Enola smiled faintly. She thought of the shocked expression on Crag Fortinbras's features as orange juice and champagne had dribbled down to decorate his tunic. She thought about how good she had felt after making that happen.

"No *inappropriate* mood swings," she said. She swung her feet nervously, like a little girl.

Huerta made a final notation, then closed his file. He looked at her steadily. "I'm taking you off the therapy," he said. "In twelve weeks, after things stabilize, we'll try again."

She looked at him blankly.

"I know your severance won't permit a delay like that," he said. "But in extenuating circumstances like these—"

Enola shook her head, making her neatly coifed hair ripple like black water. She giggled. The world suddenly seemed a brighter place. She felt like a little girl with a secret that she knew she shouldn't tell, who had found a reason why she should. "Thank you, but I won't need the intercession," she said. "I won't be going back to Earth."

Now, it was Huerta who looked confused. "I don't understand, Enola," he said. "I don't think that you understand. Your terms of employment require you to honor your terms of severance. You must go back to Earth, and you really should have the therapy before you do. Now, I can reschedule treatment—"

"I'm not going back," Enola said. The words felt good on her lips, so she said them again. "I'm not going back to Earth."

"You must," Huerta said.

"I'm not," she said. "I have secured alternate employment." She smiled tightly. "I am going to job-hop."

CHAPTER 12

THE imagineers had done their work well. The cavernous
Duckworth foundry space had been transformed since Sarrah's last visit. The outer boundaries of the place, previously little more than plastic-sealed native rock, were now
thickly layered with sound-deadening foam. So were many
of the larger reflecting surfaces in between. To preserve the
impression of raw, industrial workspace, that foam, in turn
had been painted the color of the rock and metal it clad.
Production crews were detailing that sheathing now, en-
hancing it with handheld airbrushes. Moving quickly, they
accentuated shadows and realistic-looking smears of dirt
and scarring, all under the careful eye and snappish orders
of Bainbridge himself.

"I never would have believed it," Erik Morrison said. At
her side, he shook his head. "Painting rock gray. It seems
redundant."

"There's a reason for it," Sarrah said. She spoke with a
preoccupied tone. Her right hand held the crook of his left
arm loosely as they patrolled the foundry perimeter, for
one final review of the lay of the land. "It's the kind of

thing that people want to see. The bare foam looked too fresh and new. Now, it looks like a foundry again."

Barely audible over the surrounding clatter, a heavy metal doorway clanged open. Bainbridge emerged from one of the access tunnels, did something with a piece of apparatus that Sarrah did not recognize, and then reentered the darkness. The door swung shut behind him. Mere hours remained until the Pour and its attendant live Meshcast, and the production specialist was working with frantic haste.

"It seems redundant," Erik said again. "Couldn't they mirage it in?"

"Probably," Sarrah said. She thought for a moment. "It might be a matter of economics. Large-scale miraging isn't cheap." She paused, and when she continued, she spoke with slight bitterness. "Besides, the eye is a subtle instrument. It can respond to things without knowing why."

He cocked one eyebrow quizzically at her comment, but said nothing in return.

Her skin was sweaty and sticky, heated by thermal leakage from the great furnaces built by Duckworth and by Dynamo's proprietary fusion process. They were cycling to full power now. The heat they kicked out made the air thick and rich with thermal currents that carried grit and debris on their gentle shoulders. The ambient environment would get worse before it got better, and Sarrah wondered what impact it would have on her cosmetic appliances. The imagineering specialists had assured her that they were rated far beyond human tolerances, but she had learned not to trust specialists.

They had their own agendas. Everyone did, it seemed.

"Have you ever been to the Grand Canyon?" Erik asked suddenly, apropos of nothing that Sarrah could see. She hadn't, and said so.

He nodded and continued. "Some of the most striking scenery on Earth," he said. "All it is, is a scar, really, a long hole worn into the ground by a river, over millions of years." He paused, then corrected himself. "Billions, maybe. I used to summer there."

Sarrah only half listened. Too many other things demanded her attention for her to spare much for a travelogue, even for one delivered by Erik. She wanted to know the texture of this place before actual transmission.

Since her last visit, heavy banks of equipment had been repositioned, changing the landscape within the foundry. The mounds of ingots of iron and titanium and other metals had vanished, fed into the waiting furnaces and cooking now into structural alloy. Half submerged in lunar rock, half framed by braced scaffolding, the huge cylindrical forms that would accept that alloy offered new challenges to consider in staging a presentation. Easily four hundred meters in diameter, they would serve as the wombs for the test-casts of structural casings for the great engines that would power the Ad Astra ship on its journey to the outer reaches of the solar system. Foundry workmen scurried like insects on the forms, taking readings, inspecting seams, and relaying commands to one another via ruggedized phones. Later, during the Pour itself, those same men and women would wear protective environmental suits, but for now, they suffered, like Sarrah suffered.

"It's a gash, or an incision," Erik continued. For a moment, his words became artificial and strained-sounding, as the two of them strayed too close to a suppressor that clipped the syllables. "That's the right word. It lays open the flesh of the Earth. You can see the layers there, the strata. It's not like the Moon, all gray and white rock. It's layers of color, some of the most intense hues in all creation."

The oppressive heat made Sarrah sweat some more. She tried to focus past it as she and Erik paced the perimeter. Surrounding them were angled lattices of guide cables that stretched from floor to ceiling. Along those filaments rode cameras and microphones, lights and suppresser arrays. Sarrah watched the machinery move, taking careful note of the angles and speeds. It was better to think about them than about other things.

"That's very interesting," she mumbled, without meaning it.

"No, it's not, really," he said easily. "What's interesting is, when old Hollywood made staged dramas in the Canyon, technicians felt the need to improve on nature. They painted boulders and fossils and even trees in contrasting colors, to make more interesting compositions." Now, he smiled. "That's what your people are doing here."

"No," Sarrah said stiffly. "No, that's not. They're ensuring an enhanced degree of authenticity."

Erik laughed. "Like that 'SIMULATED IMAGE' that they miraged into your feed, the first time we met?" he asked. "The eyeballs and the tentacles?"

Sarrah felt a sudden rush of new heat that had nothing to do with the furnaces. She stopped walking and looked at him. "That's different," she said. "And I made my objections, remember?"

"I remember." Erik smiled down at her. For some reason, she had never fully realized just how much taller he was than her, and she was acutely conscious of it now. "I don't like what they've done to your face," he said gently.

"I don't, either," Sarrah said. "But it's still me. All that Arreigh's people have done is move the calendar up a few turns."

Erik didn't say anything.

"He says it's to provide a better context for your friend, Hasbro," Sarrah continued. She did not like the words she spoke, but they came unbidden.

A look of discomfort flowed across Erik's features, sharp enough to look like real pain. "Enola is a friendly acquaintance," he said. For some reason, the name meant something more than that to him, Sarrah was sure. "That's all that she ever was."

"You'll see her here later."

"For the first time in at least five years," Erik said. "You seem worried, Sarrah. You shouldn't be. You'll do fine."

Sarrah took a deep breath. He was a good man, she realized. "Tell me about Wendy Scheer, Erik," she said, with forced calm.

"I can't do that," he said. "I told you that at lunch."

"Tell me what you can," she said. She looked up at him. "Not in an official capacity. Not for use, Erik. For me. Tell me what you can."

"She's the head of Project Halo," he replied. "I don't know exactly what her current title is, but she directs its operations. Since the Feds issue their contracts, I have to coordinate with her office from time to time, but I almost always deal with proxies."

"Do you know her?"

Erik shook his head. "I've met her," he said. "I don't think anyone really *knows* Wendy. Why are you so interested? Preparing a story?"

"No," Sarrah said. "I told you. It's not for Mesh use. Someone told me that I look like her."

He flinched, and looked at her closely. He had deep gray eyes that were remarkably intense, especially at such close range. He focused on her for a long moment, then shook his head slightly. "No," he said. "No, you don't."

Her heart sang.

"Except perhaps a little bit, around the eyes," he continued, as he turned away.

THE ratcheting clatter of wheels on jointed metal rails slowed as the train approached the foundry's loading dock. The conveyance had been designed for mixed use, cargo and workers alike, and its amenities were few. No food service and no drinks were provided for the short hop from Villanueva proper, and no brainware conductor announced the stops. Instead, a simple lighted display at the front of the passenger car told riders when their destinations neared.

Enola didn't mind. In fact, she liked it. She was acutely aware of just how out of place she looked, all cool and composed in a carload of grubby second-shift workers. She liked that, too. The neat attire that she wore, semicasual work dress, clearly bespoke a very different kind of work history than any of her fellow passengers. Her hair, newly styled and pulled back from her face, glossed in stark contrast to the abbreviated stubble affected by most of the plant workers.

The ride had been interesting. She had spent most of it reviewing notes and background data—all from public sources, she hoped—on her unfurled personal computer, but there had been time to bask in the attentive gazes of others, too. She wondered how many, if any, of them had seen her on the Mesh.

The clatter slowed more, then stopped as the train came to a halt. With easy grace, Enola hooked a handrail and made inertia work for her, letting the sudden stop throw her forward and out of her seat. Rising, she wadded the cheap computer into one pocket, scooped up the handbag that carried her better unit and her dress shoes, and headed for the nearest exit.

Someone jostled her slightly, and a blunt finger tapped her on the shoulder. She turned, to see a squat man with broad features look bashfully at her.

"You're Enola Hasbro, aren't you?" he asked. His face split into a broad, big-toothed grin.

"Yes, I am," she responded, delighted by the recognition and a little embarrassed by the attention. She wondered if she would need to accustom herself to such treatment.

"I told you! I told you it was!" said another passenger.

"Are you here for the Pour?" the first asked, ignoring his friend. "I saw you on the Mesh," he added eagerly.

Enola nodded.

"Will you be on the Mesh again today?" he asked. "For the Pour?"

"I don't know," Enola said, shading the truth. Her status with Zonix was still in the process of clarification, but Keith Arreigh had told her that she would almost certainly be included in today's Meshcast of the inaugural Pour.

"We're not sure yet. It's Sarrah Chrysler's feed."

"Aw, you're more fun to watch than she is," the squat man said. Then, before Enola could respond, he turned left, toward the train car exit that faced the employees' foundry entrance. Enola started to follow, then drew up short, remembering.

She didn't work for Duckworth anymore. Instead, she turned right, toward a grimy signboard directing visitors to follow its instructions. Beneath it stood Keith Arreigh and Katalin Cassidy.

"I don't *care!*" Arreigh was saying, into his personal phone. "Process it, log it, and start on the next one!" He paused. "I don't *care* if there's no next one!"

"Hallo," Cassidy said. She rolled large, expressive eyes in Arreigh's direction. "The busy man is very, very busy today."

Arreigh scowled at her but followed it with a wave at Enola. He was dressed differently than she had ever seen him before, in a logo-marked jumpsuit. She assumed that it was supposed to be a worker's uniform, but Enola was not impressed. She had seen the real thing too recently. Arreigh's outfit looked like a Mesh-designer's fantasy of what industrial workers might wear. It was of the wrong fabric, fit entirely too well, and was covered with bulging pockets and straps that would catch too easily on workplace equipment. After her so-recent train ride, and her brief conversation with the foundry worker, the inappropriate details glared at Enola.

Katalin giggled, a familiar sound. Her dark eyes flashed. "He is a bit of a poseur," she said. Usually enigmatic and reserved, she seemed buoyant and playful today, and Enola had to wonder what the reason was.

Was it because this was the first time that they had met in person since their night together? Enola hoped not. Ugly memories of Crag Fortinbras loomed.

Still barking orders to his unseen audience, Arreigh heard her. He glared again, made an impolite gesture, then snarled an apology into the phone and broke the link. "Enola, hello!" he said. He hooked thumbs with her before drawing her into a slightly clammy embrace. "So good to see you!"

"Hello, Keith," Enola said, only half looking in his direction. She noticed Katalin studying her again.

"This way, this way," he said. He stepped ahead of her then turned, shuffling backward with occasional over-the-shoulder glances as he led her toward an access ramp. "Be careful," he said. "Foundries are not the tidiest places. Don't trip. Be careful where you step."

"Don't trip," Enola agreed, half in acknowledgment and half in warning. "I reviewed the files you sent me, Keith. I think I can work with them. There don't seem to be any proprietary concerns."

"They're all public. But you won't have to worry about that much longer," Arreigh said. His feet had found the ramp, and now he had to bend his neck to look down at her. Beside him, her gaze more reasonably trained forward, flowed up the ramp. Her liquid grace was in stark contrast to Arreigh's shuffling, nearly awkward means of locomotion.

Enola had to assume that the Duckworth foundry seldom entertained visitors and didn't care to impress those few who came to call. Behind the grubby visitors entrance stretched corridors that were grubbier still, stark and utilitarian. For meters at a time they were bounded by rough rock, the legacy of hasty construction, gray and cool to the touch. The finished stretches were scarcely more refined, walls made of planed stone panels that were anchored by gray metal frames. Ceiling illuminators and the occasional hatched doorway punctuated the meandering course she trudged along.

Arreigh made most of the trip walking backward, eagerly chattering to Enola about technical specifications and feedback expectations. If Katalin seemed unusually effusive, Keith seemed positively ebullient. He spoke in rapid, short sentences, emphasizing specific points with finger-points and hand-waves. Once, he paused long enough to answer his phone, and then bark the words, "Go away! I'm with someone much more important than you!" He laughed as he broke the link and Enola laughed, too, wondering if Arreigh had ever considered being a public performer himself. He certainly liked to play to an audience.

"—your severance with Duckworth," Arreigh said. The words punched through his running monologue and commanded Enola's attention. "They're balking."

"Balking?" she said sharply. She didn't like the sound of that. The future suddenly seemed uncertain once more.

He paused in his reverse march, placed his hands on her shoulders, and looked sympathetically into her eyes. "It's almost unprecedented, Enola, at least in Villanueva," he said. "There are procedures, but they've almost never been used, and the management teams for both sisters have room for discretion. Right now, our bid for your services is being held for review. An Over-Management underdirector has raised objections, but they *will* be resolved. You *will* work for me, I promise you."

"I just don't want to go back to Earth," was all that Enola could think to say. She thought of her earlier decisiveness with Huerta and wondered if she had acted too soon.

"You won't," he reassured her. "If you were a contractor or a consultant, there wouldn't be any issue. But you're company bones, so there's balking."

"You're sure?"

He nodded. "I'm sure. Now, let's go," he said, and turned his back on her. "I want you to meet our other guest. His name is Erik Morrison."

·

SARRAH watched warily as Arreigh entered the temporary green room with his charges. The producer seemed beside himself with excitement. He hovered around Hasbro, gesturing and chuckling and touching, positively giddy as he accompanied the two women though the grubby doorway and into the stark, utilitarian spaces that Zonix had commandeered from Duckworth management.

"Here we are!" he said, and gestured again. He beamed. "Erik! Enola tells me that you two are old friends."

"We've met," Erik said. He smiled, and Sarrah had to wonder if it was the easy expression of someone who had nothing to hide, or of a man who hid things very easily. "At the Grotto. Remember?"

"And before that," Enola said, cheerfully. She neatly executed a mock-curtsy as she hooked thumbs with him, then glanced in Sarrah's direction. "Did Erik tell you?" she asked.

"Erik told me," Sarrah responded, and felt ashamed of the coolness in her voice. She was being foolish, she knew, but the chance discovery she had made about Wendy Scheer had unnerved her. Abruptly, Enola didn't seem so bad, after all. "It's a small world, isn't it?"

"Much smaller than Earth," Erik said dryly.

"Erik has agreed to make some comments during the Meshcast, Enola," Sarrah said.

"Excellent! Excellent!" Keith Arreigh interjected. He pushed himself between the three of them and clapped Erik on one shoulder. "I'm glad that Over-Management concurred with my suggestion."

"Really, I'm not sure whose idea it was," Erik said. Actually, it had been Sarrah's suggestion, made to him in his role as ALC director of communications, but tact seemed appropriate. "But this is a major milestone and—"

"Have you considered what you're going to say?" Arreigh asked. "Or should I prepare something quickly? We've got a schedule, you know."

Erik continued doggedly. "Sarrah and I—"

"I have it right here," Sarrah said. She opened her computer and consulted her most recent script. It was an articulated document, with storyboard diagrams to indicate camera setups, correlated with sequential Pour phases. She ran one finger down the screen of views, looking for the entry that she and Erik had worked on.

Arreigh craned his neck and glanced at the scrolling document. "Before Enola would be better," he said. "I want him in the booth before you introduce her."

"Enola?" Sarrah asked. The last that she had heard, Hasbro was on-site to observe only. "Have you resolved her status?"

A head shake told her that Arreigh hadn't. "But I want you to reintroduce her," he said. "A cameo should be fine." He took the computer from her unresisting hands and paged through several screens. "Here," he said. "This is best." He starred a view. "Here."

A clock display on the green room wall sounded. Live transmission was due to start in minutes, and there didn't seem to be time to argue the point of Enola's status. Sarrah glanced at the younger woman, who shrugged and smiled in response.

"All right, then," Sarrah said, resigned. "What about Erik?"

Arreigh scrolled back. "Here, I think," he said, and pointed.

His choice made sense. Sarrah would open the Mesh-cast, explain the process of the Pour, and then introduce Erik as her guest. Her prescribed, preapproved words would announce and commemorate the casting itself, followed by comments from Erik. Bringing up the close would be Sarrah's "good friend" Enola Hasbro.

"I want to see sweat," Keith said earnestly. He pulled up a diagram. "It's a standard half-dome booth," he said, and pointed. "We placed it *here.*"

Sarrah blinked. "That's twenty meters closer to the forms," she said. "To the Pour itself." She looked at him. "Is that safe?"

"It's a standard half-dome," Keith said again. His head dipped a little bit, and his shoulders came up as he gestured, using his hands to approximate the configuration. "Not fully enclosed, but enough to protect. You'll be fine." He grinned. "But I want to see you sweat."

The clock display sounded again.

"You'd better change," Arreigh said.

"Change?" Erik asked.

"Sarrah and Enola. I want to see logos on both of them."

CHAPTER 13

THE blast hit like a hammer, and the sound of its blow echoed still in the enclosed space. Not even the foam and suppressers could absorb the thunder, or even blunt its fury. It roared and rebounded in the enclosed space for long moments. Mingled in the reverberations were the ringing groans of tearing metal, like tortured bells. Overlying them all, underscoring them, were the screams.

They were still sounding when Erik came back to consciousness. He could hear them, as if from an infinite distance. A moment before, he had been walking across the foundry floor and toward the production when a giant hand had come out of nowhere and thrown him, hard, against a wheeled crane. Now, as his world came back to him, it had become a very different place.

His ears still rang as he blinked his eyes. His phones had been some protection, but not enough. Darkness seeped into the periphery of his vision, and then oozed back out as he blinked again.

Everything had changed. The world had gone monochrome. Emergency lights glared down from above, their radiance blunted by swirling billows of soot and smoke.

Everything was in shades of gray. Something had happened to the soundscape, too, or to his ears. All that he could hear was muffled thunder and distorted sounds that might have been screams.

His reality wrenched itself into new configurations as Erik gathered his feet beneath him and rose, leaning heavily on an outcropping of the crane. As he did, wetness moved beneath his fingers. Startled, he looked. The liquid was black against the gray-painted insulating foam. He blinked yet again and rubbed his eyes. Color came back, then. He could see that the liquid was red, dark under the emergency lights' harsh glow, but red nonetheless.

It was blood. It was his blood, most likely.

"God," he croaked into his phone. It hurt to talk. "Help," he said, forcing the word out, past the smoke and soot that lined his throat. "We need some help in here. Explosion."

No response came. His personal phones were dead.

He could hear screams more clearly now. Screams in men's voices and in women's, mixed with low moans. Sarrah was still on the production floor, he realized.

Erik lurched forward. The air, merely hot and dirty a moment before, burned like fire now. No matter how slowly or shallowly he breathed, each breath he took scorched his mouth and the lining of his nose. Desperately, he dropped to his hands and knees, looking for and finding something slightly cooler to breathe as he crawled forward. Soot and ash choked him as he crawled. Almost without conscious thought, he moved toward the production booth's shadowed ruins. The smoke became thicker as he moved, and the lighting became worse, but he forced himself forward.

He was halfway there when something blocked his path. Touch told him that the limp form was one of Duckworth's foundry workers, clad in coveralls and an environmental mask. Erik didn't need to see him to know that he was dead. Whatever the blast had been, whatever its cause, its concussion or aftermath had killed the other man. Erik helped himself to the filter-mask the corpse wore, donned it, and moved on.

"What is it?"

"What happened?"

"Help me, please, gods help me!"

"It was a bomb!"

The screams were dying out now, trailing off into moans. Slowly, some of those moans resolved themselves into words, each becoming distinguishable in turn as the pounding ringing in his ears receded. The sound baffles in the mask helped, too, sorting out the ambient noise and making it more comprehensible. Erik still couldn't hear very much, but what he could hear, he understood. Part of him wished that he couldn't. The sounds of suffering that rose from the broken and wounded reminded him of the red smear that his touch had left on the foundry wall. He was hurting inside and had no idea how bad his injuries were.

The realization flickered through his mind that his injuries might be mortal. He pushed the thought away. He had been a considerable distance from the explosion. Sarrah had been near its center.

Ten meters, twelve, fifteen—half crawling, half walking, he dragged himself forward. The floor was rough and filthy and warmer to the touch than it should have been. Abandoned tools and equipment littered it, and one fumbled half-step nearly sent him sprawling onto a second corpse.

As he moved, as the ability to think clearly came back to him, he tried to remember what had happened. His jumbled memories released a single image. He had seen it, out of the corner of one eye. There had been a flash of light, near the ceiling, along the lateral track. It must have been the explosion. The explosion had come from above.

"Bomb," Erik croaked, and looked up, through the soot and shadow. It had to have been a bomb, like the one in the Mall. Now, at last, he saw the source of the tearing metal sound. The shadowed mass of the great casting cauldron was stark against the ceiling illuminators. It hung crazily on its track, its angle all wrong to even his nonexpert eye.

As Erik watched, the cauldron rocked a bit, and tipped. A curved line of brightness formed abruptly at the vessel's lip, as its contents shifted and seeped over the rim. The brightness was the glow of liquid metal, seeking release from its precariously poised prison.

The explosion bomb had wrecked the cross-track and maybe the motors that drew the cauldron along it. Tons of white-hot molten metal hung precariously high above the foundry floor, with only a damaged track and vessel holding it there. If the cauldron tipped more, if it came free—

Erik tried to move faster.

THE blast hit like a hammer, and the sound of its blow echoed in the enclosed space. Time became elastic and stretched a single, split second into something that was long and lingering. The curved shield of the production booth shook and cracked as the shockwave slammed into it. It shook and it cracked, but it held, and it withstood the hail of shrapnel fragments that made Sarrah Chrysler yelp in shock and dismay. Within the partially sheltering structure, she stumbled and nearly fell, grasping a safety rail and catching herself barely in time. Hot, dirty wind washed over her as the last of the flash faded, and then time resumed its normal progress.

What the hell had happened?

A rack in the production booth held filter-masks. She grabbed one and donned the piece of safety equipment hastily, without bothering to peel off her facial appliances. The mask's outer seal caught and held, and Sarrah gulped clean air greedily. Still dazed, she turned from side to side, trying to determine what had happened.

In the emergency lights' harsh glare, she could see that ragged, jigsaw cracks now crazed the booth's contours, but that it remained whole, however barely. The instrument panels were dark, all of them. The Mesh monitors were worse than dark, they were chaotic tapestries of random signals. Their Gummis were stunned or dead.

"Hello? Hello? What happened?" Sarrah tried her personal phones and the booth intercom, one after the other. Neither surrendered any response. The concussion had gotten them, too.

Frustrated, disgusted, panicked, she looked up from the intercom, and just in time. Out of the swirling murk, something blinding and bright swung toward her. It was one of the Zonix production team's spotlights, swinging freely now at the end of a broken guideline. Sarrah yelped again and dropped back, even as the illumination unit smashed into the already damaged booth. The heavy-gauge plastic, already badly damaged, shattered instantly and completely. It dissolved into a second wave of shrapnel, bits of plastic that stabbed at Sarrah and stung her.

Someone else cried out in pain and surprise. It was Hasbro. Sarrah saw the younger woman lurching toward the production booth. Her hair was a mess, and her youthful features were pale and strained. One ivory cheek was cut and bleeding.

"What is it?" Hasbro demanded. The words were barely audible, hidden under an obscuring cloak of background noise, masked by the groan of tearing metal. The expression on her face said that she was shouting, but her words could barely resolve themselves into comprehensibility, even with the help of Sarrah's headphones. "Sarrah, what happened?"

Sarrah glared at her, alarmed at the younger woman's obvious confusion. Hasbro's frightened expression made her look like a child. "Your face!" she yelled. "You need a mask! Do you want to suffocate?" The suppressor units that Bainbridge had situated so carefully were either dead or overtaxed beyond imagination, but the words she heard still sounded broken and syllable-clipped. The mask's filtering baffles did that.

Dazed, disoriented, Hasbro repeated herself. "What happened?" she asked plaintively. "Keith said I should—" Enola's words collapsed into a paroxysm of coughing.

"Your mask," Sarrah said. She grabbed a second one and tossed it to Enola. She pointed. "Put on your mask!"

"But Keith said I should—" Hasbro said. Her voice was high-pitched and she stumbled and nearly fell.

"Your mask!" This time, Sarrah shrieked the command. "Put on your mask!"

Obediently, Hasbro complied, fumbling only slightly. A moment later, she stared out through the mask's protective lens as she said yet again, "Keith sent me out. You were supposed to—"

"Never mind that," Sarrah said. She looked around, probing the chaos. Somewhere, exhaust fans had come to life. The murk began to dissipate, however slightly, as soot was cleared from the air. Now, Sarrah could see flashing lights that indicated emergency exits. From the surrounding chaos, the cries of pain and the voices echoed.

"What is it?"

"What happened?"

"Help me, please, gods help me!"

"It was a bomb!"

Above them both, metal groaned again. The low, grinding sound was like a ringing thunder, even to Sarrah's protected ears. She looked up to see its source. What she saw made her eyes widen. Instinctively, her hand sought and found Enola's.

She could see the broken metal clearly, ragged and stark under emergency lights, their contours visible even in the swirling billows. The complex motorized guides that operated the casting cauldron had been damaged. The cauldron itself was slowly rocking, a shadowed, shifting bulk. Marking it were sullen red patches, glowing spots that testified to the heat of the liquid metal within. The great vessel rocked slowly from one side to another, shifting only centimeters at a time, but the arc of its swing was becoming greater.

It was tearing free. The overhead track had been torn asunder, and its burden was breaking loose. Even as Sarrah realized the implications, metal groaned again and the cauldron shifted more. It was a sudden lurch of perhaps half a meter, and more than enough to make the thing's contents shift and slop.

A blob of incandescence fell in slow motion, from cauldron to foundry floor. Long meters from the forms that had been its intended destination, fluid metal splashed and burned. Smaller globules of fire bounced up and out, in all directions. Someone screamed as a stray splatter found him. Enola screamed, too, and tore her hand from Sarrah's.

"We've got to get out of here," Sarrah said. She wished she had a camera. "That thing is going to fall! Enola, we've got to—"

Enola was gone. She had panicked and vanished back into the chaos.

ERIK breathed more easily with the filter-mask in place. The air that it fed him had a metallic, artificial taste, but it was clean and even relatively cool. Better still, the earpieces screened out much of the foundry cacophony. He could think again with some small measure of clarity.

Offsetting those improvements in his condition was the throbbing in his lower left side. Sometime in the previous minute or so, it had condensed from a throbbing ache into stabbing pain. Each step made it hurt more, and it was all he could do to keep hobbling toward the production booth where he had last seen Sarrah.

As he limped along, the world seemed to move in and out of focus. Twice, he nearly tripped, either over debris or the dead. Three times, he was nearly knocked to the floor by frantic survivors, unmindful of him as they headed eagerly for the emergency exits. Almost always, he kept his gaze fixed on the cauldron that hung so close to the Mesh production booth, and on the intermittent curve of white fire that the molten steel made at its rim. The glare was far brighter than the emergency lights, bright enough to punch through the haze and murk and sear its images into his eyes. If he looked away from it, its afterimage lingered on Erik's retinas and made a pale but black-fringed hole in his world. The afterimage annoyed, but the reality fascinated, so he stared at it as he moved along.

Out of the roiling fog of soot came a feminine figure. Even in the murk he could recognize the Zonix logo on her jumpsuit. Her own mask was framed by black hair, and the way that her body moved was very familiar. Headed directly toward him, she threaded her way through the confusion with remarkable grace and speed, moving along as if negotiating a dance floor. Erik remembered a woman who moved like that, a lifetime before.

"Enola?" he croaked. He reached for her, grabbed one shoulder. "Enola, where's Sarrah? We've got to—"

She hit him, striking with the heel of one hand. It smacked into his forehead, hard enough to make his head snap back. Blindly, reflexively, he swung at her and grunted as his knuckles connected. Almost immediately, she hit him again, hard enough to knock his mask free.

He fell, and his world began to go away again. He choked as the reflex sucked bad air deep into his lungs.

"Don't," he said, panicking. The pain in his side flared into new intensity as he reached for her. "Sarrah is—"

"ENOLA, we've got to go!" Sarrah shouted again. Her voice cracked. Her throat was raw and sore now. Her eyes felt like they were trying to leave their sockets, and when she coughed, she tasted metal. Whatever the mask's ratings were, she had exceeded them.

She looked around, frantic now. There was no sign of the younger woman, but it was still impossible to see clearly. Gray and black shadows played tag with one another, and with the foundry equipment and the ruins of the production booth. Disoriented herself now, Sarrah spun, trying again to sight Enola, but the only human forms wore the bulkier protective suits of rescue workers. They were Duckworth staff.

"Get out of here!" the first of them shouted, and vaguely gestured in one direction, using a flashlight like a baton for clarity and emphasis. "There's an emergency exit through there!"

"I can't," Sarrah said. "My—my partner panicked, she—"

Her own words surprised her, but their truth could not be denied. Enola had been her partner, however briefly.

"Get out!" the heavyset man repeated. He grasped her shoulders and spun her around, then pressed something into her hand. It was an industrial-grade flashlight, heavy and substantial. "Get out!" he said again. "But get out! That joint isn't going to hold!"

"That way!" the other man yelled, even as metal groaned more loudly above them. "We'll look for your friend!"

The first man pushed, hard. Obediently, Sarrah started forward. Perversely, visibility worsened almost immediately as she moved away from the broken cauldron's white heat. Billows of smoke swirled along the floor like dirty fog as they raced for the exhaust fans, only to be replaced by more.

Sarrah walked forward tentatively. She was wary of tripping, frightened of falling in this madness. Most of the screaming had abated now, and the evacuation seemed nearly complete, but the danger was still real.

The light that the man had given her helped. It cast polarized light that matched the lenses in her mask. Larger forms found new distinctness in the turmoil, and she could move with slightly greater confidence. Sarrah moved as quickly but as carefully as she could. She stepped past or over the scattered equipment and debris that peppered her path, carefully moving in the direction of exit. She had just made her way around the bulk of an abandoned utility vehicle when she heard the panicked cries.

"God! Look out!"

"It's going to—"

"Look out!"

Sarrah turned, looking back in the direction of the terrified shouts. She was just in time to see it happen.

A line of white fire drew itself again between the tilted cauldron and the foundry floor. Hair-fine at first, it quickly grew wider, and the cauldron's tilt became more pronounced. More billows of choking smoke erupted as liquid metal burned into the foundry floor. Solid metal tore, groaning, and the cascading stream of metal grew wider still.

And then the cauldron fell.

It fell in slow motion, in that gradual descent that characterized falling things on the Moon. The terror of the instant made it seem to fall more slowly still.

It fell, trailing molten fire that burned too brightly to have any color, even white. Long meters from the giant mold, the vessel tore loose completely from its track and smashed into the foundry's stone floor. Instantly, it shattered, to release a blinding wave of incandescence that raced in all directions.

Sarrah saw it, as if from a world away. She saw it as it came closer, and against it, she saw something else. She saw the silhouette of a woman, moving fast with hands outreached. She was trying to run, but the Pour was outpacing her.

"Enola!" Sarrah shrieked. Reflex made her scream. There was no way that the other woman would hear her.

The world moved in slow motion. A lifetime seemed to pass as Sarrah paused in her flight, and then she saw Enola turn to look in her direction. Sarrah gestured frantically at her with the flashlight.

"Over here, Enola!" she shouted, and indicated the bulky utility vehicle. "Here! Run!"

There was a chance.

Hasbro turned in her direction. Another dozen steps brought her close enough that Sarrah could hear her. "Where were you?" she asked, obviously still disoriented. "Where did you go? Keith said I—"

Behind Enola, the spill's wave front had begun to break up. The fire that flowed toward them busily subdivided itself into rivers, into streams, into rivulets. Behind them all was the bulk of the Pour, still a single wave of incandescence. Jagged lines formed in the foundry floor as liquid metal cut into stone.

Absurdly, Sarrah thought of the Grand Canyon.

"Here!" she screamed. She grabbed Enola's arm and yanked her to the empty utility vehicle. The vehicle was big, intended for elevated work. It had a squat base and broad metal wheels and a ladder-studded surface. Sarrah pressed one of Enola's gloved hands to a convenient rung and squeezed. "Climb!" she shouted at the dazed younger woman. "Climb! Now!"

Enola climbed. As if directed by an automated brainware system, she climbed, hand over hand. Sarrah climbed, too, if not as rapidly. Her joints hurt, and she had to force the long muscles of her arms and legs to contract. Panic lent strength, but not endurance. The younger woman moved with considerably more speed.

Sarrah was still climbing when the first wave smacked into the vehicle's wheelbase, three meters below her. She shrieked as a stray spatter of the liquefied steel found her. Even through the protective material of her jumpsuit, it seared and it stung. She clung, but shock made her relax her grip slightly.

The vehicle shifted as the spill struck it. So did Sarrah. The pain of the burn and the shock of the impact stunned her. Her hands opened. Her feet shifted. She looked down and saw a river of fire, pooling at the wheel base and seeping beneath it. The utility vehicle towered above the flood and was too big to be swamped entirely, but it shifted and shook before the tide. Sarrah screamed.

She fell.

CHAPTER 14

THEY thought that she had done it. They thought that she had set the bomb.

The thought was too large for Enola's head, too large for the tiny holding cell where she now sat. Rather than remain where it belonged, neatly nestled in the space behind her eyes, it had grown to fill her entire world. It was appalling, but could not be denied.

They really thought that she had killed those people.

Enola moaned softly. She rocked back and forth slowly on the edge of the bunk. It was the tiny holding cell's only furnishing, serving as bed and chair both. It was either sit there or stand. She had tried to pace, but the cubicle was too cramped for that. There was nothing here for her to do but think or sleep.

Enola did not want to think, and she could not sleep.

"Is everything all right in there?" The voice was neutral and uninflected and seemed to come from no particular direction. It could have been the product of a cheap synthesizer or the result of a human voice processed by a very expensive filter. Enola couldn't tell which. She supposed that was the point.

"You're awake and aware, Hasbro," the voice said. Somewhere in the cell, Enola knew, were sensors that reported her physical condition to her captors. "Acknowledge," the voice continued. "No one is coming in."

"Everything is all right," she finally said. Once, early in her confinement, she had been able to convince an attendant to enter the cell, to verify her condition. The moment of human contact, fleeting though it was, had warmed her for what seemed like long days. That had been very early in her confinement, however, and someone had been reprimanded for the incident.

No one actually entered the cell now, except on pressing legal or medical business. Huerta had made his rounds earlier, and so had her advocate, both in preparation her for the remand back to Earth. Neither had said anything to her not strictly required by professional duty. No matter how many requests she made for visitors, all were ignored.

She wondered what would happen to her on Earth. She wondered what they were going to do to her. She whimpered softly and rocked from side to side, hugging herself tightly.

The cell's surfaces were spotlessly white, mono-molecular plastic skins that resisted any blot. She could stay here for years and never leave a mark. There was no Mesh link and phone capability, no autogym. Meals were tendered through an access panel, and the utensils and vessels began dissolving as soon as she received them. They were timed plastics. In theory, they lasted long enough for Enola to consume their contents, then dissolved into ash to be flushed away. In practice, much of the food generally went with them.

Enola didn't want to eat. She couldn't exercise, and she couldn't sleep. She had made many requests for visitors, or counseling, or simple human contact. All had been denied. Alone in her cell, isolated from human contact, all that she knew was despair.

That, and one other thought.

* * *

"I think you should see her," Adkins said. He was a tall, lean man, with bushy eyebrows and a studious air that was probably the result of lengthy coaching sessions. He stood to one side of the treadmill, leaning against a counter, long fingers casually gripping an unfurled computer. Over-Management had assigned him to provide psychiatric counsel during the recovery period, and Erik was thoroughly sick of him.

Trying not to sneer, Erik glanced in his direction as he continued to pace steadily. Curving his neck even a fractional degree made the new-skin grafts there bunch, but Erik welcomed the tracery of pain. It meant that normal sensation was returning, after weeks of nerve-blocked numbness. "I think you're wrong," he said.

Beneath his feet, the treadmill's textured surface slid back and away from him, encouraging his next step. The grafts along his legs and back tightened and stung, but held. The burns there had been less severe, and what he felt now was less pain than discomfort.

Even Erik was surprised at how rapidly he was healing. The ALC had been very generous in funding his recovery, and the most advanced therapies had been made available to him. New-skin grafts, alveolar gels for his lungs, nerve-shunts for the pain, and skeletal braces to guide regenerating bone. Only a week before, it had been all that he could do to take more than a dozen steps, before fatigue and pain made him stop. Now, he could pace steadily on the treadmill for more than an hour at a time. Running would come soon.

"She asks repeatedly. It might be good for you to see her," Adkins said. "Now, while you have the opportunity."

Hasbro was being sent back to Earth in four days, Erik knew. His housekeeper's calendar announcements reminded him of it each morning. Since her conviction in Company Court, the Hasbro woman had made repeated requests that Erik call on her at the holding facility where she awaited transport back to Earth. With equal consistency, he had declined, but her persistence gnawed at him.

"I saw her during the hearings," Erik said. He picked up

the pace and watched with deliberate attention as the tread-mill's display values changed. "I testified against her."

"You saw her, but you didn't confront her," the physician said. "You spoke to the judiciary panel, not to Hasbro."

Erik shrugged, making his neck-grafts hurt some more. "You're too concerned with her," he said. "*I'm* your patient, not her."

"I'm not concerned about her at all," the counselor said calmly. He folded his computer neatly and tucked it into one pocket. "I'm worried about you."

Erik said nothing.

"You need more than physical therapy, more than just medication," Adkins continued implacably. "You were injured in the line of duty, trying to save someone who—"

"—someone who was a very good friend," Erik interrupted.

Sarrah was dead, consumed utterly by the Pour. It was still difficult to believe.

"—someone who was in the process of becoming *more* than a friend," the counselor corrected, speaking forcefully. "You're trying to put that behind you without resolving it, and you can't. You shouldn't."

"It's done. She's gone," Erik said. He thought of the eight others who had died during the Pour disaster. "They're all gone."

"We've spoken about this. And Sarrah died saving the woman who caused the crisis."

That was the difficult thing to believe. Not that Sarrah had saved Enola—enough of a surprise, itself—but that Enola had placed the bomb. Enola simply had never struck him as being that effectual a person.

Kowalski had presented impressive circumstantial evidence at the hearing, and this was backed by reports from Earth about Hasbro's troubled childhood. He had presented murky feed from a damaged camera that showed a figure with Enola's body language assailing Erik, backing Erik's own testimony. But the deciding factor had been the extensive files that Kowalski had found on Enola's home

Gummis. He had accepted the hearing's verdict, but he could not honestly say that he embraced it. The only thing that made it believable to him was that Enola had been caught in the same holocaust she had created.

"I don't know why she wants to see me," he said.

"I'm not concerned about what *she* wants," Adkins said again. "But you should take the opportunity. You're still having the dreams, aren't you?"

Erik swallowed once, and nodded. He slowed the treadmill and stepped off of it, then murmured thanks as he caught the towel the other man tossed at him. As he blotted the sweat from his forehead and shoulders, he nodded again. "The patches aren't helping," he said. "At first they did, but not now."

"Drugs have their limits," the counselor said. "The same dreams?"

"The same," Erik said. The sounds and images welled up in his mind, unbidden. He heard the screams again, and saw the fire and smoke. He felt the remembered sear of molten steel as a stray rivulet found his legs. Those memories, even in dream-state, were very difficult to reconcile with the petite, smiling woman he had danced with once, years ago. "The meditation helps more," he said. "But not enough."

"You need closure," Adkins said again.

Erik looked at him.

"And with Sarrah gone, only Enola can give it to you. Confront her. Take someone with you and do it in a secure setting, but you need to see her." He paused. "She may want to apologize."

"I don't want her apology," Erik said. He pounded the treadmill grip with one fist in sudden anger.

"I think that you do," Adkins said. "If not for yourself, for Sarrah."

"She has no apology that I will accept." Erik spoke with absolute conviction.

Adkins said nothing, but gazed at him levelly.

"I don't know if I can see her at all. She isn't allowed

visitors," Erik said. Even as he spoke, he knew that he was seizing on an excuse.

Incongruously, Adkins laughed. Even more surprisingly, the sound was welcome, dispelling some of the tension that had gathered so suddenly. "You're Over-Management, Erik," he said. "You're the ALC's director of communications for Villanueva. No one's going to turn you away."

Despite himself, Erik smiled wryly in response.

"Go see her," Adkins said again. "Doctor's orders."

"I think you're insane," Hector Kowalski said brightly. He was more animated and cheerful than he had been in days. He was in the grip of a kind of mock enthusiasm that served him in the pace of sarcasm, but to a greater degree than Erik had ever seen before. Another man might have been fooled by it, but Erik knew better. More to the point, Kowalski knew that he knew. "Really. I think you've lost your mind."

Erik said nothing, but gazed out the private train-car's window at the tunnel lights as they raced by. One of the physicians had issued him a hand-exerciser, a coil of spring steel with opposed grips and a display, and he passed it now from his left hand to his right. He squeezed, glanced at the numbers on the display and nodded, then squeezed again.

"She killed thirteen people," Kowalski said, still brightly. "Five at the Mall, eight at the Pour. She killed someone who was a guest in your home, and I was able to prove that. You don't owe her anything."

"This isn't for her," Erik said. He squeezed again. Two weeks in a hospital had cost him dearly in muscle tone, and that loss had eaten away at his upper body strength. The official reason for the exercise device was to offset some of that loss. At the moment, however, its main value seemed to be as a release for stress.

He squeezed it some more.

Kowalski was seated opposite him, the car's only other occupant. Now, he leaned forward, reached into one pocket, and withdrew a personal computer. Atypically for Kowalski, it was a plastic film unit, the kind that he didn't like because of privacy considerations. Its large display was difficult to use discreetly, but served well to present large bodies of information in a single gestalt.

That was how Kowalski used it now; when he turned it to face Erik, the flexible screen presented half a dozen views. Side by side with silenced feeds of witnesses testifying were diagrams, animations, and scrolling columns of numbers, all translucent but easily read. "Here," Kowalski said. His face was visible through the computer's membrane. "Familiar?"

"The closing arguments from the Company Court hearing," Erik said. He compressed the hand-exerciser again, feeling the muscles in his forearm bulge and flex. It got easier each time. With his free hand, he pointed at one tiled image. "I was there, Hector. Remember?"

The Erik Morrison in the recorded picture was pale, and his features were drawn. His hands trembled as he gestured, and when he left the witness stand, it was with the aid of crutches, something almost unknown on the Moon. The cut of the tunic he wore had been carefully chosen to conceal the bulge of wound dressings.

That had been three weeks before. Justice moved very fast in the ALC courts.

"Then you remember that she did it," Kowalski said. "You remember that we proved she was complicit."

"We proved that she was complicit," Erik agreed.

Kowalski pointed at one isolated view, at a testifying Keith Arreigh. "Opportunity," he said. "She was on the scene."

"No one denies that," Erik said.

"Motive," Kowalski said, pointing again. Centimeters from her finger, a weeping Narçissa Esposito mouthed silent phrases. "She had been terminated by Duckworth and would benefit from having a major news feed to call her own."

Erik shifted the exerciser to his other hand and started working that set of muscles. The wheels of the private car made clicking noises as they rolled along their metal rails.

"Means," Kowalski said, indicating the other views. They presented scrolling charts of data and diagrams. "In this case, that means knowledge." He looked at Erik, earnestly. "She knew how to concoct the explosives that were used," he continued. "Her own files prove that. Her background proves it again. Her sister died during the Czech Challenge, for gods' sake!"

That had been the biggest surprise of the entire judicial proceeding. Erik could remember full well how stunned he had been when Kowalski had presented the files scavenged from Enola's personal Mesh directories, and the various compounds he had found in her home.

"We found encrypted correspondence from the Children of Gondwanaland. Propaganda dispatches."

"She refused to confess or deal," Erik said. He wasn't sure why he mentioned it. The most likely reason he could find was a desire to make Kowalski a bit less confident in his pronouncements.

It certainly wasn't to defend Enola.

"We don't need her confession," Kowalski said. "And why do you think she wants to see you now?"

"I don't know," Erik said. "Adkins says that her reasoning doesn't matter. He thinks I should see her." They had been over this ground more than once, but Kowalski was, in his own way, very much like a dog. When he had his teeth in something, he was loath to let go.

Kowalski settled back in his seat with a sigh. He blanked the computer and set it aside. "We know that she did it," he said. His mock energy had faded into something like a scowl. "They'll get the truth out of her on Earth, at her disposition hearing."

That raised another point. "Voice/stress analysis says

that she's not lying when she denies involvement," Erik said. "So do the other systems."

"Doesn't matter. There are ways around them," Kowalski said. He paused a long moment before continuing. "Erik, it really doesn't matter whether she's guilty or not. What matters is, she's been adjudicated and dealt with."

The cool air of the climate-controlled car seemed to become cooler still as Erik pondered the comment. He didn't like it, and he liked even less how well it conformed to what he knew of Kowalski's personality.

How could he not have considered the possibility before? He had been in the earlier stages of recovery during the hearing and his mind had been on other things during the weeks that followed, but he should have considered it, nonetheless.

He thought back to the flexibility of Kowalski's standards when it came to identifying members of the Scheer network. Enola had been one of those that he had identified under those malleable guidelines.

"Hector," he said. "I do hope that the evidence you found in Enola's apartment was, in fact, found in Enola's quarters."

Kowalski looked at him and managed a grin. "That's a reasonable point," he said. "But that's not what I meant. I've been scrupulous. I had to be. The Feds will inherit my files when they take custody on Earth."

"Go on."

"I know that you disagree with some of my methods," Kowalski said. "But I think our priorities are the same. Remember the debriefing after the Mall incident? Remember Horvath?"

Erik remembered.

"We're not concerned about the deaths and injuries, Erik," Horvath had told him. *"We're concerned with the disruption and potential loss of revenues that the deaths and injuries bring. Just get back to business."*

He nodded.

"I can take steps to prevent something like this happening again," Kowalski continued. "I have taken steps to keep anything like this from happening again. But having the culprit in custody makes taking those steps easier. You need to recognize that."

The clicking sound of wheels on rails slowed. They were nearing their destination. Erik shut down the hand-exerciser, folded it, and returned it to its carrying case. "You're arguing in favor of a scapegoat," he said coolly.

Kowalski shook his head. "I'm arguing in favor of clarity," he said. "The evidence says that Hasbro did it. The adjudicators say she did it. She's the only one who says she didn't." He paused. "This visit is a mistake."

"I'm not here to be convinced," Erik said. "By you or by her."

ERIK Morrison seemed to have dwindled since the first time that Enola had seen him. The effect was subtle but noticeable. His clothes hung on him differently, and his face seemed to have lost the fleshy quality she had noticed before. He moved differently, too. His motions were more tentative as he seated himself across from her in the interview room. He moved like a man new to the Moon.

"Hello, Enola," he said. He was tense and ill at ease. Even his voice seemed different than she remembered.

The interview room was larger than her cell, but not by much. It had just enough floor space to hold a small table and two chairs. Two guards had brought Enola here long minutes before her scheduled meeting. They had seated her, made certain that she was comfortable, and then locked the restraints that held her to the chair.

Now, she could move her hands and forearms perhaps half a meter, and the guards had carefully explained that Morrison would remain beyond her reach at all times. Beyond that, neither had said a word. She had been unable to rise when he entered. The awareness that she was being rude only added to her humiliation, but there was nothing for her to do about it.

Time had slowed when Erik and his lieutenant entered the room, and it continued now at a glacial pace. Even Erik's words, two words, five syllables, had stretched and slowed to the absolute limits of comprehensibility. She studied his face as he spoke, monitored the play of skin and muscles as he shaped the words. Human contact, so rare now, was something to savor. She looked at his gray eyes and at the planes of his face, and at the narrow scar along the perimeter of one eye socket. Erik seemed to be an emissary not just from a life that she had left behind, but from another existence entirely.

After so many days of asking to speak him, the words would not come.

Behind him, his underling, Hector Kowalski, stood leaning against the wall, a studiously casual expression on his face. She recognized him from the hearing. His hands were empty, but they hung at his sides, never more than a centimeter or two from his pocket-studded belt, and his eyes never left Enola's. She had no doubt that he was using his own equipment to record the session, but she did not care.

"Hello, Enola," Erik said again. "You wanted to see me."

"This was a mistake," Hector said. His voice was cool.

She finally found the words and forced them out. "Hello, Erik."

He nodded. "Are they treating you well?" he asked. He asked the question without seeming overly interested in any answer she might give. She knew that it was a formality only.

She nodded, too. "They are," she said, her tone equally pro forma.

Then the tears came. They streamed from her eyes and burned her cheeks. She tried to cover her face with her hands, but the restraints wouldn't let her. "I'm sorry, Erik," she said. "I'm so sorry."

Kowalski snorted and rolled his eyes.

"I've been thinking," Enola said. "About what happened. About Sarrah."

Erik didn't speak.

"I—I didn't do those terrible things," Enola continued, her voice thick.

"We don't believe you," Kowalski interjected, but then fell silent as Erik gestured angrily at him.

"She didn't like me very much, you know," Enola said haltingly.

Kowalski snorted. Erik gestured again.

"She didn't like me at all," Enola said. "And she saved me. I think about that, a lot. I don't have much else to think about."

"I think about it, too," Erik finally said. He sounded curiously gentle.

"Why did she do that?" Enola asked.

Erik looked at her blankly. "Why?"

"Why did she save me?"

"This is about Sarrah?" he asked.

"I'm sorry. So sorry," Enola said. "She was a good person."

"What about the other twelve men and women?" Kowalski asked. His cool tones had become cold. "Did they deserve to die? What about the other ones who were—"

"This is about Sarrah?" Erik asked again, as if he could not believe. "That's why you wanted to see me?"

Enola whimpered and nodded.

"I had expected you to claim that you hadn't done it," Erik said. He seemed to be studying her. "That was no surprise. But I didn't expect this."

"She was a good person, and she saved my life," Enola said doggedly. This was the one piece of business that she could accomplish before she returned to Earth, and it cried out for completion. "I can't thank her, and I've taken her away from you. I never knew anyone who would do anything like that, for anyone."

"She died saving you," Erik said. "We don't know that she sacrificed herself to save you."

The point had been raised many times at her hearing. Enola made no response to it now.

"And you're not going to say that you didn't do it?" Kowalski asked sourly.

From somewhere within herself, Enola found her last shreds of anger and pride. She glared at Kowalski. "I already said I didn't," she said sharply. "But you won't believe me. Neither of you will." She took a deep breath, then returned her attention to Erik. "But I hope you'll believe me about Sarrah." An eerie calm settled over her, and the tears ceased. "I'm sorry."

There was nothing more to say.

"THAT was strange," Erik said. He half-reclined, half-sat in the train's padded seat and gazed somberly out the window as walls of the tunnel raced by. His exerciser lay in the empty seat beside him, unopened and forgotten.

"It was a mistake," Kowalski said. He chewed and swallowed.

At the detention center's canteen, he had paused to purchase Lethe water and soy crisps. "Crackly Crawlers! They're crackly, and they crawl!" the bag read, and its animated label showed images from an imagineer's nightmare. The sack was half empty now.

Kowalski gobbled down a few more of the squirming things, and sipped Lethe water before continuing.

"I accept the point," Erik said. "But I didn't expect an apology. Not an apology about Sarrah, at least."

"Don't you think she deserved one?" Kowalski asked.

Erik turned from the window and stared at him. "Of course she did," he said. He remembered a trim form striding out of the shadows and smoke, and how the skin of his face had felt when the filter-mask was torn away. "But so did I."

Lethe water gurgled, and Crackly Crawlers died writhing as another kilometer or two raced by. Finally, grudgingly, Kowalski said, "You might have a point. Maybe we should pursue it."

CHAPTER 15

THE tourist lounge at Chrisium Port was alarmingly familiar. Adjacent to the third-level concourse, tucked between
a *Fargos!* and a souvenir store, it could have been the
same watering hole that had received Erik some seven
years before.

The padded stool that he perched on now could have
been the same one that had held him then, and the recorded
images on the walls could have been taken from his memory, or from any similar establishment back on Earth.
Black condors, with penumbral wings and accordion
necks, glided through imaged skies, high above the Andes.
Erik watched as he sipped his cocktail.

The birds were images, too, of course, but entirely syn-
thesized. A mirage team with good archival footage and
better brainware simulation programs had summoned up
the species from dead history. The simulated spectacle was
breathtaking, but even the trifling amount of alcohol Erik
had consumed was enough to prompt a twinge of sadness
over the pseudo-resurrection. There were times when he
thought it would be best to let the dead rest.

"Nice place," Asreigh said. He had ordered Lethe water,

which had arrived in a souvenir glass. He gulped. As the level of the transparent liquid fell, an imaged Moon seemed to rise above its horizon.

"No, really, it's not," Erik said. "I would have preferred some place nicer, but my physician still has me on an abbreviated schedule—"

"And your physician also says that you shouldn't be drinking," his attendant said. She was an attractive woman, tall and lean, with long hair pulled back to accentuate the high rise of her cheekbones. She wore civilian clothes, but a small red cross on one lapel marked her as a member of the medical profession. Her eyes were hazel.

Erik shrugged and made a great show of sipping again. "My physician says that I shouldn't drink very much," he corrected. He glanced toward his companions, gathered around the lounge's corner table. "It interferes with the medication," he explained.

Arreigh's genial ego had led him to take the place of honor, at the narrowest end, closest to the platter of soy chips, fruit loops, and other oddments. Beside him was his associate, Katalin Cassidy. She pushed bits of food around her plate and said nothing, but her dark eyes moved constantly, attentive to her surroundings. Erik was seated opposite her, flanked by Kowalski and his medical specialist.

The attendant made no comment. Instead, with precision and speed, she plucked Erik's glass from his hand, and then replaced it with another, filled with mineral water from a communal pitcher. Erik, annoyed, shot her a sidelong glance and got a smirk as his only reply.

"No, really, it's great!" Arreigh said, effusively. He set down his glass and gestured at his surroundings with both hands. His eyes lit. "Just like back on Earth!"

"That's what I meant," Erik said. "Something with more character would have been better. Or more appropriate, at least."

"Well, schedules are schedules," Kowalski said. "We all have deadlines."

Arreigh glanced at his wrist-tattoo. "And mine says that check-in is in forty-five minutes," he said.

"Forty-three minutes." Katalin made the correction without consulting any timepiece that Erik could see. She looked thoroughly bored. With elegant hauteur, she used an olive fork to spear something that wiggled from the snack platter. It was still wiggling when she popped it into her mouth.

"I wanted to wish you both a good journey," Erik continued. "The ALC appreciates your staying this long to testify and clear up the loose ends—"

"Hah!" Arreigh barked. He seemed amused. "I wanted to work with the Mesh reporting teams, anyway." He preened. "They're taking me back in-house, you know. I'm to be the new regional subdirector for Lunar Info-Disseminative Modalities."

"What does that mean?" Erik asked.

"I honestly don't know," Arreigh said. "Staying over was no inconvenience, really."

"And, besides, there was a hold put on your return fares," Kowalski said dryly. He nabbed a salmon-skin roll from the snack tray and dropped it onto the appropriate section of his plate to warm.

"That, too," Arreigh said, still cheerfully. "I was proud to stay and do my civic duty."

A waiter drifted by, and in his passing, new drinks appeared before several of them. Erik's was vodka and orange, with a garnish of something green. Before he could raise it, however, it was gone, and mineral water had again taken its place. His attendant smiled at him, raised the pilfered glass in a mock salute, drained it. Arreigh laughed and clapped, but Erik scowled.

He returned his attention to the Mesh producer. More serious now, he said, "I visited Enola a few days ago."

At first, no one spoke. Kowalski drummed his fingers and rolled his eyes. Arreigh lowered the level of his Lethe water by another half-centimeter and Katalin paused in playing with her food as the awkward silence stretched to an impressive length.

Arreigh finally broke it. "How is she?" he asked, in a neutral tone.

"Not well," Erik said. He corrected himself. "Distraught."

Arreigh looked at him blankly. "What will happen to her?" he asked.

"Life in prison is the most likely outcome," Erik said. "She'll have a second trial, in a government court, but that's just a formality that the charter requires. There may be other charges, too." He sighed. "I feel sorry for her."

Kowalski snorted. He devoured his salmon-skin roll in a single bite.

"Sorry? For her? That's a surprise," Arreigh asked. "But you were business associates, weren't you?"

Erik shook his head. "Not really. Acquaintances. And even that was a long time ago."

"But your 'associate' knew her better than that, I think," Kowalski said. He snickered. When Katalin favored him with a poisoned glance, he snickered some more. "I led the team that searched her quarters, remember? And I'm the one who reconstructed her activities." He smiled. "I don't know everything about you, but I know everything about you and Hasbro."

"Katalin's nights are her own," Arreigh said. His words had an edge. His glass was empty now, the Moon's pale orb fully presented. As he set it down, the animated satellite began progressing slowly through its phases.

"They must have been a good match, is all," Kowalski said.

The exotic woman rested her head on Keith's shoulder in an elaborate pantomime of affection. She smiled sweetly, but her eyes showed no warmth at all.

"And I'm the one who found the Gondwanaland propaganda in her files, and my people back on Earth found the files on her sister," Kowalski continued. "So, asking me, I say she has a lot to be sorry about. She killed thirteen people and wrecked the production schedule."

"For coverage points," Erik said flatly. All hospitality had fled his voice now, and his expression, as he was reminded of the severity of the situation. "And career advancement."

"I assure you, mass murder as a ratings generator is not a strategy that Zonix management would approve," Arreigh said. He gestured with both hands. "And I can say that as Zonix's new regional subdirector for Lunar Info-Disseminative Modalities."

Everyone was looking at him now. Remarkably for the ebullient man, he did not seem pleased to be the center of attention.

"Why don't you tell us what happened, then, Keith?" Erik's attendant said. The same long fingers that had claimed Erik's drinks traced the contours of Arreigh's left forearm now, and she leaned forward and smiled. She said, "I'd *really* like to know."

Arreigh chuckled. "Well, I didn't know that anyone was going to die," he said eagerly. His words took on a momentum. "The actual bombs were placed by my associate here," he continued, gesturing.

He paused, suddenly pale. He stammered. "I-I mean—"

Katalin Cassidy came over the table in a single, liquid leap. She moved as gracefully and impossibly as water might flow uphill. She drew her legs up from the floor, kicked hard against one rung of her chair. Her left hand came down on the tabletop, her fingers forming a perfect five-point brace. The arm bent and then straightened to take the weight of her body as she came up and over and at Erik.

Her right hand still held the olive fork, and it glinted in the lounge's gentle illumination.

"Hey!" Keith Arreigh was saying now, in a voice of dumb wonder. He seemed a second or so behind the rest of his world. "Why did I say—?"

Cassidy's right hand came down in a savage arc. The olive fork speared Erik's hand, slipping between two metacarpals to grind against the table's stressed plastic top. Erik, pinned, yelped.

Cassidy was still moving. Even as Erik tried to draw back, her sandaled left food kicked out. The lightning thrust balanced her forward movement and also intersected neatly with Hector Kowalski's sternum. The ALC security officer flew backward from his chair.

Arreigh's "associate" had released the fork now. She drew herself into a tight ball as she pivoted, midair, on the brace of her left arm. Momentum carried her forward as she made a rolling mid-leap near-somersault and then unfolded herself again. Muscular thighs clamped around Erik's neck as she slammed into him.

They fell together, and as they did, Cassidy chopped backward with her left hand, driving it into the collarbone of Erik's attendant. The other woman gasped in pain as she fell back and down, too.

Through it all, even amid the impact and confusion and even as his world started to go dark, Erik remained remarkably aware of Katalin Cassidy's expression. Her strong features had remained quiet and composed, perfectly calm as she moved to kill him.

Great pain hammered Erik as his shoulders and back struck the floor. He brought his own hands up, instinctively, groping for the Cassidy woman's throat. He groped, but her hold would not permit him to reach. As he tried to struggle free, she brought her hands back and up, lacing the fingers and preparing to bring them down again.

He knew that he was about to die.

Before that could happen, however, a metallic dart abruptly sprouted from the alabaster skin of her neck. Electricity buzzed. Katalin's eyes rolled back, then closed. Her jaw hung slack. She convulsed and went limp.

The entire sequence of events had taken only a few seconds.

"God!" Kowalski said. He gurgled as he spoke, and flecks of red appeared at the corners of his mouth. "I've seen feeds—but in person, I've never seen anyone move that way, *anyone*." He lowered his dart-gun and lurched forward, a set of elastic restraints dangling from his free hand. "But once I get these on that Hungarian hit-bitch—"

"Never mind that," Erik said. His ears rang, and his

shoulders ached, but he scrambled to his feet and turned to face his companion. "She'll keep. She's down, she'll keep. What about—oh."

Keith Arreigh, looking at once worried and confused, was busily helping the other woman to her feet. She seemed unhurt, but suffered his attentions patiently before acknowledging Erik's concern.

"I'm fine, everyone, really. But thank you," Wendy Scheer said.

EPILOGUE

"ERIK was the target all the time?" Enola asked. Even now, she still sounded confused.

Wendy nodded. Her flowing hair, red today, rippled and glossed beneath the office's indirect lighting. Not for the first time, Enola recognized that her hostess was a woman of considerable natural beauty, with the type of classic, matter-of-fact good looks that aged well. Except for hair color and minimal makeup, she only rarely wore facial appliances. She would have done very well as a Mesh newshead, Enola realized, at least under prevailing audience preferences. She would have been strong competition.

Not that it mattered anymore.

"Yes," Wendy said. "Or, he was one target. There's some evidence that the Gondwanalanders tried to kill him on Earth earlier in the year." She paused. "He's a prominent man, Enola, and he will be historically important. I'm certain of that, even if he seems blind to it sometimes."

They were in Wendy's office, in the Halo complex at Armstrong Base. It was a place that mirrored much of

Wendy's demeanor, attractive and efficient, but unprepossessing. That quality was still novel to Enola, especially considering that the office belonged to the federal enclave's highest-ranking official.

"But Arreigh—"

Wendy shrugged. "Arreigh confessed. He's not sure why, but he did. He wanted a larger audience for his feeds. The explosions alone would have given him that. I don't think that he realized the extent of Katalin's assignments." She made a delicate, ladylike snort. "That speaks poorly of his worldliness. Terrorists like her always have agendas, and they're never small ones."

Enola knew the rest of the story. Arreigh had sponsored Katalin Cassidy's presence on the Moon. On the truthful foundation of their genuine partnership, they had built a superstructure of lies and deceit. Enola's recruitment as a newshead had been predicated, in large part, by her basic, physical similarity in height and build to the Cassidy woman.

Cassidy, for her part, had built upon that similarity. She practiced perfect body control and intimate study to mimic Enola's body language. That was why Erik had thought that she was the one who attacked him in the foundry, and one reason that Kowalski's "physical dynamics" analysis had identified Enola in the Mesh security tapes. She had planted the two bombs while in reasonably close proximity to Enola, at the Splinter and at Duckworth's foundry, using access tunnels to conceal her movements.

"Villanueva is a rat's nest, in more ways that one," Scheer said. "It has a maze of access tunnels and maintenance spaces that most don't even imagine exists. But someone with her training, and her mind-set, could master them well enough to do the job."

The files and other evidence discovered by Kowalski in her quarters had been Katalin's work, too, and Enola even knew that she was to have died, too. She was to have been found dead of injuries on the foundry floor, with more evidence planted on her person. Only Erik's struggle with the terrorist had delayed her long enough to keep that from happening.

"What happens to her now?" Enola asked, already knowing the answer.

"What would have happened to you. Deportation to Earth, life in prison," Wendy said. "But I suspect that there will be more. She'll be analyzed for genetic modifications, at the very least." A look of distaste flickered across her features.

"I didn't think that people could move like that. She must have been enhanced." Enola shuddered. "She must be a monster. And I was so stupid."

"Don't feel bad. It's over," Wendy said kindly. "Keith told me that he had developed misgivings about the situation fairly early, but too late to change course. He really thinks highly of you, Enola. You tested very well with Mesh audiences."

"Did he really say that?" Enola asked.

"He did. He was very forthcoming during interrogation." Wendy dimpled. "I think he likes me. But, at any rate, there may be work for you on the Mesh, yet."

"But not now."

Wendy shook her head. "Not now, no. Zonix has lost tremendous prestige within the ALC over these incidents. They were in the process of rehiring someone who turned out to be a saboteur," she said. "Management disavows all knowledge, of course, but I'm not sure who believes them."

"And I was part of it."

Wendy nodded. "You were convicted of being a saboteur and murderer. That can—*will* be changed, but people remember."

Enola remembered. Long weeks in the white room weren't something that she would ever forget. She bit her lower lip. "So, what do I do now?" she asked.

"That's why I wanted to see you," Wendy said. She leaned back in her chair. "You don't want to go back to Earth."

Enola shook her head emphatically.

"Zonix doesn't want you," Wendy said. "Duckworth is done with you. You could try to find work with one of the other ALC sisters, but that's not very likely."

"Erik said he would try to find something," Enola said. Her voice caught. "He says I've suffered enough."

Wendy laughed, a bright tinkling sound. She touched Enola's hand with a neatly decorated index finger. "I can hear him saying that," she said. "He has a flair for the dramatic."

"He does," Enola said, eager to agree. She had seen feeds of the incident at the spaceport lounge.

"And he blames himself," Wendy continued.

"Why?" Enola asked. Other, similar comments had been made during the past few hectic days, and none had been explained.

"And it's why you're here. He thinks he owes you a favor," Wendy continued, not really answering. "Would you like to work for me, Enola?"

Enola blinked. The idea of taking a federal position had never occurred to her. She had a healthy skepticism about Project Halo.

"I—I don't think I'm qualified," she said slowly. "I'm no scientist. I don't know anything about Halo."

"Not Halo. Me. You'd be working for me," Wendy said. She leaned forward, so close that Enola could feel her breath. "You'd be my personal envoy, my representative." Wendy paused. "My proxy."

Enola was dubious. Simple pragmatism prompted another question. "Where?" Enola asked. "Where would I live?"

Wendy laughed again. "Villanueva," she said. "I only go there under special circumstances, but with a livelihood, you'll be able to come and go as you please. With you as my eyes and ears, I could accomplish more from here." She took one of Enola's hands in hers and smiled more widely, more warmly. "You may not understand it, or even believe in it, but we do important work here. *I* do important work. You'd be helping me tremendously."

"Well," Enola said, and then she smiled, too. "I'll accept. If it makes you happy."

Coming August 2005 from Ace

Camouflage
by Joe Haldeman
0-441-01252-3
Two aliens have wandered the earth for centuries. One
has survived by adapting to other life forms—the other
by destroying anything that threatens it.

Age of Conan: Songs of Victory
by Loren L. Coleman
0-441-01310-4
Volume Three of the new *Legends of Kern* series
in which Kern must seek out an ancient weapon that can
kill any man, beast, or god.

Also new in paperback this month:

Raven's Strike
by Patricia Briggs
0-441-01312-0

Changing Planes
by Ursula K. Le Guin
0-44101224-8

Available wherever books are sold or at
www.penguin.com

Don't miss the first book in the
Inconstant Moon trilogy

HUMAN RESOURCE
by
Pierce Askegren

All Erik Morrison wants is to earn enough as
EnTek's new Site Coordinator so that he can
return to Earth as soon as possible. But he's about
to uncover a shocking revelation on the moon's
colony that some want exposed—and that some
will do anything to keep secret.

0-441-01079-2

**Available wherever books are sold or at
www.penguin.com**

A322